Under
BRIDGE

Immanuel James

ELEVIV PUBLISHING GROUP
Houston, Texas 77082

Under Bridge

ELEVIV PUBLISHING GROUP, TEXAS

Under Bridge Credits:

Book Layout & Art Direction: Eleviv Publishing Group
Cover Design: Eleviv BrandX
Photographer: Peter Oboh
Cover Image: Peter Oboh

Published by Eleviv Publishing Group
Houston, TX 77082
USA
www.elevivpublishinggroup.com
1-832-328-7935

ISBN: 978-0615989129

To Emilio Poloni,
boss as friend.

To all children of broken homes
Caught
In-between parental punches
And abandoned
To parent themselves
From squalor to grandeur.

And to young people everywhere
Bold enough
To question
Convention.

Acknowledgments

Gratitude is a poor currency for repaying radio host, multiple entrepreneur and motivational speaker, Vivian Elebiyo, my US publisher, for the roles she played in this work. Never has a fan been so audacious in staking resources to promote someone else's talent. Never!

Tchidi Jacobs, one tall broadcaster and writer, led me by the hand into the world of overseas publishing, and spent long nights with me as we sent over thirty poorly written query letters to literary agents. His belief in the work supplied me with needed hope in moments of depression. Thank you, brother.

Ayodele Olofintuade, my 'foul-mouthed' critic and editor, made sure she insulted the work enough to make it better. And Prof. Unoma Azuah, my second editor, followed in her steps, until we 'quarreled' to enact a healthy writerly relationship.

My recent meeting with Onyeka Nwelue at the Bogobiri Bar, Ikoyi, yielded the most honest pieces of advice on how to make this book happen. The current title of the book was a response to Chambers Umezulike's criticism of the old one, after he had read a manuscript he so admired. May success stalk you guys like it had nothing else to do.

There was Lillian Chioma Nwosu, that intelligent young lawyer whose debates with me helped the dialogues on homosexuality and religion. Vivian Osekwe typeset the first drafts of my handwritten manuscript until I learned to type faster solely with my middle finger. Efeilomon Idowu gave a lot of support, just like George Amakor, my friend for life.

Ikhide Ikheloa, who "would love to have a peep" into the manuscript, later encouraged me with positive remarks. Thank you, sir.

To Lanre Yusuf, my social media guru; Collins Nwodo, that good friend of mine; Macsimeon Simeon, a good colleague; Ekene Okoro, journalist-friend and critic; Nonye Okpala, a dedicated fan; Stanley Anyanwu, my amiable younger brother; Chisim Chukwu, an avid supporter; Olusegun Soyemi, who taught me Critical Writing; Chinedu Ozordi and Cheta Nwanze, my editors at The Nigerian Telegraph - thank you all.

I'm grateful to others too numerous to mention, whose support or lack of it catalysed my resolve to realize this dream. May God bless you all.

"The individual must find within himself an Identity, an independent, firm source of joy, one not too subject to the world's troubles. After wealth is lost or shaken; when death snatches a loved one; when evil attacks things that make life beautiful, one must fall back to oneself — to one's Identity — that somewhat permanent asset which only death or extreme infirmity can take away. That Identity is what is entirely our own of all things, namely, a strong, impenetrable will; a belief in self — a belief that one still has the spirit and resource to re-establish oneself; a disdain for material things and the possession of a soul firmed up in learning and wisdom; a certain great passion for the soul, like love for the arts or something abstract; and for theists, a belief in God. Without Identity, the individual is to be pitied at the strike of misfortune, since his happiness is hinged on his material fortunes."

Under Bridge

Table of Contents

Wanted- A Divorce Party

Life is an imposed opportunity to exist: No one asked to be born. Existence was thrust upon all of us by force. One could become very wealthy, or become more famous than sex, yet being unborn would probably have made a better choice, since there would be neither gain nor loss. For those whose bread is buttered by Fate, life is a blissful imposition. It is incarceration to those at the other side, whose lives are hell placed on an early rehearsal. But they have a choice: a good rope and a willing neck. Wait! Yonder is such an uncertain alternative. Both hell and paradise are curious places: the first is said to be a continual dedication to suffering; the other projects an endless monotony of bliss.

For a larger part of my thirty-one-year-old life, I've been thinking about these and other life issues. My life is one big bag of mixed experiences. No, it's not necessarily another grass-to-grace story with a happy-ever-after ending, because I'm not yet particularly happy despite having achieved a few little things many young people like me would wish for. At first I wanted to keep my story to myself, believing that one has to be very arrogant to think that one's story would matter out of over 7 billion others. Autobiography is the synonym of hagiography, and both run the risk of incredibility. But then I felt that if I don't share my story, it's no special virtue either, since many others, possibly far greater than I, have not shared theirs too.

My name is Victor Ekwueme. In 1980, I was born in one tiny village called Umuege, in Ngor-Okpala, Imo State. As the first child among four siblings, I was naturally seated very close to the scene of endless domestic wrestling between my parents. At eleven, I had grown to define parents as those adults whose unions are validated by local boxing.

I cannot so easily forget how the lump on Father's eyebrow came to be. That Sunday afternoon, he came back from his married sister's place in the next village, and demanded his lunch. His sister hated Mother. Clad in a singlet tucked into a wrapper tied round his waist, he sat in the veranda on a wooden stool set before a worn-out table whose fourth leg was disabled, only supported with a piece of brick at the base to guarantee balance. Mother placed two covered plates on the table and checked the disabled table-leg to be sure the brick support was doing a proper job. She then opened the plates, cut a wad from the fufu, sank it in the soup and stirred the soup with it, before swallowing.

Father would not eat the food if she didn't taste it.

He stood up and adjusted the huge knot he had formed below his navel with his wrapper and sat down again, scornfully looking at the meal. I watched him from a corner, and saw that he did not touch the meal before his thunderous voice cut through the air.

"Nwugo! Nwugo! How many times have I told you not to serve me Ofe Ede? Come and take this nonsense away! Look at the face of the soup, like babies' shit!"

Mother emerged from the kitchen a few meters away, looking displeased.

"Mine, but in the morning you said you had not eaten Ofe Ede in a long while...."

"And so? I don't want to eat it if it has to look this miserable!"

"You've eaten in your sister's place, that I know," she said, as she took the plates away, mumbling, "Nwoke nke a enweghi mmeta, tufiakwa!" – This man is so unappeasable!

"What did you just say? Come back here! Stupid woman!," he blustered, bolting towards Mother, who was walking away rather leisurely, daring the threat in his voice.

His slap came from behind her. It took her unawares and she staggered, the plates slipping off her hands and their contents turning over. She turned facing him and held the huge knot of wrapper formed above his crotch, tugging it furiously.

"You must kill me today!" she cried, as Father sent out further punches all over her body to weaken her hold and prevent her from stripping him naked. She held even more firmly onto the loop, ignoring the rain of blows, clinging to her only source of strength in the bargain – the knot of his loincloth which was the apparatus to unveil nakedness. Father realised, suddenly, that his blows lacked advantage, and bent over to disengage her hand from the knot. They staggered. I started crying helplessly. Then Mother reached for his face, and buried her teeth in his eyebrow. Blood! He recoiled, a hand clutching his wrapper to salvage what was left of his near nakedness, the other hand cupping the source of pain above his left eye, as he yelped repeatedly:

"Witch! She has eaten my flesh, ooooh!"

By then Mother had already taken to her heels on sighting the heavy flow of blood. Her feet were clogged with marsh from the soup that poured on the ground, trod into a mud by their feet. Concerned neighbours gathered and later took him to a hospital.

Father had a most enigmatic persona. A warped sense of reasoning and an extremely wild temper were all his, coupled with a loquacity that made him report his domestic issues to whoever cared to listen. That always embarrassed us, but no one dared complain to him. Within his complex was equally a morbid fear of death, which made him superstitious. His siege mentality made him to always suspect co-workers, relatives, Mother, and I. And he sought safety in the attendance of numerous spiritual churches where his worst fears were always confirmed in mendacious prophecies. There was no predicting him as he liked and disliked the same thing depending on the whims of his current lunacy. He was a junior worker in an oil firm in Port Harcourt where he lived, while Mother, my siblings and I lived in the village with his aged mother, Mgbeke.

How my parents managed to have four kids amid a routine exchange of vicious fists remained a mystery. Whenever Father visited us in the village, there was always trouble. A fight could break together with dawn between him and Mother, sustain itself through the day, and heighten at dinner. Nights never brought a ceasefire, as heavy punches in the bedroom, yells, and the clatter of domestic weapons held sway. Mornings were free of commotion only if some external event had overrun the simmering rage, or if Grandmother's mediation had earned a reprieve. Peace was a rare guest.

One day, the silence of the evening was shattered by the clattering sound of an okada that pulled up in front of the house.

Father alighted from the passenger seat and plunked his un-
wieldy suitcase on the dusty ground, hurriedly settled with the
okadaman and charged into the house. A sprightly man in his
fifties, he stood very close to the ground in size. Mother approached to help with the bag but he snubbed her, with a frown
that virtually extended to his neck. Quarrels and grudge-keeping
had been shared hobbies in their twelve-year-old marriage.

His visit to the village that evening held much suspense. His
earlier visit was only two days old, and since Umuege stood for
diabolism for him, he scarcely came home. No sooner had he
freshened up that evening than he slouched into a lounge chair
under a mango tree in front of the house, sullen. It was not out-
of-place to see him in that mood but he appeared to have
something very serious this time bothering him. The ogogoro he
brought along with him from Port Harcourt sat by his side in a
small bottle. Soon the bottle was planted on his mouth and its
entire content was emptied. A thorough rinse, then a singular
gulp and the mouth was free as the liquid hurried down his
throat. He grunted, as if to scrape down remnants of ethanol.
His head was bowed. There was this impression of a man who
had to take alcohol to be able to take a tough decision, or action.

Umuege lacked electricity then – in the early 90s. And due to
the ubiquity of vegetation and shrubs around, darkness often
arrived earlier than normal. At that time no one there was rich
enough to afford a generator. At night, homesteads were animated by the poor luminance of paraffin lamps, or live embers
that warmed cold hands during the Harmattan. Though Father's
house lacked the trappings of a decent apartment, it came off as
a reference for higher status given the predominance of thatch

roofs and mud houses. That he worked in an oil firm was a hard currency on its own, regardless of his position at his workplace. Besides the 'luxury' of brick walls and corrugated iron roof that defined our house, the living room and the other rooms had ceilings. Ceiling was not a fitting born of necessity but of grandeur.

But my room was marginalised in the application of this asbestos sheeting. The carpenter's estimation was wrong so a fraction of the room was left out. And by some funny set up in the room my bed was directly under the opening. The ceiling formed the footboard for the frequent gyration of two hefty rats at night. In the height of their noisy flirtations and sexual violence the animals often fell through the hole and my little sleeping body always helped to cushion their fall. They would scamper away leaving me startled and miffed every night.

The routine continued until I resolved, one night, to slay the mischievous couple. I stayed awake and took position, cudgel in hand, reading their footsteps mentally to be able to synchronise their descent with a malicious strike. The rascals seemed to have known their limits, as they held themselves back on many occasions from careening through the hole, each of the time making me strike at the void. The drama persisted until I slept, from fatigue. I planked against the wall, the weapon loosely held. Just as sleep recorded some penetration the duo landed right on my forehead, left some bleeding scratches there and vamoosed triumphantly. I surrendered. The next day the contested space was closed with a wooden panel and all hostilities ceased.

The curiosity in Father's return was further heightened by his affectation towards Mother the following morning.

"Mine! We'll visit your maiden home tomorrow morning. It's been long I visited my in-laws on a happy note," he told Mother, beaming.

"Hmmm! I can't remember the last time I heard such from you," Mother replied, looking phlegmatic.

"I didn't bring home two bottles of Schnapps to start up bar business in the village."

Mother smiled. "So you have such a noble thing in mind yet you've worn a long face since you came back yesterday?"

"I had a bad journey. Pick-pockets stole my money yesterday at Osisioma Park in Aba...Victor! Come and have some biscuits," he added.

He gave me a crisp ten naira note in addition. For the first time in my eleven years of existence, I saw a very excited Father. Mother was very impressed. She sang happy songs rapturously as she did chores in the kitchen.

Like Father, Mother had temper issues, and talked too much. She was deemed wicked due to how brutally she punished us, her children: an errant child would be stripped of all clothing and locked up in a room all day till the next morning, hungry. She held linear canes in contempt, preferring complicated branches that multiplied a single stroke by ten. Come morning and victim would be jerked up from sleep, his violations read to him again. Cane would be administered on every part of the body. Wailing redoubled her anger and made the whip land more ruthlessly. The whip would break into pieces and her limbs would conclude the job. I was often the specimen in those flogging sessions.

Later that morning, my parents left happily, for so it seemed, for Mbaise, to 'greet' Mother's people. In less than two hours, Father was back home alone, locked in a monologue of insults.

"God punish them! I don't take nonsense! I've had enough! However they want it I'm ready, idiots....It's over!"

He uttered the words again and again, moved about the compound in a frenzied manner. Suddenly a van thrust into the compound and disgorged Mother and her cantankerous siblings. Rancour, as expletives flew from every corner.

"Hopeless man, you'll suffer! Let me see the woman that can tolerate you."

As the mudslinging continued, Mother's things were already being flung into the van by her siblings. Villagers gathered in their numbers, more out of spectatorship than of concern. Unable to catch up with Mother in the war of words, Father resorted to repeating the same line of insults a thousand times:

"Ashawo! Go and marry the men that have been sleeping with you! Ashawo! You say they told you I'm fucking an Ikwere woman, aren't you fucking around in the village? Ashaaaawo!"

I became utterly embarrassed seeing my peers and school-mates snicker at the unfolding drama. They always taunted me for being too effeminate, for pounding pepper and sieving fermented cassava for Mother, tasks meant for girls. Mother never allowed me to play football or indulge in other boyish pastimes. If there was no domestic work, she would create one for me or have me memorize and recite an entire unit in Imo Reader:

Edet lives in Calabar

He is eight years old

Every morning he goes to school
In the afternoon he stays at home....

I hated this drudgery of recitations. I wanted the freedom enjoyed by other children in the village. Caged as I was in the house on her orders, I would watch fellow kids jealously as they squandered liberty in playful abandon. From the window I would watch them hurl stones at an orange tree to bring down a 'ball' for soccer, form the teams and chase the object about right there on the main road. Occasionally the ball bursts between a collision of feet and another is hurriedly plucked from the generous tree and the game continues, in defiance of the persistent rings from the bicycles of market women. Soon another burst and plucking and the aged owner of the oppressed tree sneaks into the sporting arena, walking-stick in hand, nabs and beats up an unlucky footballer, as the rest take to their heels, laughing noisily. I envied them.

From the moment of the divorce my life took an uglier turn. Proper divorce rites had not yet been effected. But since Mother left with all her belongings, coupled with the fact that the marriage never worked, I knew she wouldn't come back.

Mission accomplished and Father was set to go back to his base the next day. I mobilised my younger ones for a hunger strike to demand our mother's reinstatement. Father was piqued by the impudence of such a rebellion.

"So you want to go your mother's stubborn way eeh? I'm not surprised; a snake must always beget a longish thing," he roared at me.

"But Papa," I stammered, "Look at the other families in the village. I'm only trying to make peace, after all when you married Mama I was not there, I was not consulted..."

"Enough! Oh, you have grown wings already to challenge me! I'm going to make you suffer, idiot! You have taken sides with my enemy...."

In a swift moment he pulled his belt from around his waist and launched heavy strokes on me, as I ran out of the house towards the backyard. He chased me down there till I gained a safe distance. He shouted whatever threats he could think of, how he would withhold upkeep funds and make sure I was thrown out of school, how he would curse me to marry a bad wife, etc. The following morning he left for Port Harcourt. It was clear that the new enmity was now between him and me.

For days, my tears did not stop. I knew that the future that lay ahead was one of agony. I imagined the denial of upkeep funds and a schooling that hung in the balance. Grandmother was too frail to take up the motherly role. I knew of my impend-ing role to my siblings, that of a human trinity comprising a father, a mother, and an eldest brother. By the sheer tacit power of Father's dictatorial decree, Mother was banned from either visiting us or giving us anything. "She'll poison you, stay away from her if you want to live. If I hear reports that you keep in touch with her I'll kill you," he warned us before he left.

In my tearful ruminations, I wondered why divorce was not made to be as colourful as wedding ceremonies. Like, regulation demanding compulsory divorce ceremonies for parting couples, an event to be accorded the same, if not a greater enthusiasm, than the wedding pomp: printed invitation cards displaying a couple's discovery of long-sought happiness just at the exit door of marriage; an appeal to well-wishers to come share in this eureka feeling, with plenty to eat and drink. "If only there were divorce party", I mused. Ordinarily too naive to engage the topic, I had already been honed to an early manhood by the mental and corporal drilling my parents gave me. I wept so bitterly till it became a tearless humming, a humming whose instrumentation lurked in the future ahead.

The first batch of Father's torture programme was announced some months later: he abdicated responsibility for my education. Prior to the divorce, I had just completed my primary education, and was waiting for the result of my Common Entrance exam for secondary school enrolment. Suspecting that I could commandeer the money meant for my younger siblings' school fees, Father withheld all allocations to the household finally. Trouble had just begun for me, I knew. I hated him. From that period I no longer called him Father, unless in his presence. In his absence I called him by his name, Ekwueme, a name that carries a tinge of arrogance and impunity – it means the one who fulfills whatever he says.

Ogba N' Azu Aka

An Igbo epithet for a soup lacking substance, so watery it
escapes through the back of the hand towards the elbow
- be ambushed by an agile tongue.

Months after Ekwueme turned his back on us, I emaciated
due to endless brooding and poor nutrition. Abject poverty had
finally arrived following his withdrawal of financial support from
his family. For close to a year he had not visited the village.
News of his romance with an Ikwere woman kept idle village
gossips busy. A hilarious version of the story, though sarcastic,
went that he did not stop at eating the woman's love potion; he
was said to have had a thorough bath with it and, having not
used a towel, the water, with details of the charm, dried into his
body. The effect of that all-round juju penetration was a zombie
loyalty. The woman, daughter of his landlord and single mother
of two, had just found a cash cow. His month-end envelopes
went straight to her to ensure that no notes found their way to
Umuege. It was not certain whether he was truly under a spell,
but his abandonment of his mother and children on the heels of
a divorce lacked justification, such that any allusion to juju
earned instant credibility.

Signatures of poverty permeated the entire household. My
siblings acquired huge heads on spindly necks, with baskets of

ribs as stomachs. Due to late cultivation the previous year, yields from the cassava farm were poor.

Grandmother took everyone to the farm to harvest the last batch of cassava one afternoon. Silence, save for the fall of hungry feet, as we trod on a convoluted pathway that cut through a bush of mighty shrubs. She trailed at a short distance, unable to catch up with our pace. Poverty had worsened the effect of age on the 85-year-old woman. She got to the farm minutes later, and I was already busy with the harvest, as my younger ones chased locusts all around the farm.

It did not take long for me to get the tubers off the ground and have them aligned in the cane trunk we came with. I noticed that Grandmother was lost in thought where she sat under an acacia, having called her twice without her response. I knew she was worried, and went over to talk with her. Her head was bowed, and she would not look up even though she knew I was now by her side. Face down, she burrowed through the folds of wrapper around her waist and fished out the tip of her cloth where her snuff-box was ensconced inside a knot, and brought out the container. A few finger-strokes landed on the box to settle down truant bits of tobacco. Slightly she opened the box. A small pyramid of the substance was shovelled into a waiting mouth with her index finger, and brushed generously across a set of carious teeth. A gob of tobacco-ruined saliva was ejected, and she sneezed. Her eyes were teary when her face became visible. She had just attempted to feign artificiality for those tears by taking tobacco.

"Nne you're crying", I said. All her children and grandchildren called her Nne, an Igbo word for mother. For us, it sounded fonder than its synonyms.

"No my son. You should know that tears and sneeze come with taking snuff."

But I was wiser than that. I knew that tobacco was not guilty of the emotions in her voice. She had to explain that.

"Sit down, *nwam*. I'm not bothered about myself, *mba*. I'm already close to my grave. I'm worried about you, my children. This is the last set of tubers from this farm. Our new farm will yield in eight months. How will you survive when I die?"

Tears. Her efforts at restraint had broken. I listened as she continued to bemoan a tomorrow in starvation. Her crying was infectious; I joined.

"You won't die, Nne, God forbid! Nooo, you wooooont!"

My voice was tremulous. Tears, previously held back by what could be termed a manly resolve, fell freely. The sobs became louder as we hugged - a hug full of inner strength and a resolve to live and repel sorrow, to call the bluff of a common enemy and assert the hope of triumph. The other tip of her cloth unsoiled by the eye-harming contamination of snuff emerged to wipe tears in our eyes. Consolation for each other followed and we all went home to process the cassava.

The garri from the harvested cassava did not last long. Ordinarily the farm would have sustained us till the following year when the young cultivation would mature, but much of the yields had been sold to raise upkeep money. After exhausting the garri, what lay ahead was an infinite stretch of hunger. My worries redoubled, though I no longer spent hours crying in privacy. I braced for the challenges of a premature manhood thrust on me by fate. I had to devise resourceful means of survival by taking whatever menial jobs that came my way. Child labour was not much abhorred at that time. In fact it was deemed a sign of proper upbringing for kids to undertake commercial tasks meant for adults, and such kids would enjoy a reference status from parents whose kids were less physically industrious.

But most adults preferred child labour out of a selfish desire to exploit innocence. A certain man turned me into a work toy to accomplish underpriced tasks that were eventually never paid for.

The man was a naughty drunk who had lost virtually all his teeth to frequent okada accidents often caused by his drunken recklessness. He first made history in the village when he abandoned his wife in a far-away party: as soon as his wife dropped her bag on the rear seat of the okada as they were about leaving for home, he zoomed off, mistaking the thrust of the luggage on the seat as her sitting down. And he spoke all the way to the luggage in a supposed chat without suspecting the lack of response to his monologues. He had a classical intelligence to manage insolvency. If you came in the morning to demand that he should pay up his debt, he'd complain how debt-recovery was ill-suited for mornings; afternoons he'd say were too sunny for one to be confronted over debt; evenings were too late. If you refuted all the foregoing, he'd remind you how your father owed him for five years before the Biafran war and he didn't bug him, or how he rendered a similar service to your grandmother for free. On a certain day on which he had earlier on promised to pay up, my expectations and domestic calculations were disappointed: he flung out the inside of a thread-bare, dirty trouser pocket, rescued a half-chewed bitter kola into a waiting mouth, chewed it noisily and said:

"Children of nowadays are too money-conscious. When I was at your age, Victor, I didn't know the colour of money. He who dies from monetary greed does not reincarnate!"

The debt was just like that literally swallowed with the bitter kola; I gave it up.

Every morning, together with my siblings, I would go pick fallen palm fruits and nuts in the bush before going to school – I had managed to enrol in a community secondary school. We had to go early enough lest we would be beaten to the picking by rivals. Availability of the nuts and fruits depended on the season of the year, the poverty level of the palm-tree owners, and on how punctual rival nut hunters could be. Poor palm-tree owners hardly allowed their fruits to ripen and fall off, when domestic budgets would have been predicated on those fruits at the first signs of ripening, if not earlier than that. Regular inspection ensured that ripening was quickly followed by harvest, such that not a single drop of fruit would take place. Nuts came from non-harvested palm fruits whose oil essence had rotted and dried up, fallen by wind or marauding squirrels. But the abundance of poverty in Umuege meant the poverty of nuts.

It was not an easy job defying the morning dew and prickly leaves, the menace of snakes and the danger of stepping on dry and wet faeces, discharges of many villagers who had no latrines. And despite that it took several weeks to gather a sizeable heap, manual processing and low commercial value reduced the whole effort to torture.

Setting bush traps was another survival invention. Virtually every young man in the village owned trap lines. My traps had caught a few rabbits and glasscutters – and those were the only occasions that the household ate meat. Meat was a privilege more imagined than enjoyed. It was a solely Christmas goody now inserted in some other months of the year by the offerings from trap-setting. Nothing more explicitly described the elusiveness of meat than how my younger sister, Ebere, treated moments of meaty enjoyment: she would clutch rabbit limbs in her palm for the better part of a whole day, gnaw at the meat, biting off but atomic bits once every hour, when the rest of us would have since excreted our own rations. Occasionally she would rub the oily palm on her little gown, or wipe her wet nose with the back of the same palm. We eyed her and her possession enviously, rueful at our lack of her kind of discipline for savings. That was the little girl's idea of prolonging an exclusive occasion, one whose repetition lacked imminence or guarantee. Sometimes she'd fall asleep, meat in hand, and the other naughty two would carefully pull the matter out of her palm and eat it. She would wake up later and beat them thoroughly as if to make sure that whatever nutrition they got from eating the meat was lost through tears.

I did not take trap-setting seriously until my trap nabbed an antelope. It was a very happy day. The congratulations from envious faces that saw me on my way back from the bush with the animal draped over my shoulder, my own sense of achievement, and my siblings' excitement at the prospects of protein, all reinforced the viability of the occupation. I soon expanded the geography of my traps to distant bushes. One day, however, the hunter became the prey.

That morning was rainy. As I walked by my trap-path on inspection, I noticed that the next trap's hunching stick that usually held the device in a tensile position was standing erect. That was an indication of a catch or a miss. When I reached the mouth of the trap, the evidence was there –rabbit furs and blood stains everywhere, but the animal was not there. Given over-whelming proofs of trap strangulation and animal death, there was no buying the theory that the rabbit had extricated itself and escaped. I had to examine the scene further to know what really happened. Human footprints! A punctual thief was on duty, and had left with the catch. There was a general familiarity with that kind of theft among industry players! I was angry, arms akimbo. I then lowered my machete and bent to re-set the trap. It was often a task for two, but I had a way of coordinating setting the trap all by myself. As I got to the last stage where I had to properly adjust the mouth of the trap, the wooden lever, central mechanism that activates contraction, was mistakenly pushed down. And the trap caught the tip of my left thumb. I screamed helplessly as the cable wire dug into my flesh, gradually sinking to slice off my thumb from the base of my nail. There was no one to help. There was I yelping in excruciating pain, watching a part of my flesh being gradually separated from me. In a sudden burst of desperate energy I latched onto the tensile rope with my right hand, somehow, quickly suspended the tension between my hand and the hunching stick, and rescued the unlucky thumb. Ceaseless bleeding. Left palm caught hold of Independ-

ence Leaf, forcefully drew off and squeezed the leaves and
released chlorophyll on the wound. That was the local first-aid to
fresh wounds. It took months for the thumb to heal. The
incident put an end to the trap vocation.

But the trap vocation merely gave way to another drudgery
called *ohia eju*, that nocturnal hunt for snails. The bushes and
compost that separated one house from the other provided the
moisture and humus for snail habitation. Trouble was the fear of
ghosts or evil spirits, real or imagined. Owls and other eerie
creatures heightened the morbidity of nightfall with their
outlandish noises. Unconfirmed stories of encounters with night
spirits at that period by a certain lady who had gone for the hunt
were enough to discourage everyone. Soups went barren from
that period.

Given that the household had completely run out of cassava,
garri was no longer a common staple but a luxury. My earnings
from a welter of menial jobs did not add up to anything to buy
enough of the item to serve the household. The odd jobs were
not even on a steady supply to guarantee funds for fairly decent
soups. Matters got to a head and there was no longer money to
make soups, and neighbours began to contribute same as much
as their humanity could go. I had a sense of shame that impelled
reluctance to accepting such gestures, but hunger leaves little
spirit for keeping principles. I was brought up to refuse meals
from other kitchens. Each time I received such offers something died in me. It was the spirit-being of human dignity, that
thing that always died. I was now a twelve-year old man, not a
boy. Troubled by this feeling of shame, I had to invent a concoc-

tion to make sure that stomachs were always filled up, even if with useless but eatable matter.

The garden at the back of the house was green with vegetables. Shredded pumpkin, salt, onion, and palm oil were the ingredients for the world's latest cuisine, the one I had just devised. Just little water, to enable the vegetable have the upperhand in the formation. The cooking followed a special procedure: onions first took a plunge into the simmering oil, sizzling to give off neat clouds of smoke and an aroma that deceived the outside world; then the vegetable - shortly after the onions had cooked only for a short while so they could retain that crisp, sharp effect in mastication; after salt and little water, the half-done, bland vegetable broth was ready for consumption. Hands would present bowls as I would scoop spoonfuls into them. Eating was either with spoons or with hands, to ferry dripping leaves in a separation of chaff from water, into famished mouths that chewed voraciously. It went without eba. The remnant water, coloured more by chlorophyll than by oil, would be drunk as a post-meal beverage. It made the stomach murmur within as one moved around. The youngest in the house usually made a mess of the whole thing. He always sat on the floor confronting the phenomenon with bare hands, as the soup seeped through finger spaces towards his elbow....

For me, the culinary creation was a big relief. For many months, ogba n'azu aka was a daily hunger solution. Whether the meal was tasty or not was inconsequential, so long as the organs within had matter for their own functionality. The vitality in the vegetable content of the meal helped add new flesh to blot out the prominence of those ribs around.

Such improvisations did not end in the kitchen, as every other department of life was lived by significant reduction. My school uniform, for instance, summarised my destitution to the school community. I was too playful and rough. And because of the lack of a spare, my uniforms wore out too quickly. My shorts bore large perforations behind, with shoddy patches that were a riot of colours and material. My shirt was always flown out to cover the corruption behind and save me pokes from mischievous peer fingers.

But that also left me at the mercy of prowling senior students for the charge of improper dressing. On one occasion I was tossed out of the crowd during a dressing inspection in the assembly, flogged mercilessly by Moustache, a self-styled brutal teacher so nicknamed due to the child-frightening brush of thick hair above his upper lip, and asked to tuck in my shirt. I did, and the assembly was thrown into an uproarious laughter when I went back to the crowd walking backwards. It was better baring my mutilated behind to fellow students who were already familiar with it, than to a colony of insensitive teachers on the platform.

But despite my limitations, I did well in class. The youngest in my form two class in the nineties when it was prodigious to have a thirteen-year old at that level, I was a very shy, smallish student. Unproductive teachers found exoneration in my excellence in subjects that recorded mass failure. The four years that followed, however, witnessed the evil remaking of a once well-behaved boy to a delinquent.

The economic pressure at the home-front had reached a boiling point, that watershed where hunger turns aggression, the very threshold of either crime or redemptive religion. Such was a daunting social challenge heavier than the psychological containment of a teenage boy. The bulwark of religious socialisation and proper parenting was absent, and in its place was that teenage propensity for deviance. I was ready for crime given my personality cast in poverty, anger and parental negligence. All that was needed was the criminal foresight of a godfather to enlist me for misdemeanour. Waganto, my classmate, volunteered on behalf of the devil.

He began by teaching me how to smoke cigarette and how to womanize. By the time we both got to form six, truancy, pilfering and vandalism of school property, and appetite for violence had become part of us. Waganto did not earn five expulsions from five different schools in Ogoni, Rivers State, for nothing. A full-baked crime teacher that would leave Oliver Twist's Fagin green with envy, he had relocated to Imo State to break new grounds for the devil. He was tall and handsome, and owned a large chest of muscles, and was rather over-aged for secondary education having lost so many years to the dislocations in his schooling. One could hardly reconcile his handsomeness with his devilry. Greedy for crime, he was always the first to reach any robbery scene at the highway overlooked by the school. He would defy the danger of stray bullets, skulk in a corner to watch the robbery, and come back to dramatize his lessons on fellow classmates: "You! Your money or your life!" He finally ended up in the creeks of the Niger Delta as a notorious militant.

My nickname was scrawled on every available space on school walls: "Ganja On Top! Ganja '96 Was Here!" Waganto fought in school too often and earned himself peer respect. I wanted to be like him, so I craved for fight. My schoolbag drooped with the weight of weapons. A small axe, a small knife, and two empty coke bottles were in there. A tiny jotter was tucked away somewhere within the armoury. I sought every opportunity to use those weapons, especially the axe. I would sharpen it every morning at home, brandish it gleefully in a mock frenzy, and put it back in the bag playing deaf to Nne's anxious queries about this strange possession. I had not been able to put any of the weapons to use in the many gang wars that broke out in school.

I finally did, but not in a gang fight. My class had just finished a mock exam in Agriculture in preparation for the Senior School Certificate Examination. The large hall was littered with cocoyam tubers used as specimens in the exam, thrown randomly about by students. The whole place was noisy. The subject was the last in the series of mock-testing and created a false sense of final triumph, one whose celebration was in the indiscriminate hurling of tubers. I could have peacefully left the hall but I didn't, wishing that my body would just stop a flying tuber and thrust a victim on my laps. It happened. I did not need to know the culprit. I quietly opened my bag, took hold of my knife, and held a female classmate by the neck.

"Who threw the tuber at me?" I shouted.

Mortuary silence. The whole noise was instantly switched off by this vocalised menace. The fire in my eyes and my ominous clench at the girl's jugular were noise enough. Everyone watched in fright as I released the blade from its fold.

"Please it's not me! It's Christian!"

Short, stout, Christian was another mature student with an imposing presence. The crowd watched in speechified muteness: Will Victor back down in fright? Will Christian beg this small troublesome boy? Christian braced up and moved towards me.

"Yes I did, and what are you going to do about it?" he replied bravely.

An arena formed itself immediately as people moved away from the two of us as if to escape from the possible splash of blood. I sprang to my feet and pushed him back forcefully. He came back furiously towards me and was repelled by a thrust right into his belly.

"He has stabbed him!", yelled the crowd.

Christian charged towards me the second time if only to wrest the knife from me. I stabbed him again right below the navel. Stampede, as people ran for dear lives from an apparent lunatic. Blood trickled down the floor from my blood-covered stabbing fist. Christian fell down. A fellow rushed to the scene to force the weapon out of this butcher but had his wrist pierced. I saw the pool of blood, perhaps for the first time, regained some humanity, felt some immediate remorse, and fled through the bush. As I struggled with obstructing bush, my heart broke repeatedly when I heard the commotion emanating from around the scene of the fight. I feared that Christian had died.

I ran all the way home and looked like someone who had lost his mind. Nne's questions about my flustered look and my unusual early return were ignored. I quickly changed clothing and went to the back of the house where I climbed a kola tree. Lost in the foliage of the tree I started thinking about the whole incident and its possible results. Then I felt deeply sorry. I swore never to fight again or indulge in unruly behaviour if I should ever get out of the present trouble. But remorse is the wisdom that walks backwards, remedying little or nothing. Right there on the tree I began thinking deeply about my entire life, tearful.

My thinking was interrupted by the sound of a car that squealed to a halt in front of our compound. A middle-aged, stern-looking man in white cassock got off the wheels, as two policemen were sprung out of the back doors. The man in white was the Catholic priest in a nearby parish with whom Christian lived. The policemen pulled Christian's limp body out of the car and placed him on the ground, his entire abdomen soaked in red. I watched from the tree and almost fell off in trepidation. Nne rolled on the ground screaming as loud as her aged voice could go, attracting neighbours to the scene.

With the intervention of some elders in the village, however, the matter was settled without further police involvement. They offered to bear the medical cost. I only faced disciplinary action in school. It was my final year in secondary school and since Ekwueme refused to send me money to register for the school certificate exam, I missed out.

Life after school in Umuege was a bore. Days, weeks, even years just came and left, held neither any promise for, nor demanded much productive action from, a seventeen-year-old boy. I hated farming, the only useful thing that could keep one busy there. Most of my peers had been taken to the city by their guardians or older siblings. Ekwueme had no plans for me, so I wasted the subsequent three years as a village layabout playing draughts and chasing village girls. I had quite a number of such girls from neighbouring villages, and always ran into Nne's trouble in the course of my escapades. Nne was an unrepentant spoil-sport between young boys in the village and their girl-friends. Whenever she sighted a girl and a boy walk into a room, with her walking-stick she would trudge into the same room, find herself a seat and begin taking her snuff, chipping in one or two useless remarks in your conversation. It did not matter, the look on your unfortunate face, your angry silence or even protest. She would sit permanently in the room until she was sure that she had successfully aborted the sexual preparations of the pair. Soon her obstructionist mission became public knowledge among village boys, and they found a way to beat her to the game, either by dodging her surveillance or by shutting the door behind them immediately after entry. The latter did not always work. Shut your door yet Nne would wait at the thresh-old, breaking off and dumping her melon shells there. And your girl had better prepare for embarrassment as soon as your door was opened. Nne would greet her and ask her how the siesta went.

The fifth year of waste was just about to begin. In the past years Mother had kept away from Umuege in deference to Ekwueme's order, only sneaking in on occasions to see us and give us gifts whenever she sensed that Ekwueme's informants would not be around. The fear was that Ekwueme would beat me up as was always the case whenever he was told she visited. He had begun visiting home once in a while just for Nne's sake and nothing more, dropping a paltry sum for our upkeep. Mother was very worried that I had nothing doing after school, and decided to enrol me as an apprentice for spare-parts trading in Mechanic Village, Owerri. For me who, in the course of the little positive changes I experienced after school, had begun nursing ambitions for further studies, becoming a trader was totally out of the question.

"I'm not skilled in that kind of job. I don't know how to convince people to buy what they don't want, Mma. I want to go to the university," I protested.

"Do people go to school on credit? You have to grow up and face reality, there's no money for such a huge project," said Mother, in her Mbaise Igbo dialect.

I frowned, feigning anger. She cajoled me, assured that I would still go to the university later, reminding me of how most of my age-mates who were once in the village were now either apprentice traders in Onitsha or practising welders in Aba. She mentioned their names, how they would soon become rich and drive big cars while I still wallowed in the village.

"No one has said you won't go to the university. They gave an old woman a baby to cuddle and she complained of a lack of teeth – was she given the baby to bite?"

"Mama I'm not ready for your proverbs today."

"I've already concluded arrangements, my son. Your master is a nice man. He's your namesake even, a very successful young man. You can tell a lady's future looks from her mother's present appearance. His station wagon car is on lease to a driver who plies the Owerri-Okpala route, raking in a daily income for him, don't you envy him?" she asked, imploringly.

"Hmmm. So when am I to go start learning?"

"He said I should bring you to his shop so you can assess each other for two weeks. After that, both of you would know whether to sign agreement or not."

"No problem then. I'll be ready to go by next week."

She smiled. I put my things together in the following days and on the scheduled day, she and I went to my new master's shop. The shop was one of the many wooden shacks filled with all manner of greasy automobile junk known as tokunbo parts often imported from Europe, extracted from dilapidated vehicles there. Every space in the shop was filled with metal: shock-absorbers, crankshafts, brake-discs, radiators, axles, etc. The only free space was the about two-feet-wide-two-metre-long centre of the shop where bargains often took place. Floor was plain earth blackened by the accretions of grease. My master was quite hospitable. "I like him already", he said repeatedly as Mother smiled to that compliment. My face was merely wooden, for, right within me I knew I would not fit into the whole arrangement. My interest lay in education and nothing else. I just needed to be on the lookout for plausible excuses.

The excuse came in the realisation that the same shop strewn with European junk reeking of condemned oil and grease was my bedroom. A flat, dirty carton which stood for mattress would be spread on that space at the centre of the shop at night. The moisture inside was an invitation to cockroaches and other insects that hate man. They would creep into a sleeping body from under clothes, caress, bite, shit on it until the sleeper, startled to consciousness, would frantically slap parts of the body and shake out the invasion.

"Oh c'mon it's a normal thing here," said Master when I complained after the first night, "Do you know how long I slept in a much worse condition as an apprentice? Seven good years! You spend only one night and you're complaining! Every apprentice here sleeps inside a shop. Some don't even have where to sleep."

"No problem sir, I'll cope well. I guess it's a matter of time," I said, unwilling to push the matter further.

"Now you're talking. Keep your mind on the privileges of becoming a master in the future and you'll see how easy you can contain these things."

My master had a fair secondary education and was thought quite educated among his trading folk. Most of them were well-rounded illiterates. As a result, he held so many leadership positions in the market unions. I pretended to have settled into the business, praying that the two-week probation period should just end quickly. He liked me, especially with the fact that he needed an apprentice to take care of business so that he could concentrate more on his main source of income: a fairly rich mother-of-five restaurateur in the market was his lover. His daily meals came from her, plus other perquisites of gigolo romance. He stayed there often, spent nights with her in a room at the back of the restaurant. The woman's husband, a poor driver, had given up on her after several attacks on the duo strengthened rather than end the relationship. Master, with a head that looked like a volleyball placed vertically on the neck, was shamelessly stubborn in the matter. The two lovebirds were deaf to gossip.

After two weeks, I was set to return to the village to go pre-pare for the contract agreement so that the apprenticeship could commence in earnest. Master gave me a list of the things to bring along: two crates of soft drink, three crates of beer, a bottle of gin for traditional prayers, kola-nuts, etc. I stuffed the list flippantly into my travel bag as he bid me goodbye.

"Come o, your bag is full, why are you leaving with all your things if you truly intend to come back?" he asked.

"I surely will come back, Master," I assured, "These clothes are dirty, I need to wash them. Besides, there's not much space in the shop to drop things around sir."

"Okay then, I just hope you'll come back. I can always get you a better place to sleep if the problem is your sleeping in the shop."

"Aaah, no sir, I'm already used to that. I'll be back; it's in my own interest."

I left. There was no coming back. Mother felt very disappointed in me and fulminated about what she considered my lack of manly fortitude to face life. She had to find another economic engagement for me before the year ran out because she hated the fact that I had no means of survival.

Christmas for the current year came round, a very remarkable one – the new millennium was seven days behind it. Urban dwellers trooped in, and many who had not visited their village folks for years, broke the jinx. One of them was my aunt Ann, Ekwueme's niece who lived with her elder sister, Monica, in Lagos. The latter and her husband were said to be very rich. None of them was on good terms with Ekwueme, so they were unaware of the goings-on in his household. He was not in support of Monica's marriage to the man because the man had another wife from our town.

"So you mean you've been wasting away in the village for four years now and your father feels unconcerned?" Ann queried.

"Well the last time he came home," I said, "he promised he'd sign me on for apprenticeship to a mechanic in Port Harcourt but I refused because I'm not good at mechanical things. He got angry and said I was not serious with life."

"But you know your father, why would you refuse? You should have followed him, at least to leave the village."

"Was he even serious? He just said that because he knew I wouldn't like it. When I later accepted he fled and has not been seen in the village since then."

"No problem, Victor. I'll drop with you our address in Lagos so you can come and join us there. Monica's husband owns two companies; there should be a space for you."

"I'll be very grateful auntie," I cheered.

"But hey, I have to first tell Monica that you are coming. I think she'll accept."

I was overjoyed. I sent Auntie Monica a letter through Ann, stating the state of affairs and when I would come to Lagos. There was no concrete idea about what I would do there. Lagos is a big city and must have many offerings for all cadres of people, I thought. I would get a job, go to the university, put my siblings in better schools, and place Nne and Mother on a monthly grant. I would have enough money to build my own house and bring Mother back, to shame Ekwueme. A glimmer of hope had just peeped through, it seemed.

Umuege had a boring morning routine: A cacophony of crows would herald the arrival of dawn, a dawn that usually crawled in by phases of clarity. With so many trees in the vicinity holding back the sun's glance on the village, rays had to first, force their way through the treacherous spaces between serried kola leaves, and later through door crevices and roof leaks, sometimes terrifying the eyes of late risers. Hollow sounds of wicked pestles would tear through the air, alerting the world to someone's early cooking. Houses were separated by sparse vegetations of maize, pumpkin and Abakiliki yam. Every morning the palm-wine tapper's butt would go up, his pouted lips whistling away traditional war chants. His gourd would run errands up and down the palm-wine tree fetching the cream liquid, sometimes with corpses of drunk, drowned insects in a disgusting floatation.

I had my last share of this monotony one beautiful February morning in 2000, as I left for the terminus of a Lagos-bound bus service. There was a sense of excitement and anxiety. I was anxious of how Monica would receive me since she did not reply my letter authorising the visit. But the situation at hand demanded no pessimistic probing into the vagaries of the future. I seemed to have lived despair to its limits and nothing worse could lie behind it. My youthful exuberance had fizzled out since I left school and became more thoughtful about life. Much as I tried to suppress the thought of a hostile reception, that possibility haunted me throughout the duration of the journey.

The old luxurious bus finally chugged into the most chaotic city I had ever seen. Ojota's night economy was buoyed by restless Lagosians and energetic nocturnal hawkers, most of who doubled as thieves.

I was set down at Oshodi by 11 p.m. Whoever I approached for clarifications on the direction to Mafoluku either ignored or insulted me. A sarcastic fellow simply opened her mouth and pointed a finger in it and said, "Mafoluku dey inside here." For over twenty minutes I stood by my luggage crestfallen, till a Mafoluku-bound commercial bus arrived, the conductor's husky voice croaking out the destination of the bus. I hopped in.

From the last stop I boarded an okada to Ewu Street. We got there minutes before 12: 00am, and the commercial motor-cyclist was denied entry to the street by a vigilante group. I had to trace the address on my own. The numbering was random. Another half hour went into the search, and finally, I located the address. Repeated knocks at the gate and a pair of disembodied eyes cast a thorough inspection through a chink. Questions. A visitor's form was slipped to and fro the hole and the guard vanished for what seemed like an eternity. The hole was flapped open again and the eyes returned.

"Who you say you wan' see sef?"

"But I've already given details in the form...."

"Stay there dey argue", retorted the voice as its owner scoot-ed off.

Apology was shouted across to the faceless voice at the other side, the eyes returned again and all manner of accreditation followed. How are you related to madam? Does she know of your visit? When last did you see her? Why are you coming this late....?

Finally, the gate creaked open and I went in. My luggage went up on the guard's shoulder, who led the way through a walk-way that was fenced in at both sides. He kicked open a second gate to the sight of a large house that sat in front of an array of cars. A part of the open space in the compound was a lawn a little smaller than the size of an average football pitch. Two poles stood at the longitudinal ends of the lawn, with nets that had no bases tied to their tops. I wondered what all that was for – I had never seen a volleyball pitch before. A gesture showed me a vacant seat in the porch as the edifice swallowed the luggage-bearing guard. I waited. It was now 1 a.m. and I had eaten nothing all day. The guard seemed to have lost his way in the belly of the house and stayed put wherever he was. Soon, a man of hairless head in a red robe, barefooted like a rabbit, appeared, grinning.

"You are welcome my son. Come along let me take you to your room."

I followed him. The living room was so exquisitely furnished that it was scary. Through a few turns I was led into a room and the man with gorimapa left. An acrid tang of incense was the air for inhalation. The next room vibrated with the tramp of feet that danced to cacophonous jingles. I was convinced that I had fallen prey to the occult, as Monica was nowhere around. My mind went back to the guard's many questions at the gate, how he gave the impression that I was in the wrong place. What with two huge gates leading to the house! The barefooted man later appeared with a plate of stewed rice and water, giving assurances that Monica would soon show up. That the food could have been drugged made no sense to me as I was very hungry. A prey has no use of caution in a predator's belly. I prayed and the food was mowed down to the last grain, followed by a wakeful, watchful resolve, a resolve that gave in to the first incursion of sleep. Knocks at my guestroom door at dawn and a short, very beautiful woman sauntered in. Her fair, radiant skin offered a rich contrast to the black crops of hair on her chin. That was Monica the great!

"Good morning Victor, I was conducting a midnight prayer when you came, how is Nne?"

"Everyone's fine auntie, I thought I was in the wrong place. The whole place looked strange and they kept saying you were coming to see me," I answered.

"Oh, I understand. I run a spiritual church.... Anyway, I got your letter; I could have sent you a reply if not for my tight schedule."

"I thought as much."

"You see, eemmm...my husband will not allow your staying here; you'll have to go back to the village tomorrow morning."

I was numbed at that statement. That all the troubles of the journey had come to nought, culminating in having to go back to the village, left me speechless. My fare was even borrowed by Mother from a church cooperative. Monica sounded impervious to contrary, sentimental reasoning, her body language echoing finality. She left without waiting for a response, returned later with some money for my transportation back home, and met me as I was crying.

"Listen, don't think I'm callous, I don't want Ekwueme's wahala please. Go and make peace with him and take up the job waiting for you in an oil firm."

I looked up inquiringly, wondering, what job?

"Yes, the Lord revealed to me when I was praying this morning that a Good Samaritan would come pick you up to Port Harcourt for the job, in less than 21 days."

The prophecy went on and on: a job, a good car, an overseas training....The whole thing lacked credibility. I had been in the village for four years and this Samaritan held his peace till now?

"Can I at least get a direction to Ajegunle, Auntie? I have a kinsman living there who might help. I have his address."

"Oh, you don't believe the word of God? Suit yourself! I'll give you the direction."

My kinsman, Okey, lived in Ajegunle. He visited Umuege a month before for his traditional marriage, and gave me his address when I told him I had plans to migrate to Lagos. He might be of help, I thought.

The journey to Ajegunle that morning put a lie to all the reports I had heard about a beautiful Lagos. The molue bus choked with a surfeit of stinking, vociferous humanity. On the driver's naked back lived a community of healthy rashes nourished by the moisture of dirt and sweat. A half-drunk sachet of Chelsea gin that powered his mental engine dangled from his large mouth, as the vehicle roared its way to hell. Between two rows of seats was a space for standing passengers, who had only a rail above their heads as their only support against the jerkiness of the motion. The space was maximized to the last inch with a tight, linear bundle of humans. The conductor squished in-between bodies as he collected the fare. A fellow standing in front of me would not pay, and the conductor would not accept that.

"You dey show yourself abi? When I come back again make you no pay, you go see yourself."

"Mi o ni owo!" retorted the defaulting passenger, a young man in his mid-twenties, with sufficient scars on his body as his own profile statement in street hooliganism.

The conductor came back to him later, his demand more forceful, more pugnacious. The defaulter repeated his excuse of lack of money and the conductor stretched a blow onto his lips. Blood, and a fight was birthed. Each of them had only a fist and a foot for use, as the other hand for each was holding the rail above, one leg for each also steadying their footing on the floor respectively. They traded punches. Commotion. Some passengers received stray blows in the scuffle. I got one, and took it calmly. There was no escaping such deflected blows given the nearness between me the fighting duo. My shirt was stained with blood and sweaty dirt from contact with the bleeding young man fighting with the conductor. Curiously enough no one cared to separate them, and the driver acted like he did not hear the ruckus, and kept sucking his gin. At a point the fighters got tired, and the conductor left the bleeding chap promising to come back in a jiffy to push the fight to its logical conclusion.

"You go die for my hand today!" he assured.

"You no fit do anything!" rebuffed the battered fellow, still dripping blood from his mouth.

I was moved by pity and gave the beaten chap the exact fare so the matter would end. He did not thank me. And he would not pay up either! I felt stupid to have wasted my charity. The conductor came back again and they continued from where they left off, till the bus got to my stop in Ajegunle, and I alighted.

At that bus stop, another distraction caught my eyes. A danfo bus pulled up by the side of the road, and a woman hopped down from the bus and sprang towards the trunk area. The conductor raised the hatchback with one hand, with the other hand aided a basket to emerge and sit on that woman's head, as the bus rolled forward. Then from nowhere a uniformed fellow appeared, cane-in-hand. His white shirt was deemed white only because dirt had not yet completed the imposition of brown on that fabric. "Owoda!" he growled, a hand stretched towards the conductor, who was now hanging from the doorway of the slowly moving bus.

Fellow barked his demand for money, formed and brandished a left fist, running alongside the vehicle. Conductor was unmoved, his wooden countenance confirming his familiarity with that kind of threat. Angry, Fellow ran to the driver side of the bus, apparently to yank off that side of the mirror, prospective confiscation for default of payment. Shit! No mirror, perhaps his kind had smashed it in the past during a similar episode. He bolted towards the other side mirror, that one was intact. He struggled with the pull, and suddenly realised that the mirror was actually stiff at the joint where it could be tilted from, and was facing the front rather than its default position from which it should reflect rear images. It was of no use to the driver in the first place, so confiscation would be good riddance. No wonder the conductor did not put up a fight.

But he couldn't let go, Fellow. Bus was still moving slowly to enable new passengers get in. Conductor was engrossed in that guttural affair of shouting out the vehicle's destination, veins worming beneath throaty skin with each scream that made him gesture his neck like a crowing cock.

The wipers were not there, otherwise Fellow would have taken them. They were detachable, so the conductor, knowing that Fellow and his ilk were always interested in wipers, must have earlier removed them, to cock them back whenever it was raining. But there was one more prospect for seizure - one of the seats, now detachable from disrepair.

In a swift moment Fellow grabbed the long wooden panel that stood for a seat, hung it on his left shoulder, and walked briskly away, triumphant. A game-changer: conductor was stopped in the middle of an uncompleted shout, and then got down to catch up with Fellow. Arguments. Negotiation. They both walked back to the bus, still arguing. Fellow reinstated the precious piece of wood, joined the conductor to hang on the door, as bus was now moving a bit faster away. Both still haggled from their own quarters, heads above the roof of the vehicle. Finally, notes exchanged hands, and Fellow fetched a marker from a trouser pocket, and from where he was hanging stretched a hand to the windscreen, and scrawled a mark - a sign of exemption from further harassment for the day.

Now, Fellow needed to get off the bus, but bus motion was now much faster. He playfully dangled a leg towards the ground, brushed a foot on the tarmac, perhaps to test if the speed was convenient for a jump. Driver fired on, deliberately, to help make the jump as deadly as it could get. But Fellow was made of harder stuff. Suddenly he jumped down backwards, slapping both feet on the tar alternately for seconds, and the threat of harm disappeared in the sheer art he made of that sport. Another bus came around and Fellow began Episode Two...

It was later on that I understood that Fellow was a motor-park tout, member of a larger department of social malaise called Area Boys.

Ajegunle was a contrast to life, a euphemism for the lack of it. People, infrastructure, even the air itself all contradicted meaningful living, for which the city could earn an unopposed nomination as the king of slums in Nigeria. Everyone there was angry. Little delays or hitches over change from the bus conductor for fares paid resulted in expletives.

It was not difficult locating Number 8 on Ashafa Street. The road was untarred and busy. Street soccer and the noisome loitering of jobless boys and girls held sway. At the frontage of my prospective host's house, a scene was created by a couple that threw tantrums at each other. "Yeye man! Na drink and Baba Ijebu go finish you, otobo! Come cut my breast chop, you de hungry, mcheew!" The lady mimicked the sentence "I dey hungry" contorting her face in the effort. She slung her verbal assault from afar, as the crowd cheered. The man could not earn crowd support with his drab flaks, and so resorted to violence: he glanced around, picked a nearby stone and lobbed it at her but it went over her head. "Over the bar!" chorused the crowd. A naughty fellow ran commentary for the duel: the man he called America; the lady, Iraq. The lady chased the stone, caught it, and sent it back to source. Crowd ran helter-skelter as the stone flew menacingly to crash on anyone. I was standing opposite the house and waited for a safe moment to move into the building.

When I entered the building, I spotted a pretty young lady leaning on the doorway from one of the rooms. We exchanged glances severally, and smiled.

"Welcome!" she said.

"Thank you, good morning. Please I'm looking for Mr. Okey, a newly married man..."

"That's his room behind you, knock at the door," she said.

The communication cut off the formality between us and she stepped forward to help with my bag, as I knocked on the door.

"Thank you, I can carry it. It's light," I said.

"I know you can carry it, let me see if I can carry it too," she said. We smiled again. I let her have the bag.

"Iyawo! You get visitor!" she shouted, knocking a bit louder on the door. Okey's wife was inside. Her husband had gone to work, but was expected back that morning – he was on night shift the day before.

"Anyway, I'm Victor. What's your name, my friend?"

"Nse."

At that point Onyinye, Okey's wife, opened the door, and Nse left. In that short moment I looked at her quickly as she walked away. With the vibration that emanated from her back-side, I knew there was trouble ahead.

Okey's abode was the first room in a structural contraption that was no more than a dual stretch of rooms separated by a long, dark corridor. No, it was not a single room; it was double: the living room consisting of three worn-out sofas and a tacky centre-table, stopped at the opaque partition of a curtain. Behind that curtain was a room within a room, the venue of the couple's covert bedtime activities. Not that the regular moans at night from that quarter did not puncture the pretensions of that obscurity. The corridor that led to the room was cluttered with all manner of things, and served as make-shift kitchenettes to tenants. Tenants were entitled to the spaces behind their door-ways as cooking spots mostly on top of food cupboards. But no one dared leave food in those cupboards even if the largest padlocks were on guard. Most rooms had up to ten occupants, and the corridor served those who came back late from work, who could not find sleeping space in their rooms - and these were practised food thieves. Soup pots left in that corridor could be mopped thoroughly by skilled fingers till Made in China showed up.

I was well received in Okey's house. Even with a new wife and a poor income, his hospitality was amazing. It was no little sacrifice accommodating a young man in a one-room apartment. Onyinye did not particularly like my intrusive presence but she played the good wife in contrived gaiety. I understood that she wanted her marital privacy, understood that it was sheer magna-nimity to cede that privacy to indefinite, inconvenient hospitality. Those sturdy treads on my sleeping body on the floor when she moved about at night were statements of anger. I accepted the righteousness of her sense of deprivation. I needed a job as fast as I could get it so as not to overstretch my host's toleration of the burden I constituted, but I didn't even have a school certificate to start with.

It started with eloquent frowns, the waning of my reception, culminating in other forms of silent lynching. I had already spent six months in the job search and no employer seemed interested in a young man who claimed 'Awaiting Result' as the only credential. Okey's coldness issued from my refusal to take up his kind of job - he worked as a guard in a security company.

"You need to get off your high horse young man," he said to me one day, shrinking his fat face in the effort. Two parallel lines formed on his forehead, his special trademarks of deep frustration.

"With my influence, you won't be required to provide any credentials in Noble Guards, except what you already have - broad shoulders and a useful height."

Okey had a fair secondary education but seemed quite allergic to big dreams. Dehumanizing living conditions were normal and just fine to him, just as lofty ambitions were idealistic. I did not like the emerging situation of being thought lazy and useless, and decided to seek employment in the security company.

Noble Guards was a slave-driving firm that exploited the massive unemployment rate in Lagos to harness cheap labour for cut-throat profits, under working conditions that glorified the ancient slave regime. The cosy official premises with a large space for parades, a potpourri of armoured vehicles and sleek security uniforms decked with ornamental fripperies were mere constructions of organised corporate falsehood to belie the labour terrorism going on in there. I had submitted a handwritten application and was scheduled for training the following morning.

I reported a bit late, as the fresh band of slaves was already on parade.

"Left! Right! Left! Right! Faster! Faster! Faster! Faster! Stop! Fall like a tree! I said fall flat, fools!"

The military travesty was being conducted by Moses, the operations manager. Overzealous, fat and lousy, he looked like a huge bag of meat held in place by erect bones. As he raised one booted foot after the other during the parade, I noted how his K-leg looked like the legs were wrongfully inserted in his waist, left for right. Smoke-ridden saliva formed bubbles around his lips, spattering with every speech - and Moses never spoke, he barked.

"I was a commandant in the Nigerian Army; I give you military training because that is what you need. You are a real soldiers and must behave like ones...."

I watched from a corner together with some other boys that came late too. I was both amused and frightened, amused over the free entertainment in his poor grammar, and frightened over the despotism of the parade. Suddenly Moses saw us, perhaps for the first time, and growled:

"What are this fools doing here looking like morons? Join the parade or get lost!"

We all shuffled into the lines immediately.

"No no no no! Are you even fit to join us? Oya you, take a walk let me see your gait."

A fellow among us fidgeted, walked straight towards the gate but Moses shouted at him.

"Go home! You're walking like a crab! The next!"

Another adjusted himself and walked forward.

"No! You too go home! You're walking like a crab!"

Chuckles. Two more crabs and it was my turn. I already knew what Moses wanted to see, and I gave it: I bounced with exaggerated treads, springing my chest with arms floating sideways in the air. I did not walk too far else the crab crap would thunder down on me. I turned facing Moses, took a few steps, slammed my left feet on the ground and saluted. Applause! An obviously flattered Moses smiled. "Join the parade!"

After a week-long training, I was handed my work paraphernalia: a pair of fake, ugly boots; a beret; uniforms – a brown short-sleeved shirt and a black pair of trousers full of funny designs and decorations; and a whistle tethered to a lanyard, all of whose cost would be deducted from my first salary at source. I clad myself in the new identity and a sense of humiliation gripped me. The uniforms were oversized. My eyes grew misty from sad emotion.

I reported to the office that evening at Ebute-Metta for onward despatch to my beat for a permanent night duty. I opted for a permanent night duty so I could use my free daytime job-hunting in the meantime. The security job was to be a temporary pastime to enable me organise my life properly: to enable me have access to some personal funds, sit for GCE exams, and look for a better job with the O Level result to be acquired, before going for further studies. My beat was the residence of a

rich miser in Victoria Island, the managing director of a commercial bank in Lagos.

The most eccentric species of humans are lodged within the
rank and file of the security workforce. Happy fools, deviants,
crooks, thieves, decent persons - all are represented. I had three
colleagues in my beat, though I met only one on duty the day I
resumed - Reverend Akpabio - the others were on day shift.

"I'm an apostle of the Most High", he declared, as he saw
the surprise on my face when he introduced himself as "Reverend." A man in his mid-fifties, Akpabio was the father of
thirteen children from three wives. "The Bible does not forbid
polygamy, I'm a reverend my son, I know better....Children are
blessings from God, no one should ever try to curtail God's
blessings, He has a purpose for them... It is God that trains
children, whoever thinks he can fend and cater for them on
account of his own planning is a liar from the pit of hell...Any
man wey no like woman na mumu." Akpabio had a specious
defence for everything. At a point I decided not to waste intelligence anymore over a man that had obviously elected to die with
his foolishness intact.

Night, and work, began. The rich miser had gone to bed -
after collecting the ten naira change from Akpabio from the
purchase of a Sunday newspaper a week ago - and we took
position. I was at the back gate while Akpabio was at the front.
Shortly, he left the front gate and walked up to me where I sat at
the back of the house.

"You know why I like this beat?"

"No, reverend."

"For night with small money, person go just carry one of these ashewo girls wey dey waka up and down come for this backyard, fuck better fuck put for belle!"

I smiled. Akpabio was happy that I smiled. He wanted to find a sinful solidarity in this newcomer, a new being that seemed to argue too much about ethics. A prostitute later came and 'anointing' began.

My other two colleagues, Billy and Ayoola, were just as intriguing. Just for a wrap of weed, Billy would take up anyone's duty. He never boarded a bus to work from Mushin to Victoria Island, a journey of up to an hour by bus. A loaf of Agege Bread, a measure of alcoholic Agbo, and his weed were his usual solace after each day's trekking to work. Genius of awful meal combinations, Billy could eat jollof rice with bread, or pour a short of ogogoro in his tea. The result was his perpetual farting. Right in the middle of some serious discussion among guards a fart or two would escape from his butt. Everyone would laugh and he would join in the laughter – which would make matters worse: laughter would set his anal muscles free and a set of successive farts, equally explosive, would be unleashed, the sound imitative of a throttled motorcycle.

Billy's degeneration began with paroxysms of unprovoked laughter and a rapid loss of weight. He later died on his forty-fifth birthday, single, a loss I mourned for long because I saw him as the only honest person in the lot. "He died of AIDS", said Akpabio, to taint Billy's avowed chastity and make it seem like everyone were implicated in the plight of sexual addiction. Later medical reports proved lung disease and depression. "He died of Noble disease," I retorted, claiming that the inhuman work conditions in Noble Guards led to whatever led to his death.

Ayoola was the braggart in the fold. His father was always either some rich late politician or a late prince of some Yoruba kingdom. His girlfriends were all graduates, just like him. He was working as a guard "only in the meantime." That 'meantime' stood for 'indefinitely' since he never left the job.

But Billy's sickness and eventual death had a more putative ancestry than the shallow causality established in lung disease. Six months before his death, there had been a robbery incident in his previous beat. It was a small residential estate of two gates manned at night by him and another guard only. They often took turns to patrol the premises every fifteen minutes. Objects of surveillance were mainly the exotic cars of residents usually parked outside their houses in the open. With the long history of safety and absence of security breach in the estate, they became less faithful to the fifteen-minute routine-check. It happened that some thieves had been lurking around noting the guards' laxity.

One night, they had a field day, the thieves. Billy and his man were snoring away and the prowlers crept in and pillaged about fifteen cars in one fell swoop. Headlamps, rear lights, car stereos, bumpers, some dashboards, and whatever they could conveniently gorge out from the vehicles were carted away rapaciously. Perhaps the guards were engrossed in the fantasies of a dream world that offered more pleasure than they had ever gotten in their real lives and they were not in a hurry to return to reality. Or they were part of the robbery. Those were the permutations given. For, it was difficult to be convinced that such degree of plunder could be carried out without sufficient noise

to wake up any normal person. The bottom-line was that Noble
Guards was made to pay to the last kobo the cost of the repairs,
and the company held the guards responsible for the liability.
Their monthly salaries put together in three years would not
yield anything close to the expense of repairing the vehicles,
most of which were posh Mercedes-Benz and BMW cars. Moses
believed that the guards were the real thieves, and must be
tortured to extract confession.

As a former senior military officer, he had a measure of impunity. For three days he locked Billy and his colleague in a
secret cell within the company premises. The so-called cell was a
flattering name given to a four-feet-square brick store with no
window. Air sneaked in there in random generosity through
door crevices and through some spaces below the roof since the
place had no ceiling. The detained guards had mostly their
revolving stench for air. They only ate once – two little plates of
rice each – to instil little stamina in them to enable them contain
the gruelling doses of inhuman corporeal punishment Moses had
hatched for them. Clubs and kicks landed maliciously on knuck-
les, elbows, ribs, and wherever. In one variation the legs were
tied together just as the hands, and then tethered separately to a
high horizontal bar from which their sloping bodies dangled.
The blitz of pain first settled heavily on the shoulders. Then the
spine crackled from its pressured slope, and the neck ached
excruciatingly from being kept painfully upright to avoid the
concentration of blood in the head if left to hang loosely down-
wards. The whole body became an entire territory of pain. Pain
can extrude guilt from innocence. And guilt is often easier to
establish than innocence, whether by proofs or non-proofs.

Billy's colleague 'confessed' to the crime in the lack of further fortitude to bear pain, admitting that they conspired with the thieves. Asked of the whereabouts of the accomplices and the loot, he said the thieves had since disappeared with everything. Moses was too blinded by the delight in the success of his brutality to notice the incoherence in that guard's claims. For the guard, it was better to live in imposed guilt than to die in unproven innocence! His guarantor was made to pay his own part of the liability after which he was sacked.

His 'confession' made matters worse for Billy, whose continued claim of innocence infuriated Moses. Every possible contrivance of his brutish intelligence was deployed on Billy to destroy that innocence, which, for him, was criminal perseverance. Billy stuck to his guns in about two weeks of detention crying, begging, swearing to uphold whatever was left of a battered innocence – but never admitting. His poor, illiterate relatives were too inferior for the challenge, and could only beg Moses. Moses was not touched, even as his victim fainted twice. He was intent on breaking him, for the victim's containment of pain sort of ridiculed his callousness. Billy could not die and so the matter could not end. The managing director of Noble Guards later got wind of the case and interviewed the accused. He did not only believe Billy was innocent; he also ordered that he be reinstated after treatment.

But the treatment was never done professionally. Internal organs appeared to have been damaged in the course of administering torture and Billy was never the same again till he died six months after.

Billy's story got me worried about the job. We worked together only for a month before death redeployed him finally.

For the third month running I had saved nothing from my five thousand naira salary, a pittance that lacked value even in the Nigeria of 2001. I wept bitterly every night on duty, bemoaning the cycle of work-induced poverty that lacked a tendency to end. Later I worked out a plan that enabled me save half of my salary: I had to trek half the distance to work, pay ten naira to stand in molue buses to cover the other half, eat once a day and cut off all other expenses I could do without. I just needed to raise money to enrol for an external exam to obtain O-Level credentials.

Sometimes I trekked to work even if I had some money for transportation, despite that it was dangerous doing so on the expressway, occasionally worried about the storied incidents of vehicles careening off their tracks to knock passers-by off the road. Still I trekked. The distance offered accommodation to thoughts that began from questions about the human condition, to my own personal predicaments. In the main I composed poems mentally, or stumbled upon some witty mental sentences in that abstract exploration - sentences that became premises of future theories and philosophies about life. Thinking, or rather musing, made trekking very useful, made distance seem like the latitude to stretch thoughts to their logical conclusions. Sometimes too, long distances became suddenly short, reduced to insufficiency by the greediness of thought. It was often sad getting to the workplace without having concluded a piece of contemplation, interrupted by the intrusion of co-worker pleasantries and work demands. During work at night, I would find a lone spot to continue my thinking, or read a book. The beat offered the right ambience for night reading and I exploited that. But that would soon land me in trouble.

Moses always joined the night patrol team of Noble Guards supervisors. Regulation demanded that all guards must be at alert at all times, dressed in full regalia of the security uniform. Even the bottom of the trousers must be tucked into the silly boots else one would be penalized for improper dressing, and five hundred naira would be docked from the package, the value for about three days' work. The black tie sewn with plain material, same colour as the trouser uniform, must be worn also. The patrol vehicle usually pulled over at a distance to the beat to enable the supervisors walk in by stealth and nab sleeping guards.

One night, I was reading in a corner at the front beat by 2 am when Moses crept in with his men.

"Shon Sir!" I saluted.

"What do you think you're doing, reading on duty?"

"It keeps me awake sir, so I can do my job well."

"That is not allowed! If you can't do your job on your own then get lost!"

"Noted Sir!"

"And why didn't you wear your tie?"

"I thought it was meant for only day guards."

The operations manager's eyes widened in surprised anger.

"Don't be silly! Did I told you that?"

"Sorry sir, but imagine if you catch a thief and he holds you by your tie, who's under arrest between you and him?"

Moses wore that he-has-a-point kind of facial expression. He bent over the table in the security booth to sign the log book. The upper rim of his dirty boxer-shorts peeped over a skin as dark as tar. His trousers sagged from the treachery of a flat butt, his branded vest made dwarf by a greedy bulge of abdominal flesh. His breath stank of ogogoro, giving off a nasal torture which I stomached with duty-bound stoicism.

"By the way, I understand you are not on duty yesterday, why?"

"I went for medical check up sir, and my colleague was able to stand in for me."

"Your colleague was on day duty. And you make him continued like that on night shift when you knows he'll still be on day the following day?"

His English always came down in blundering spurts.

"I paid for his service sir."

"Whaaat? You mean you paaaid him?"

"Not in monetary terms sir: I prayed that he shouldn't take ill as I did. Besides, I didn't want to bother you about sick leave sir."

That was not true. I had paid Billy by bread and by the monetary value of two wraps of weed. Billy was alive then. My confession of payment was a slip I had to correct immediately, but Moses had an egoistic hatred for such smartness.

"You think you're smart abi? You have to come to the office tomorrow to answer reading on duty then. Come with all your bags and baggages. Stupid!"

Akpabio nudged me to beg Moses but I refused. I was not comfortable with having to salute my own humiliation by massaging the oppressor's ego.

Everyone feared Moses. He grew into a divine complex from the offerings of slave courtesy he enjoyed from guards and other operational staff in the company. One did not have to commit an infraction to be booted out. Getting sacked depended on Moses' mood, perhaps on what he had for dinner the previous day and the state of affairs in his home. Despite the poor working conditions in Noble Guards, a company whose name must be understood in its very contrast, no guard ever wished to be sacked: if poverty held on this possessively to men that had jobs, what would it do to those who hadn't? That was the rhetorical summarisation of guards' economic dilemma, one which Moses perfectly understood and turned into his own source of power. Sack, its threat and indiscriminate punitive deductions from guards' meagre salaries were his tools of fascism and personal enrichment. A sack could be reversed with a bribe, and threats of job termination were issued to galvanize pecuniary inducements for attenuation of offence. Those who wished to be posted to juicy beats like oil firms and embassies could give him as much as an entire month's salary or more, depending on the size of the prospective pay package. Not that such bribe guaranteed anything. It was merely a token in an entire scheme of competitive slavishness. Give the bribe, outdo others in eye-service, and pray to whatever deity you believed in. If Moses did not post you to that beat of choice after bribing him, you still had to be thankful; at least he had not sacked you. More willing slaves were out there wishing to be employed.

Your sack would be their breakthrough. You had to thank god-Moses in all things, whether good or bad. You had no choice. The few guards who had the semblance of a cordial relationship with him, who were seen publicly laughing and shaking hands with him, were demigods. Privileged slaves to petty salaries exchanged for maximum efforts. They had immunity, or rather, impunity. No, both. They were the beat supervisors, collective prefects of capitalism who absented from work at will, who reported their fellow guards to the fascist authority for a pat on the back or a share of the king's hollow grin.

The next day at the office, Moses barked endlessly. Explanations rendered in good English infuriated him and I continued to annoy him unwittingly. The subtle apologies I offered were even with utmost condescension. I had much self esteem and pride, a sense of self that bothered on arrogance. The difference between him and me was that my own arrogance was borne out of purpose and conviction, an arrogance that hated arrogance. Moses fumed even the more:

"You dey speak grammar dey show yourself abi? You no go last for this company. You're hereby redeployed to Eagle Bank at Oke-Arin where mosquitoes will teach you a lesson. Resume there Saturday evening."

That Saturday turned out to be a day I would never forget in a hurry. It was a day for the Adamu Orisa Play, a day set aside to mark the popular Lagos Eyo Festival, a tourist event which often featured stick-wielding, white-clad masquerades that moved about the nucleus of Lagos Island in festive frenzy. The stick was supposed to be modest, often the base part of coconut frond, mainly a cultural prop in the masquerade's enchanting dance. There had been reports of Eyo masquerades beating passers-by who had any prohibited items on them, items like worn footwear, smouldering cigarettes, etc. An ordinarily colourful event rich in cultural display and grand rituals, it yet suffered corruption by the riff-raff who would wear the Eyo mask, get drunk and bludgeon whoever they saw to a pulp with sticks big enough for murder. Frequent warnings by the state government asking masquerades to desist from beating people were a waste of words to those riff-raff, the so-called Area Boys.

My new beat was around the venue of the event, where thousands of the masquerades were cached. I was still new to Lagos and did not fully understand the pros and cons of the festival, what was forbidden, etc. I had my sandals on. On my way to the beat, I passed through where many of the masquerades were quaffing alcohol. As I walked innocently past their congregation, one of them came from behind and unleashed an impressive slap on my chin with a flat, heavy stick. I recoiled in pain, grabbed him and tried to snatch the stick from the faceless attacker, not having understood the motivation behind the battery. While I engaged one masquerade in a brawl, tonnes of others thronged the scene with even bigger sticks, pummelling me pitiably with whatever malice they could muster. My body was virtually shared by the beaters, each concentrating on a part in contributory beating. I ran, shrieking helplessly. But the drunken feet of my attackers were faster, and I was soon brought down. Passers-by screamed for mercy, others bawled at me to yank off my sandals. I was too soaked in pain to hear anything, other than the twang of huge sticks landing on my body. I did not know how the sandals left my feet, and the men

finally abandoned my sprawling body on the ground. Sympathis-
ers came around and soothed me, dusted up my clothes and
cleaned up the blood stains all over me. I could not stand, let
alone walk. The masquerades knocked the sandals off my feet
with their cudgels and rendered that part temporarily useless. My
helpers massaged the feet, tugged, and tilted it to re-adjust the
dislocation I felt there. In the end I managed to limp to my beat,
more enlightened than before.

The new beat was a dumping ground for guards sentenced
to death by working. The bank was stuck somewhere within the
rowdy Ebute-Ero market, occupying the ground and first floor
in a four-storey building. The veranda upstairs was the only
space for night guards. With no booth for the storage of uniforms and other personal work effects, guards had to stuff same
in polythene bags hidden from the reach of rainwater. The
market was the capital of dirt. Burst waste pipes from upper
floors urinated faecal effluent on guards at every flush of waste
matter. Drainage stench produced an atmospheric pollution that
kept noses regularly clenched, opened only out of respiratory
necessity for the inhalation of life and death. Guards sat helplessly at the open veranda when it rained at night. The environment legally belonged to mosquitoes and they repelled every
human encroachment. Hands were buried in long, thick stock-
ings, heads in wool scarves punctured at the nasal point. Hardly
was any bodily space uncovered, but the syringes that pierced
knew no barrier. Heat from thick clothing was the alternative to
mosquito bites.

But despite the deplorable working environment, the bank's
branch marketing manager added to the harrowing experience of

the guards. A tall, handsome personification of pomposity, he felt too big to share humanity with people of lower social status. He bullied everyone, sent guards on private errands without any sense of gratitude for such favours. He was said to have studied in the US, and he flaunted that with an annoying, nasalised intonation filled with profanities. I had stomached his abuses for too long and soon prayed for an opportunity to dress him down and earn manumission for myself and my colleagues. I was being driven by a certain knack for purposeful rebellion. We were contract staff and were not answerable to the haughty man. The operations manager, overall boss of the branch to whom even this American wanna-be reported, was most humane and friendly to everyone. People, including junior bank staff, grouched about the high-handedness secretly but no one was bold enough to end it.

Not long enough, Providence presented me with a chance to speak some sense into the bully's head. A lady came looking for the Yankee manager by 7 p.m., when work had officially ended and all staff but he had left. I called his office via the intercom to be authorised to let the lady in but rather received some bashing.

"Haven't you seen that lady before, are you so daft? Asshole!" He hung up on me, and I consequently denied the young lady entry so that the bull would come down from his upper-room office. He charged down to the gate thumping out more intimidation.

"If I worked for you in your house sir, and let every familiar guest in without your authorisation, would you feel justified in paying me?" I asked.

"I can't even employ you," the manager sneered.

"I can't even work for a corporate tout," came my reply.

Totally humiliated by the tout tag in front of a lover, the manager rained abuses on me and threatened to report me to Noble Guards, to which I simply riposted: "With this whole vibration and hollow mouthing, haven't you proved me right that the title is truly yours?" It was as if more fuel were poured into a raging fire. Lover-girl pulled her man away from possible use of fists. My colleague was only too happy, closed his mouth in furtive laughter in the excitation brought about by the whole drama. The next day nothing happened, no one had been reported. The manager seemed to have had some quiet time at home, and resolved to go on transfer to another branch, or perhaps fate helped abbreviate his shame by creating space elsewhere. He left and the matter ended.

Voyage into Self

Onyinye's silent hostility tore me apart. Her smiles disappeared whenever I entered any scene where she was. I had begun making monthly contributions towards upkeep funds in the house but she was not impressed, and continued to scoop the top of soups to disallow substance in my rations. She sat idly by all day and I would have to return from work each morning to a barrage of domestic chores, from dish-washing to even making the bed where she would lie with her husband at night. Okey appeared to have noticed the covert enslavement going on in his house but he was too steeped in love to caution the lady, who was my junior in secondary school. With Onyinye and Moses meting out hatred from both ends, I lacked peace.

Apart from sitting for the external O Level exam which I passed excellently, nothing else had been achieved, not even sufficient savings to rent my own apartment in my two-year sojourn in Lagos. If I had to continue in that job saving half of my monthly salary, I needed about five years to be able to rent a ramshackle single room in Ajegunle given the prevailing cost of housing. There was yet an imminent threat of accommodation loss judging from Onyinye's now constant spitting, the very sign of an early pregnancy. Her mother would have to visit Lagos for Omugwo, and my sleeping space on the floor would soon have a new owner. Life for me held no promise.

I sat one afternoon at the back of the house brooding. I still had some time left before leaving for night duty. Suddenly from one of the shacks that stood for a bathroom she emerged, covered in beads of bathwater. A piece of scanty, light-tissue wrapper ran from her cleavages down to the neck of her smooth thighs, making very explicit revelations in the wetness of the cloth. Buttocks were well-rounded projections that swung in seductive circles with assisted freedom, as Nse wriggled them provocatively. Right from that first day I came to Okey's house, I felt deeply attracted to her. She was beautiful and intelligent. I could not woo her given the many worries I had to contend with at the time. But that evening she looked sexier than before. Her presence monopolised my thoughts from that moment. Nne's oft-repeated mantra rang in my mind: money is like the cooked head of an animal, and women are like the ears attached to that head; he who has the head already has the ears.

I had lived in celibacy for long and Okey taunted me too often for that. He 'promised' to drill a hole for me in the wall of the back fence. He said he would lubricate the hole with okro soup so that I could satisfy my sexual urges there:

"I saw it again early this morning while you were sleeping, your erection. It stood exactly like a gear lever. I'll soon fulfil my promise to a brother", he'd always say, laughing noisily.

"I'm not keen on sex right now, oga. I have bigger worries", I'd reply.

"Make I hear word," he'd always counter, "Konji wan' kill you, you stay here dey talk of bigger worries, na only you get problem? Still your boxers dey grow horn every morning."

Konji is the slang word for sexual starvation.

Nse and her okada-rider elder brother lived in one of the rooms in the compound. She was waiting for university admission.   Whenever we ran into each other in the compound she would smile and roll her eyes in that shakara fashion. I would struggle to suppress my excitement, smiling. My liking for her grew. We had a bond, unspoken. Sometimes when Onyinye was not around, Nse would visit, on the pretext of wanting to borrow a home video cassette, always clad in attires that flaunted her curves. We silently sought opportunities to say hello, and smile to each other.

She had left for pre-natal care that afternoon, Onyinye, and Nse sneaked in as usual, having dressed up after I earlier saw her leaving the bathroom. This particular visit seemed like a chance for me to say something concrete.

"Bros, do you have any past GCE question papers?" she asked, smiling as usual.

Without waiting for an answer, she sank into a sofa facing me, and I was just in the right mood for anything. Her mini skirt shrank further to bare more luscious details of her fair, spotless thighs partially spread to show her underpants. My eyes shone and my boxer-shorts revealed my bulge. She saw it, and stood up. A hug. Her tongue found my left earlobe, tickled it and made its way down to the back of my neck. Gently she lowered me on the sofa and we kissed each other with all the passion in the world. Her flicking tongue made its way from my hairless chest down to my thighs, and elsewhere. I hmmed and aahed. She moved from one erogenous zone of my body to the other, until we finally got locked in the tangle of carefree sex. A relationship had just been consummated. The episodes were repeated a dozen times whenever we found the opportunity, sometimes at the risk of being caught pants down. Nse gave all: love, sex, Calabar meals. She became the only source of joy in my troubled world.

The joy was short-lived, however. Nse got pregnant. Abortion was the only option open to us but I could not afford the ten thousand naira demanded by the quack doctor – Noble Guards had not paid salaries in three months. I had lent my little savings to a friend who promised refund in a month but defaulted indefinitely. Two months yet nothing had been done about the pregnancy and she became increasingly worried. I decided to confide in Okey and seek financial help. Okey's reaction was a burst of derisive laughter and "Happy father's day in advance." The same person who had been pushing me to have sex had turned around to mock me because I did. A lesson was learnt.

A colleague at work finally came to my aid and the pregnancy was aborted. Post-abortion bleeding with stomach upset became yet another hurdle. Nse lost much weight and became sickly. Suspicions. Her brother was fed with all manner of gossip by neighbours concerning her affair with me, and he subjected her to endless questioning. Her health further deteriorated and one afternoon, she passed out. The secret was blown open by the doctor after her revival at the hospital. Her brother came back from the hospital to fight Okey's household. Altercations, verbal exchanges ensued.

"Wey that Victor guy? If them send am to come destroy my sister make he tell them say him no see her. Make he come out here now!"

People gathered. Onyinye was just too happy that a prima-facie case for my eviction had just been established. It was all in her countenance, that God-don-catch-you kind of expression. I was engulfed in shame and frustration, and hid myself somewhere around. The abortion matter was later settled by Okey, who would continue wearing a long face such that I was assailed by the fear of eviction.

Okey was said to have evicted his childhood friend before he got married. He had lived with the friend for several years in that compound. A little misunderstanding broke out between them and he asked the said friend to leave the house by the end of a certain month. The other, who thought it was a joke, came back from work by 11.00 in the night on the day the ultimatum expired, and met a shocker. He was kicked out at that time of the night. He had nowhere to go to that night, and was walking aimlessly on the streets of Lagos until he spotted a bachelor's eve party going on somewhere. He mixed with the crowd and the next day, he joined a community of beach squatters on Lagos Island.

When Nse, after recovery, told me the story since she was around when it happened, she was being very apprehensive in the light of what Okey was capable of doing. She felt equally awkward being caught up in the midst of the whole situation. But I was unmoved.

"I'm no longer bothered about that, Nse. I can withstand anything that happens," I bragged.

"You're just acting the superman, how will you cope if you lose the roof over your head?"

"See, if it does not happen it'll be good; if it happens it'll be better. I'll get a mosquito net and will be sleeping on this corridor."

"Can you imagine what you're saying? How could it possibly be better to lose your accommodation?"

"It'll be better because it'll sweeten my story in the end; it'll add much flavour to the experience I shall recount someday. Not that I'd like to go through such an ugly experience, no. But one must always find a positive side to every challenge. It helps to keep one moving."

She nodded. She was my angel at that period. Despite all what her brother did to stifle her interest in the relationship she never budged. But she later earned admission into the University of Calabar leaving me totally heartbroken by her departure. With her leaving, I became instantly orphaned: there was no one to talk to, no emotional support to help in my life struggle. I was lonely in the midst of people, thought so much that I took ill. It was a life that had no substance in it, completely vacuous in the present and in the future. I began to ask introspective questions, making attributions to spiritual diabolism. Misfortune is the father of superstition. My woes must be spiritual, I concluded.

The spiritual churches I visited varied and amplified my confusion. I was lost in the labyrinth of prophetic declarations. At one place, I was told that Ekwueme had spiritually sealed my destiny; at another, that there was an ancestral curse upon me. A third said my paternal uncle had shot down my star spiritually. Prayer after prayer. Fasting and seed-sowing, yet nothing changed in my life. A fellow prescribed yet another spiritual house. "It's the final bus stop; stubborn shackles are loosened there by our father in the Lord." My spiritual shackles appeared to have been forged with something stronger than iron since there was no breakthrough after a visit to that church. All I wanted was a change in my circumstances, a better job to enable me rent my own abode, and pursue higher education. So I could not understand why God would not look into my petitions, ordinary as they were. I had now become extremely despondent; my mind had reached a critical state of despair. Finally, I was fed up, and gave up on spiritual solutions.

With my fair O Level result, I thought I would be able to get a fairly decent job so that I could quit the security one. The female vendor that had a newsstand at a junction close to the house was of help, so to speak. Tuesday editions of The Guardian newspaper had columns for job vacancies. I could not afford the paper, so the vendor would allow me skim through for twenty naira. I inadvertently alerted her to that aspect of the business such that in no time she started offering the same service to erstwhile free readers. Job seekers came in droves to pay to skim through vacancy editions. For long after so many attempts, I could not get any response from the firms to which I submitted application letters. The lady observed that I kept coming while some others had stopped, having gained employment through the medium.

"God go do am, you hear? Him don already settle plenty people from this stand", she assured.

"Amen. I don de tire sef. I hear say most of the vacancies wey them dey advertise na just camouflage. Them don know who them go put for the jobs already. The advert na formality."

"Na true sha. But atimes na matter of the kain result wey you carry. And the school wey you go. Where you graduate from?"

I could not answer the question and quickly changed the topic. That was the last day I ever went to that newsstand. It dawned on me that I needed to be more educated to stand a chance in the first place, that multiple credit passes and a few alphas in GCE were too ordinary to get me a decent job just like that. I had to adopt a new strategy.

It had to do with registering with an employment bureau. Usually the bureau would help one get a job and take the first month's salary as recompense. After closing from night duty each morning I would journey down to the agency's office at Ojuelegba to know if there was any placement for me. It was beginning to take longer than I expected and the lady at that office had got tired of my importunate demands for placement and my plaint about waste of money on transportation, especially given that I had refused taking some offers in the past.

"Gentleman I suggest you drop a phone number. You don't have to come down here everyday, do you?", she snapped.

"Well if only you'd got me a job by now I'd have bought a phone."

"If only you'd taken the offers we gave you before..."

"What offers? One was the job of a houseboy. The other, that of a salesman for a Lebanese firm. I didn't have to pay your agency and come here every morning if I wanted to be a slave. The day you cajoled me to register you made it seem like I'd soon be bombarded with job offers."

She went mute, but visibly angry. Her hand rummaged through her sleek handbag, brought out a small mirror and a tiny duster, and she started applying make-up. Every woman is an artist. In that short instant a new layer of borrowed beauty ran over her face in a smooth garment of clay worn over facial potholes and bumps: the duster would go down into her make-up kit, pinch the clay powder and caress her face; it soon moved to another powder case in the kit whose substance was redder, mopped it, and made a funny, round impression on her cheeks – they call it blush. I watched the artistry in suppressed rage. She inserted crisp black lines on her bald brows, inspected the perfection of her craft in that mirror, and distended her lips into a pseudo smiley so that the lip gloss could be laid evenly. She began the process all over again. The image in the mirror probably fell short of costuming standards. Her fair face wrinkled with displeasure, either from the failure of her creative task or from my redundant presence. I was beginning to lose my cool, but yet managed to talk to her in a courteous manner:

"Why are you keeping quiet, madam? And what am I supposed to do since I don't have a phone number and can't be coming down here daily?" I queried.

"What else do I say? You don't have a degree and you're being too choosy."

I was ostensibly galled by that statement but I held myself back from flaring up. At that point the lady's superior who overheard the argument from an adjoining office came to the scene, asked her a question in Yoruba and told me to sit down. There was a question about this or that file and finally, a company name and address were scribbled on a piece of paper and handed to me.

"Go and check out this company," the superior said, adding, "If you're free you can go this morning, they need an employee urgently."

"Thank you sir."

"Don't mention. Good luck."

At first, I was taken aback by the address of the company written on the piece of paper: Railway Line, Ijora. That part of Ijora did not seem like where a serious-minded company could be sited. Against my doubts I set out to locate the address. At the particular spot on Railway Line where the said company was supposed to be, I could not see anything that looked like a corporate building. I went back and forth looking for number 14. There was a house in a total state of disrepair that had "14" on its wall but that could not possibly be a corporate office. No one seemed to know the name of the company I was asking for, so I had to approach the ugly, wretched house to see if its occupants could clarify if there was old and new numbering.

The people I met there were busy: a lady with a long pestle was turning amala in a huge mortar; another was thumping ewedu in a bowl with broomsticks; yet another worked on the fire embers to worsen the plight of the ingredients in a large black pot that sat on the fire. Some other ladies that were dressed like waitresses dusted up the plastic chairs and tables arranged at a side of the building in the manner of local canteens. A stinky drainage channel ran just by the side of the makeshift kitchen. Unpainted walls, a dirty floor, and the buzz of houseflies around a few unwashed dishes all enhanced the flamboyance of filth. I sighted an older woman that seemed like the owner of the place and walked up to her. So fat and round, her massive buttocks filled up the virtual square-metre space of a plastic chair, with a large remainder of pelvic flesh protruding at both sides. The lady at the fireside scooped into a bowl a large piece of meat, about the size of a puppy's head, amid a small stream of stew and presented to Madam to have a taste and pass culinary judgment. Madam gnawed at the meat, swiftly threw it down into the bowl, blowing air onto the scalded fingers, as the meat effused smoke. More oral air settled on the beef and she lifted the luggage for a second attempt. Teeth could not sink in and she threw it down again. "Ah, e never done, Dupe. O ga o, na woman cow be this." Female cow is said to make hard beef. But she would not let the meat be. A third attempt, only half of the meat was now visible, the other half shut in by a clench of teeth. Her head went back, as her hand pulled the dangling arterial beef to forcefully break its elasticity. No way. She persisted, eyes shut, and facial nerves prominent in muscular exertion as the pull became an Olympic affair. I stood in her front, unable to make inquiries from a woman that obviously lacked peace. Madam continued. The last pull took longer, and longer, until her gums lost fortitude to bear the heat, and her teeth were about to be uprooted. She could no longer bear the pain and immediately released her hand. And the meat was forcefully slung onto my crotch!

"Jeez!" I screamed.

"Ah! Sorry oo,aaaahh!"

I was short of words. She apologized a dozen times, brought water and detergent for me to clean the mess. That done, I smiled. And everyone burst into laughter.

"Anyway, ekaaro ma", I said.

"Ekaaro o, omo mi, ki le fe? E ma binu o."

"No wahala ma."

All the while that I had been in Lagos no matter how hard I tried I could not understand Yoruba beyond the greetings and of course the insults, and a smattering of common conversational lines.

"But maami, mi o gbo Yoruba o," I said, still smiling.

"You no understand Yoruba still yet you dey speak am", the woman remarked jokingly.

"Mummy I'm looking for C & C Ventures Limited, it's supposed to be on number 14 but I can't see any structure or signpost to identify it."

"Hahahaha, signpost ko, sign-field ni, omo Ibo, you don' reach where you dey go o jare."

"I don't understand ma. I come from an agency in Ojuelegba for work matter. Them say one company, C & C Ventures, dey find male worker. Them no talk say na canteen."

"Woo, me I don't know o. See that wall, wetin them write there?" she asked.

I turned towards the direction she was pointing at and saw "C and C Ventures Limited" written there, made partially invisible by the overlay of smoke.

"Oh,oh,oh, na you them send for us? We tell them say we need male workers. Hahaha, you sef no fit do the job, you wey be like bomboy", she quipped.

I was shocked! Madam and the other ladies in the canteen made jest of me in Yoruba, laughing mockingly at the whole situation. When I protested at the agency the following evening, the lady guffawed to the point of annoyance, claiming she did not know about the company's specialty since its name did not suggest anything. While I argued with her, through the window louvers in the next office I saw that her superior was counting a few bundles of money. The man looked thoroughly fulfilled – it was another good day. That was the day's harvest from an ever-growing army of unemployed Lagosians, who constituted a lucrative industry to be harnessed through organised thievery. The man sat there smiling in sheepish joy, flipping dirty notes contributed from even dirtier menial jobs: a finger would touch his wet tongue, run briskly over the notes, and soon get stuck in a lack of friction. The tongue would crawl out again to lubricate his manual system of corrupt-money accounting, literally. There he sat, the man, a human evidence of human predatoriness, thriving in his cannibalism of helpless minds, feeding fat from the commercialisation of external poverty. I suddenly realised my victim status and resolved never to go back to the agency again.

At work nothing had changed for the better. On my way to work one day, I stopped over at the open stalls that sold rusty books under the pedestrian bridge at CMS, Lagos Island. Dirty, classical works dotted with cockroach eggs were displayed for sale at ridiculously cheap rates: Plato's Magnesia; Ovid's Meta-morphoses; Karl Marx's Philosophy of Misery, etc. There were also works by Rene Descartes, Tacitus, Homer and more. A certain fat volume had the simple title Essays. Those other grand titles like Theistic Humanism, Epistemology, The World of Forms, and so on, seemed too complex for my naive mind. I wondered why anyone would buy such perplexing titles – but later in the future they would become objects of my intellectual gormandizing. With one hundred naira, I bought Essays by a

French writer and philosopher, Michel de Montaigne. I was struck by the statement in the preface, where the author claimed that his book was "a vain subject which no one should bother himself about." I later discovered that to be a mark of the usual sense of intellectual humility and modesty for which philosophers, especially those of Socratic conviction, were known. Large as the Bible, Montaigne's Essays had a word for virtually every concept: Life, Death, Poverty, Wealth, Anger, Wisdom, etc. I was stuck. More and more visits under the pedestrian bridge and I became the proud owner of a massive collection of classics.

The reading offered a special kind of pleasure totally inexplicable in its seductive charm. I had found something comforting that gave me insights into life, and made me genuinely think for myself. Days became enthusiastic pages in knowledge acquisition. Nothing else mattered but intellectual pursuit. I cherished the opportunity of holding discussions with ancient sages by flipping through the pages of their written thoughts. Gradually I became a master of my own thoughts, and world. From classical to medieval philosophy, then to sociology and law, I read everything I could find. The spirituality that just elapsed became a source of self-ridicule and retrospective humour. I noted the partial vindication of that Marxian claim that religion is the sigh of the oppressed creature. I had finally discovered myself within the rottenness of Under Bridge, and explanations to my predicaments were offered in the sociological context of a dysfunctional family situation and a humdrum national economy, both of which trammelled proper parenting and productive employment. There was nothing spiritual about my misfortunes, I dismissed.

Under Bridge, that Nigerian metaphor for squalor, marked the paradox of a triumph scavenged from ruins, of finding essence in debris. That triumph was inward, that point when my real self erupted from within me, and led the way to higher pursuits. I no longer saw inhibitions on my path, no longer gave poverty the privilege to harass my soul as it did my body. Philosophy became a positive distraction from an earlier fixation with material worries, an inner passion for making love to life at a sublime level. My being content with life and being happy without any physical stimulation for the feeling were of surprise to many, who converted that surprise to a mockery of what they saw as self-delusion. They could not understand how someone could find exciting substance in merely reading tasteless volumes scripted by dead, mainly unknown, thinkers; how intellectual orgasm could be reached in the mere invocation of Fanonian ethos, or in the appropriation of that Cartesian pride:

"To live without philosophising is tantamount to keeping one's eyes closed without ever trying to open them."

Under Bridge was the point of embarkation into self.

The spiritual experimentation of the past ignited in me a new thirst to study religion, that closed-minded system by which groups hate one another in eye-service to God. There began a search for Truth, one that took me through many Faiths, from Islam to Eckankar, Krishna, Hinduism, Christianity and even traditional religion. I tried as much as I could to be objective in my search, invoking that Husserlian doctrine in Phenomenology of putting one's old beliefs in brackets and approaching an investigation with a mind free from cultural interference. Temples of each of these religions were visited in feigned innocence, as a new convert who had come to learn Truth. At some point I inwardly scoffed at the arrogant certitude with which each claimed the monopoly of that Truth, each refusing to concede validity to others. I found myself breaking the Husserlian rule of not allowing previous knowledge filter into the investigation. Some religious teachers seemed to me as ignorant folks who read just a single Book and were all over the place asserting absolute knowledge. "They're under the illusion of knowledge. Part of the problem with religion is that the Holy Books are made available to every trader and artisan, to people lacking the intellectual eligibility to understand Truth. Fanaticism is often more fertilized by illiteracy," I thought.

My investigation led me into further doubt rather than conviction, for each Faith had question marks in one thing or the other. I began doubting the existence of God, tinkering with the thought that the Early Man must have invented Him as a morality construct to wean people from evil? Beyond the accounts of religious literatures, parental indoctrination and perhaps some subjective metaphysical experiences, is there possibly any empirical evidence of His existence? I needed to settle my doubts outside the walls of recorded history. Some atheists have contested the logic that man cannot exist out of nothing on his own. They hold that if God, a more complex Being, could exist on His own, how come man, a less complex one, couldn't? And those revelations in abiogenesis, thermodynamics and naturalism did not totally lack appeal in their demonstration that Life was brought about by an Impersonal Cause.

There was yet the suspicion in how all dominant religions had to come from outside of Africa. Are they part of imperial cultural expansionism or sheer coincidence? I needed definite answers.

Answers were needed to that central question: why did man come to be? Not just Who made man but why was he made. If creationism is true, why would an omniscient God create the devil and man, knowing how they would turn out in the future, only to regret so doing later? It's not as if He needs man for His own validation, or does He? Why create man when He could stay in the world as He met it, enjoy complete peace, and not get disturbed by endless requests, and angered by recurring sins? Why bring His beloved children into the same world where the devil already is, and let them slug it out with that rascal? Then He opened two books, of life and death, to register candidates for heaven and hell depending on performance, when all that trouble would have been saved by simply not creating? Some theists argue that He created man out of love, out of a wish to share His divine nature with His creation, and that He gave man a free will to choose between good and evil. But I did not choose to be born in the first place; He made the choice for me, so where is the free will? Then the concept of Hell negates the very idea of free will: if someone threatens that he'll harm you forever should you fail to do his bid, how are you free in the circumstance? I needed answers to all these. I was allergic to accepting things without investigation.

Put in brackets was that account in most Abrahamic religions that God created only two people in the beginning. It was way too curious to accept that the Igbo man in my native Umuege, the Chinese, the Indian, the American, etc., are all the progeny of that aboriginal pair, yet these offspring lack appreciable biological, cultural and religious connections other than the fact that they are all humans. What racial identity were the first parents? What racial imagery do we have of God, white or black?

But atheism had even more question marks. The ontological question of how man came to be and how phenomena evolved has not been properly addressed. Creationism seemed as weak a theory as evolutionism: the former left the issue of the evolution of the First Cause, God, totally to what seemed like superstition; the latter left it to the ramblings of the dubious science of organism metamorphosis or molecular interrelationships. The two schools of thought were enmeshed in the flaw of infinite regression: in the evolution theory, what caused that minutest form or organism from which evolution took off? In the other, what caused the first creating Being? And then how does one explain miracles if God does not exist? If spirituality is true, that source of juju and miracles alike, then it follows invariably that supernatural dualism is real. That is, there are both evil and good forces, not complementary but antagonistic to each other, the spiritual modules of God and devil. My head was virtually spinning out of my neck! Nothing but the invocation of that Kantian example of limiting knowledge to make place for Faith seemed more like it. And Montaigne's paradox mocked at the entire effort in that defeatist submission:

"Inquisition is the beginning of all philosophy; confusion the progress, and ignorance, the end."

I was lost in the maze of the pursuit of certainty, and concluded that since both philosophy and science lacked definite answers to the questions I had, I must embrace faith to supply whatever was missing and leave matters at that. I set aside all my doubts, designating them as belonging in the province of Mystery, to be unravelled if not in life, then, in death – or never at all. While I granted that man lacked the justification to make objective – absolute – Truth claims, I accepted that the quest to scavenge for Truth must be kept alive. For, to totally resign from such inquiry is indolence; to assert absoluteness is to play omniscience. The middle-point position, which I later learnt to be close to the term Fallibilism, seemed quite appealing to me.

I therefore, finally embraced Christianity afresh – as a rational Christian theist.

Socratic philosophy cautioned against giving in to bodily pleasure and pain. The word was moderation, or indifference. I became born-again into this new conviction, became unmoved by the stark economic realities around me. Nothing more than The Lord's Prayer was enough for the day, for I believed all necessary supplications were contained therein. I felt that no craving should be so important to the individual that he should surrender his human dignity to the authority of a piece of want, and make him turn praying into physical gyrations and voluntary seizures. Indifference to the euphoria of material things and one would be truly free. I had no material possessions in the first place, so whenever I dismissed materialism, my new colleague in the Oke-Arin beat would criticise me for condemning something simply because I lacked it. Just as rich people who preach disdain for money are accused of selfishly discouraging others from having what they have. But deep down in me there was now a genuine contempt for material things.

I soon groomed an unwavering spirit to challenge convention. Opinions, practices and norms no longer earned validity on
account of majority backing, but only after satisfactory evidence
of objective truth. I incurred the hatred of many for questioning
certain religious and social practices. Not that I cared. It is
always difficult for men to contain attacks on established values,
no matter how rationally sound such attacks are. Emotions are
often chosen over reason. Society has a herd mentality, so the
individual proposing a counter-culture, even if his proposition is
superior to the firmly entrenched prevailing tradition, is on a
lonely trip.

I became a very happy man in my world of lack. I did not
hate economic wellbeing, only its flaunting. With a mind firmed
up in learning, I decided it was time to recreate my socio-
economic life. I needed to make money first to be qualified to
despise it. But that required vision which, I recognized, was non-
existent in my life.

A clear articulation of vision is often the take-off point in the
drive for self-actualisation. To live life without a mental picture
of the tomorrow which one desires, without a demonstrable
architecture of how that tomorrow will come into being, is to be
a foolish, indolent dreamer. The individual who does not wake
up every morning to the thought of some noble ideal which he
labours continuously to bring into pragmatic being, by which he
intends to earn his own little space in history, is occupying the
world's space, depleting its resources and contributing to its
problems, for nothing. His validation ends only in his status as a
market variable in the statistics of consumers. Without vision,
human life holds little difference from animal life. For, it belongs

to goats and birds to wake up every day without a construct about life, only to eat and procreate. I felt, therefore, that to live just to work and eat, raise children, train them and die is to under-utilize the human self, to have about the same aspiration as lesser animals.

Vision must not necessarily be about the invention of some new, unprecedented type of jet engine from the blues, or the creation of new theories of science. Let it be anything that adds value to life beyond the self, which registers the individual's earthly presence in the hearts of fellow men; a life-surpassing validation of life. Yet a vision, even with the accompaniment of a framework for its attainment, is a mere intellectual exercise if the individual does not have it entwined in the frame of his daily consciousness. Moments before sleep at night, in the morning before the day's engagements, on the bus, in the toilet, in fact every idle moment in life must be filled up with thoughts about one's vision, everyday. I designed a vision of moderate wealth and extensive humanism; a life of lofty intellectual accomplish-ments and charity, one that would guarantee me some exemplary space in history and a richer attunement with God. For me, humanism was part of Godliness.

Having sent out so many job applications in the past with-out success, I appeared to have reached a cul-de-sac. But my focus remained to study hard and religiously save two-thirds of my salary no matter how hard in the meantime while I took time to think about the next step. My resumption time at the Oke-Arin beat was 6p.m, and most of the bank workers would still be around by that time balancing accounts and closing vaults. The operations manager of the branch, superior to that overbearing

Yankee, had been observing me for some time. There was a job opening for a teller in the bank. He called me into his office one evening to discuss possibilities of employment.

"You called me sir," I said, holding a copy of Wole Soyinka's The Man Died. He asked to see the front of the book. Compliments and all what not about the writer followed.

"Oh, you're still standing, sit down....What's your qualification?"

"School Certificate sir."

"Hmmm, you mean you've not gone to school? Not even an OND?"

"No sir. But I'm passionate about study. I've been looking for a better job to have access to more funds to go back to school."

"I see. I actually called you thinking you had some tertiary education. There's a job on ground. I wanted to recommend you to HR at the head office. You sound more educated than you really are."

"Thanks for your interest in me sir. But is there no way you could still recommend me given your position in the bank? I can do the job if I'm inducted."

"I wish I could. Policy says minimum of OND. Unfortunately our system does not circumvent policy and protocol."

I was downcast. This certificate issue kept popping up as if all those out there who had university education were employed. For some seconds both of us remained silent until I felt irrelevant and stood up.

"Should I go now sir?"

"Oh yes you can. You have the right spirit towards life, my friend. One thing I can tell you is this: associate with the right crowd."

"Thank you very much sir, I'm very grateful."

As I left that office, the sentence echoed in my mind. Associate with the right crowd. I recognised that as yet another fundamental imperative in the quest to find self, and vision. The individual sailing on the voyage to actualise dreams does not need the company of those who do not understand the mechanics of, or even need for, navigation. Such company would be as useful to him as an aerophobic lot would be to an astronaut on a space mission. Cynics, arm-chair analysts and the like are not to be in the crowd the manager talked about. If one cannot find the right crowd in real life, one can delve into relevant literature to explore the company of like-minded thoughts. The noblest of feats are often those that lacked kindred support at the beginning, those which the hero tugged out through a compost of sneers – the case of triumph catalysed by external doubt.

Back home in the village things had changed but were still the same. My younger sister, Ebere, was now mature enough to take care of the other two boys and Nne. There had been reports of her wayward living and that bothered me. I feared she could bring shame to the family if she didn't change. I wrote her counselling letters yet the bad reports kept coming.

Nne was always on my mind. I missed her every day. I needed to change my fortunes, gather some money and travel to see her. I would buy her Akwa George or Hollandis, noble wrappers of rural women. I was emotionally attached to her more than I was to my mother. Back in the day when Mother used to beat me up mercilessly Nne was often there to save me. Whenever Mother locked me up in a room and denied me food in punishment, Nne would smuggle food in there for me, much to my mother's chagrin. She had sold all the sublime wrappers in her cloth-box to raise my school fees at critical moments in the past after my parents' divorce. She was old, yes, but that would not stop her from tying the prospective wrapper to do *inyanga* in one of those women meetings East of the Niger. If there was no meeting, she would wear them to church, to that Baptist Church at Umuege junction where she was baptised Grace by a white missionary. She loved her Baptist church so much that she never missed out on any programme. Association Meetings, Lydia Women gatherings, Workers' Meetings, she attended all, usually carrying her Igbo Bible whose single letter she could not read. It did not matter whether she could read or not. Did the pastor not often say that angels attended all meetings, taking record of punctuality and Bible possession? The last time she sent a message across to me, she asked me to buy her maxi and sweat-er, that she had not worn new clothes in a long while. I felt the urge to do something tangible for her now that she was still alive. But that was not to be.

At the age of ninety-three, Nne died. I grieved with a pro-fundity that got everyone worried. The sense of loss for a loved one is often not totally mitigated by the exhaustive age of the deceased. Reminiscence begins to sadistically dangle imageries of what is truly lost: services of friendship and humanity - nothing is actually lost but these. On the day I left Umuege for Lagos, Nne had seen me off. In the cup of my palms she had blown gusts of saliva, that traditional seal of geriatric blessings that always capped prayers or libations for success in any journey. Together we had wept in each other's arms before I mounted the okada that took me to the motor park. My head turned severally while on the bike to behold Nne, as she stood ruefully watching the image of her beloved grandson peter out of sight. I was deemed the reincarnation of her first son lost to the Biafran war. She mostly called me by the late son's name. Oftentimes, she would scrutinize my body, noting what seemed to her as the exactitude in the replication of birth marks and scars. She'd shake her head after such inspection, flick her fingers, and mutter: E ji alo uwa alo, chai! - 'Reincarnation is real, wow!' That myth of reincarnation was the soul of the special love she had for me. I grieved not only for the recollections I made of her life, but for the fact that I had done nothing in reciprocation of her perfect love, if not the little sums I sent her occasionally.

Nothing afflicts humanity like the fear of death. Such euphemisms like "passing unto glory", "a glorious exit", etc are merely man's inventions to tame the morbidity of death, a demonstration that what is feared is not only the concept but also its wording. But that fear itself is a function of man's arrogant greed for everything that Nature can give. From having life thrust on him without his request, man continues to make greedy arrogations of the tenure of his life, riding especially on the blandishments of religion. He does not feel convinced that long and short life are, by death, reduced to the same thing, that nothing is long or short in a thing that is no more. The dying old man and the dying lad share the same sense of loss, since what is lost is not the past or the future, but the present moment, this fleeting moment. They are both dying the present death. It is the living that bother about length of life, as if that would have any impact on the circumstances of the deceased. Let a man live as long as he could, he'll die still having some unfinished business. Just as life is an imposed opportunity to exist, so is death the loss of a privilege given by an arbitrary Luck.

Nne's death reinforced my dedication to making money, if only for the sake of my younger ones. A huge gap had been created in their lives. My studies veered off to motivationals, but much of the preachments in those books were sheer idealistic concoctions whose prescriptions lacked substance in practice. One must seek counsel in relevant literature for every undertaking to which one applies oneself. Many of the motivational works available did not recognise that one man is different from another in skills, cultural orientation, and uniqueness; that what works for one might not work for the other. And that given the dynamics of man and society, approaches to solving problems are in constant evolution. In many of such books, there was also a lack of appreciation of the fact that settings do not all respond to efforts in the same way, that socio-cultural conditions differ; that straight-jacketed rules for wealth-making should not apply. Some even went as far as recommending businesses for readers. Not bad, but to what extent has the theorist explored the advertised businesses? And what would happen if everyone were to dabble in those templates? Let the entrepreneur reach into his creative being and rummage for ideas, and apply himself to any which offers him fulfilment and convenience, which fills a need in society, rather than get lured by the touted profitability in popular prescriptions.

However, my frustration ended when a friend gave me a copy of The Richest Man in Babylon. In Arkad, the lead character, I found the humanization of theory in simple, classical literature. The rules in the book were even, with a broad applicability. Arkad became my new religion for money-making. My two- year savings had been appropriated by my treacherous friend who would not pay me the money I lent him; I had to start saving afresh. Two things were of essence: money and time. I had the latter since I worked only at night. I stuck to my savings plan, but another challenge was what to invest in. It had to be a business that did not require the lease of a shop or other conventional infrastructure, and one that could cope with little funds too. My concern was just to create an additional source of income, without regard to the size of profit.

After much feasibility studies, I settled for the supplies of construction and engineering hardware, though the business card I later printed boasted 'General Contractor' as a means of incorporating everything that had the prospect of profit. I was able to wring out more funds to print invoices, waybills and letterheads, after registering my business name. I was banking on Okey's assurance to sponsor the execution of any supply order that would come. Okey's new posting in Noble Guards offered a daily reward of generous tips from car park users where he was stationed. In a few of months of working in the car park, he had bought an okada, a brand-new 14-inch television set, and a tokunbo fridge. "My wife carry beta luck come," he'd tell whoever complimented him for his new status as the richest man in the compound. Most other rooms had merely archaic, humongous boxes with frightening knobs for television sets, usually bought at Westminster, that notorious market in Apapa for fairly used electronics. Roguish traders often ripped off unsuspecting customers there by, sometimes, selling them electronic boxes filled with hard mud as non-tested TV. Okey's fridge harboured loads of drinks from neighbours, drinks usually redeemed on Sundays to entertain guests. Not that owning such appliances was exclusive in a 21st century Lagos. Poverty had reduced people in most parts of Ajegunle to mere spectators of life, to whom even the most ordinary possessions were status markers.

Having put together all the provisional stationery for my new business, I braced for marketing and contract-sourcing. First I realised I needed a new look. A visit to CMS and some cheap, fairly used corporate shirts went home with me. The two pairs of tokunbo Italian shoes I bought at the Tejuosho market in Yaba needed just a little cobbler's touch to balance out the uneven soles. I soon started daily visits at corporate offices in Apapa, dropping my business cards, collecting those of company procurement desks, and striking up other necessary overtures for business relationships. My presentations were not always impressing to most technical managers but at least I spoke fairly good English with nice airs that won attention.

After six months of continuous scouting on the commercial streets of Apapa, not a single order had been made from me by any company. I had a daily vision of a rewarding future whose realisation would spring from the crucible of the present moment. My thoughts, whether on a transit bus or in the toilet, centred on my dreams. My target was to drop proposals in three construction companies in Lagos every day, for thirty days. I imagined some of the likely challenges that could come up in the course of marketing, and proffered solutions beforehand. Thankfully enough I had not given up my night job and it did bear the financial burden of my running around. My dedication to my dreams was unflinching, despite Okey's derisive remarks:

"Shey person wey go give you contract no get brother wey dey find work? Person go just dey deceive himself, dey hang him bag where him hand no go reach to collect am", he'd often say.

"If my hand reach to hang the bag, e go reach to collect am." That was always my standard reply.

I had grown immune to all negativity, even subsuming the anxiety that Okey's wife would soon have a baby, a veritable threat to my continued stay in that house. The daily transportation cost to Apapa on weekdays had eaten into my savings and had placed me on a poor diet. Cooked corn, soaked garri, puff-puff, etc, went down as proper meals, consecutively for days. One morning, Okey came back from an occasional night duty and met me as I was demolishing a bowl of soaked garri, decked in my corporate being, in readiness for the day's hunting at Apapa.

"As you wear shoe and shirt like beta person now dey go Apapa," he said, "person no go know say na garri dey your belle. Imagine your embarrassment if something should puncture your belly on the road with the garri gushing out."

I laughed and ignored him.

My schedule of visits for the day was to start with a branch of Universal Trust Bank in Apapa. I headed for the place after the meal. Inquiries at the gate and the guard showed the way to the branch manager's office.

"Good morning sir, I'm Victor from Famalec Limited. We deal in office equipment and stationery... Fantastic prices sir... May I sit down, sir?" I said smiling from ear to ear. Since it was a bank, I had to offer a deal in office equipment and stationery, rather than in my main interest of construction and engineering hardware.

The creature I addressed that sat on the swivel chair opposite me had the eyes of an owl; they pierced. A fifty-litre stomach that was poured into a French suit sat below his chest in the partial obscurity of a laptop on his table. At a corner of the office was a pretty young lady thoroughly garnished for sex appeal. The black owl was incensed by the intrusion that appeared to have scuttled the desires of that sinister twosome, or the anger was just out of that stupid mannish tendency to impress a lady of interest by humiliating a fellow man, to flaunt some authority.

"We're not interested, Mr. Man!" he roared. "How dare you come to see me without an appointment, you must be a very foolish man! Stupid! Get out! And call me that stupid security man at the gate on your way out, you two must be twins!"

"I'll go!" I retorted. "Look at your tummy: If you lie face-down, I'm sure your head and legs would never touch the ground because of your huge stomach!"

I quickly moved out feeling triumphant to have diminished his pride in front of his lover, as he did to me too. The lady only chuckled. I heard his voice rattling away as I left walking faster to leave the premises, the lady's voice urging forgiveness.

As I left the bank premises, I felt somewhat dejected over the failure of this first call for the day. Only the previous evening, a teenage female bank customer at the Oke-Arin slave beat called me a "bank dog" during a minor misunderstanding. My spirit had been deeply wounded too often in the course of my duty as a guard, and now this job that seemed like a noble one also had some humiliation to offer. I rebuked the urge to go home for the day, if only to debunk that superstition that when a day starts on a bad note, it would have multiplier effects on other things. I found an abandoned bus at a corner of Creek Road and moved into it to have a quiet time. Then I slept.

An angry sun parboiled Lagos that afternoon. Several sweat tracks snaked from my hair down to my dirty collar, as my head hung on the headrest of a worn-out bus seat in an awkward position of sleep, mouth agape. My waking followed the giggles of school children who watched from the bus window the perching and re-perching of flies around my face to sip the salinity of sweat. The children had thrown cooked groundnut shells at my open mouth but the shells were too light to follow the instruction of their hands, landing rather on my chest. A clatter of their running feet in triumphant giddiness when I got startled left me livid.

When I got off the stationary bus, I spotted two trucks moving out of the next official premises. The inscription Podrecca Nigeria Limited with an emblem of construction business gave indication of a prospect for me. I walked up to the security man at the gate and demanded to see the Project Manager. A form travelled back and forth and I was let into the company's reception office, which was four rooms away in a stretch from the PM's office. A voice shook the earth from that office, venting the autocracy of its owner, amidst heavy strikes of hands

on the table. The recipient of that vocal violence ran to and fro
with frantic automation, either bringing in the wrong document
from the one demanded or nothing at all. Louder went the voice
till its owner choked and started coughing.

"Sorry sir!", said the errant staff.

"Sorry la melda! Dai cretino!"

There was calm. Shortly the vocally harassed young man
came from that charged office to the reception.

"Are you the man from one Famalec Limited?"

"Yes sir."

"Now go see Mr Luigi fourth office by the right."

My heart beat faster. How would I face this man of implacable temper?

Mr Luigi was the tallest white man I had ever seen. An Italian in his mid-seventies, he had a baldness that looked like the
frontal arc of a building – or was it a prototype of some construction design etched on a towering human as a living file? He
was some kind of a masochist whose self-hate manifested in his
preference of shouting to speaking, so much that he screamed
his eardrums to pieces. There was a permanent moss of cotton
in both ears to keep tympanic medication in place.

His discussions with me were cordial. A few more visits and
the first order was made: I was to supply ten pieces of 32mm by
50cm Punch Jack-Hammer Chisel. I had no idea what the
material was but I nodded. I was very happy, and hurriedly went
home to share the good news with Okey, my potential sponsor.

Okey was happy with the development, or so it seemed. I
made inquiries on the cost of the material and tabled my findings
to him, for the release of funds. His first gimmick was his

deliberate avoidance of home whenever I was deemed to be there. Podrecca Nigeria Limited had a policy of revoking orders that were not discharged within five days, and Okey's trickery had eaten up two days. He could not hide for too long so on the third day, we met. The moment he sighted me, those two notorious lines formed on his forehead.

"Well, the little money I have is kept for a purpose. Not even my father's death can make me touch it," he said conclusively.

I was shocked. I could not figure out any reason for his change of heart. Besides the fact that we were kinsmen, his accommodating me at the expense of personal convenience qualified him as my genuine well-wisher. I reminded him that there was appreciable profit in the transaction, promising to even give him the lion's share, but his mind was made up. I realised that to judge men merely by their acts is to be shallow-minded. The man who has exhibited bravery, generosity, love, hate or any other attribute could have been prompted by the accident of circumstance, and not by any inner conviction or trait. And for disappointment, I realised that it comes when it is least expected, especially from the person most qualified not to give it. No one was willing to lend me seventeen thousand naira to set forth the actualization of a dream I had put in so much to nurture. 'If only you had asked last week I would have helped.... My children's school fees have flattened my purse...My business has been standing on its head for long now.... Excuses flew out from every lip. All my efforts to raise money failed, and the order elapsed, officially. I had no telephone line to receive Mr Lingi's likely queries, nor could I go to his office to face him.

Failure as the first impression in a new business prospect could be quite inimical, I feared.

On my way to evening work the next day, I stopped over at Ijora at the spare parts shop of one of my kinsmen who had offered me encouragement sometime in the past. Chima did not wait for any persuasion. A man in his tapering youth, not only did he provide the money for the transaction interest-free, he took me to Agarawu market, the Lagos hub of technical hardware, conducted the bargains, and gave me tips on how to approach the tall menace at Podrecca. Surprisingly, though the supply was made two days after the expiration of the order, no eyebrows were raised. Everything sank in perfectly, opening the door for more and more orders that raked in handsome profits. Chima was too willing to sponsor all, without demanding any share from the proceeds.

Everything went smoothly well with the first supply but that was not to be the case always. Technical requests often had a lot of problems. If the man of the site writing the requisition used a professional name for the needed item, chances were that tools merchants might not understand what it was. There was also the problem of not supplying to specification, given the scarcity of many of the regularly specified models of construction hardware. Some rigid foremen at the site might reject supplied materials for as flimsy an excuse as the faintness of the colour of a brand emblem, though most times that was a sort of blackmail to get the supplier to bribe them. With time I learnt the techniques of the business, but I could not have envisaged how an Igbo trader's mispronunciation of the 'r' letter could cause me some trouble.

Luigi's request said Supply 10 pieces of 4" Fubora. I turned over the whole plumbing materials market but no one understood the material I wanted to buy. I was just leaving the market for Apapa back to Luigi to get clarifications on the use of a Fubora when a trader accosted me, claiming knowledge of the item.

"I get am sir. Footballer," the trader averred.

"Not footballer, Fu-bo-ra! Fu-bo-ra!"

"Ehen now, Fu-bo-la!"

"Oh my gosh!," I cried, "You can't even pronounce it well, are you sure u know it?"

"Na to pronanse am be the main thing abi na to see am? I dey tell you say e dey you dey speak Engrish. Follow me go shop."

We got to his shop. He drew a face towel out of his jeans back pocket, flicked it on a dusty wooden stool and motioned me to sit down.

"Make I go bring am from store, wait small I de come."

"Oh, you want to waste my time like the others did, going from one shop to the other looking for it since they didn't have it? No I'm leaving! I can't wait."

"This oga na waa, shebi na to bring Fubola for you?"

"Not Fubola, it is Fu-bo-ra! Fu-bo...! Whatever! Just don't waste my time else you won't meet me here."

Shortly he was back, with ten pieces of what looked like footballs fixed unto a plastic lever threaded at one end.

"Na im be this," he declared.

After the haggling I paid and took the items to Luigi, who erupted like one who just saw a heinous abomination.

"Wetin be this? Porko-Deo! Deo-kani! You are not competent! You bring me ball-valves instead of Fubora! You lie that you know the job, you know no nothing! No no no no! Bring back my order! You waste too much time!"

The fuss went on and on. I took the items back to the trader, called him names and got back the money paid. On my way out of the market I ran into a friend and narrated my ordeal to him. The friend, who worked as a plumbing engineer in a building firm, chortled loudly. He knew the item, knew where to get it. All was settled when Luigi saw the replacement and burst into laughter, saying, "That first time e be like say you never chop then."

The last encounter with Okey had dented the relationship between us. His constant frowns were but a mafia approach to the suppression of an inner guilt, the expression of an arrogance that could not concede apology. The silence between us heightened the war at the psychological terrain. My fortunes had improved in relative terms but not enough to earn me a personal accommodation and still leave some money in my coffers for business. But then I did not want to leave Okey's household with grudges. It would be ungrateful of me to blot out his earlier gesture and sentence him for the present, as if that past had not provided the foundation for the fortunes at hand. I had to find a way to make peace rather than continue to keep grudges with a man in his own house. I had come to recognise that everyone is an only child in their own world, that external concern is merely part of the freebies of human relationship. The impression was already beginning to emerge that my little fortunes had gone into my head and had routed my sense of respect.

The opportunity for peace finally came: Onyinye had a baby. The euphoria of the moment united everyone. That her mother would soon be on her way to Lagos to take over my sleeping space in the room did not matter to me. There was no present plan for my own accommodation but there was this tremendous confidence and a feeling of peace within me, that ownership of self that comes when a man has a living hope or a dependable source of income, a sense of competence for the immediate challenge. I consolidated on the peace that had been attained to make up with Okey, doing all I could to reassure of no hard feelings.

Nothing relieves more than the cathartic discharge of grudge to usher in forgiveness, the emotional reality that immensely rewards both the offender and the offended by its cleaning up of the burden of a negative consciousness. Forgetting is a different thing entirely. To try forgetting something is to further entrench it in the memory, and to urge one to forget is to admit ignorance of the workings of the memory. Wrongs should be forgiven but could be retained even unconsciously, as cautionary lessons in human relations.

Before Onyinye's mother arrived, I had begun making efforts at getting an apartment. Okey was fully involved. I did not want to live in Ajegunle despite that cheaper offers were available there. That environment lacked any form of encouragement both in the quality of its humanity and in the conditions of habitation there. I wanted a neighbourhood whose relative glory would constantly remind me of the poor value of my achievements and propel me for greater exploits. The man who has big dreams should do everything possible to dodge the flattery of men who see mediocrity as heroism. My choice area of Lagos hardly had one-room apartments, but I believed there must be some landlord in that middle-class setting who would not be rich enough to build flats. A decent one-room self-contained apartment would be just fine for a start.

It was like the hunt for a sterling treasure. Property agents ripped me off as much as they could: they would call me on phone to come inspect an apartment, even though they knew that the option did not fit into the description I gave them. I would hurry down to the location, protest my waste of time and money at coming to examine some tacky house; they would apologise, and demand more money to enable them conduct more searches, money that would soon fill up the purse of the nearest pub dealer. As soon as the apology they gave the last time expired, they would yet place another call for more money. More protests and more extortion, and the agents finally got a suitable place.

The landlord was an old journalist whose children lived abroad. The compound was spacious, had two bungalows: one for the old man and his old wife, the other bungalow housed two units of mini-flats, both of which were vacant. The old man had an addiction with nature exhibited by a plethora of greenery in the premises. I grinned as one of the agents led me into the serene cottage of sorts, with buildings fresh with paint and surroundings perfectly clean. I mentally allotted myself spaces for reading and lounging, greedily lusting after the pleasure and comfort that flirted around in the scenic splendour. The cost might be higher than average but that was not to be a problem.

What was to be a problem was the aged piece of trouble that owned the apartment.

Bespectacled with overgrown white hair that looked like a bloom of virgin cotton, the short, dark landlord had a very active spirit for bickering. As soon as the agent introduced me as the prospective tenant, the retired newshound took off his eyeglasses and dug a probing gaze into my eyes for some passing seconds as if he were reading some esoteric message on my face. Taking off the eye-glasses exposed the involuntary wetness that formed in those eyes, one of whose corneas seemed impaired. The glasses went back to their beat and the old man began administering an unwritten questionnaire:

"What's your name?"

"Victor, sir."

"Nice name. Why do you want to rent my house, what happened to where you were living before?"

"I currently live with my brother and his wife. A baby's on the way and it's a one-room apartment."

"Hmmm. What kind of job do you do?"

"A small-scale contractor, sir. I provide support services to construction firms. I also work as a night guard."

"Night guard? You mean you are a *maiguard*?", he gnarled scornfully.

"I don't know the meaning of *maiguard* sir."

"You don't know the meaning of *maiguard*, are you not in Lagos? Anyway, when do you close from work? Because I lock my gate 8:00 pm everyday."

His English was crisp, his words dropping slowly with geriatric finesse – that phonetic consciousness that ensures that words are pronounced to the last consonant or vowel for proper effect.

"That's ok by me sir. Because by that time I should be at my night duty post," I stated, looking a bit nettled by his pedantry.

"Good. And I hope you know you don't bring in anybody to live with you, except your wife. And since it seems you're not married I don't want girlfriends swarming about the whole place."

"I'll live alone sir."

"Good boy. One more thing: It's easy to say you'll do this you'll do that. If you break any of the rules I'll kick you out right away. The last person that left that apartment lived only for two months. She messed up and I refunded her accordingly and showed her the way out."

I was already feeling huffed at the whole drilling, and immediately decided to call his bluff and leave. I needed to be polite with the insult that circled around my tongue.

"I'm ok with your rules sir. When do I park in?"

"Park in for what, have we discussed money?"

"Oh, am I to pay money for the house?"

"You want to live in my house rent-free, are you ok? Agent, where did you bring this man from?" he woofed.

I did not wait for the agent to say anything, and simply cut in:

"Well Baba, the rules sounded like you run a prison, not a house for free humans. And no one pays to go to jail!"

The agent snickered as I stormed out of the scene and banged the gate. Baba hurled invectives at both of us in Yoruba, monologued about how Igbo people lacked respect and all. The agent ran out as Baba called him names, cursed him for bringing a mad boy to his house. "Serves him right", said the agent to me when we both met outside. "That Baba own too much. That's why him get two mini-flats wey dey empty for long now, nobody gree pay. I happy as you take talk to-ram."

After that episode I was just fed up with the accommodation search, and resolved to edit my taste to suit the kind of houses that were available. Onyinye's mother had arrived, and I was temporarily squatting in a neighbour's room. Not long another apartment was on offer and I paid. The cost was far higher than the Ajegunle options and reduced my business funds considerably, but the amicable relationship with Mr Luigi gave assurances of prompt replenishment.

My new home was not as decent as I would have liked. Onyinye's mother's presence had placed urgency on the accommodation hunt, and made a strict adherence to taste unnecessary, coupled with my lack of toleration for the extortionist schemes of property agents. The houses in the compound were all detached two-room structures built shabbily from the advance payments of the tenants that lived in them. The landlord was a happy old drunkard who acquired the property when the going was good. The only appeal was that the number of tenants was much lower that what obtained in Ajegunle, so the amenities did not suffer much pressure. But again, poverty lived in all the rooms. I had only spent two days when one of the neighbours accosted me.

"Bros na you be the new tenant wey enter?"

"Na so my brother", I answered.

Fair-complexioned with black spots all over his face and a head of yellow hair, Oyibo, as he was fondly called, smiled mischievously and walked away. His baggy trousers that had shrunk high up to his shin flapped noisily in tandem with his undersized thong that left his heels to kiss the ground. His heels bared irregular calibrations from harsh weather and unsatisfactory hygiene. I was not about to let him go without the suspense cleared.

"Wait! Wait! Wait...! Any problem, my brother?"

"Noooo! I just dey ask.... shey you be Igbo?"

"Yes bro. Imo State."

"Sake of say you be Igbo like me, I go tell you. People dey wan pack comot you dey enter. This compound be you like where human beings dey live?"

I was speechless. I could not understand the whole puzzle.

"Brother please make you explain to me, I no understand."

"If you wan' make I tell you, I go tell you: people way live here no dey progress. The landlord don submit everybody luck to him yeye secret cult. Na so him dey bury dog ,goat and other orisirisi for compound make we no for see road prosper. I know how I be before I enter here, everything don dabaru. Look around, you see anybody wey dey breathe from him nose?"

I thanked him and left, and dismissed the information as pure hogwash.

Oyibo was a local plumber who did no more than household plumbing repairs. He often stayed at home. The other tenants were all menial workers who had no serious ambition other than prolific child-bearing. None seemed to have a viable spirit or equipment to face life let alone have a vision, apart from hollow wishes of prosperity whose vehemence ended at the end of vigorous prayers. This man of superstition already had a jobless live-in lover who would rent and watch not less than five home video films each day. For a man with such a choice further limited by his own myopia, his luck would have been submitted wherever, and everything for him would dabaru.

But Oyibo was not the only ludicrous poverty institution in the compound. There was another man, a taxi driver, whose car regularly started on its own, especially at night. The vehicle was nothing but a sheer moving nest lacking the least pretensions of comfort. A mangled stretch of fibre was the dashboard, and seats were mere skeletons of iron with thin tissues. By error the man, one day, dropped the car key in a hole at the back of the driver's seat. His short hand, no matter how he stretched it, could not reach the depths into which the key had fallen. Somehow he bore a hole under the seat and tried catching the naughty metal from there but it slipped into the dark mechanical jungle of the car floor and stayed there forever. Efforts to shake it out were a waste of time, curiously. The next morning, he was found peeping at the exhaust pipe – to think he actually thought the key could have been ejected from there! He was not just a taxi driver. He was a mechanic, an auto-electrician and a panel-beater, all in one, skills he necessarily acquired through his daily experience in personal repair of all kinds of his vehicle's break-down. After losing the car key, ignition became the marriage and separation of two wires. At the end of each day's work, fatigue would make him forget to part the wires completely, and chances were that the car would start on its own. Most times the sound of generators in the compound would muffle that of his running engine. "Chai! My fuel don burn finish," he'd exclaim in the morning after each experience.

He was my laughter therapy. Part of the penalties of living in the midst of uneducated folks is that one would be cursed to suffer perpetual audience to irrational viewpoints on politics, religion and life generally. Their analyses of current affairs were often very annoyingly flawed. "Obasanjo rig the election abeg; that population census wey him do two years ago you think say na for nothing? Na the census he take rig this election. Thank God them no count me join...All these plane crash na these yeye politicians dey cause am. Na ritual sacrifice to take win election...."

In the Citadel of Nailing

Behind the exotic huge gate was a world of organised physical beauty. A neatly paved road, policed by a line of well-pruned flowers at both sides, led into a lively new earth of ubiquitous greenery and stylish architecture. Lawns, mown by small motorized contraptions, bordered a court of green cage which fenced in two men in white as they playfully batted a ball at each other with youthful zeal. At the other side was a swathe of marked park showing off the automobile possessions of men. Sleek walkways were the arena of hurried feet that chased down different engagements at business centres, lecture halls and staff offices. Fat, slim, tall, short, ugly, good-looking species of humanity animated every space, clutching books, baring cleavages, laughing, frowning, exchanging banters, etc. There was a general impression of serious life and commitment to purpose.

But the beauty ended at the threshold of the next classroom. Large as the lecture halls were, a rowdy sea of heads filled up every space, not without the presence of late-comers giraffing from high window louvers to be part of the lecture. The sheer number of students reduced the efficacy of proper ventilation. Heat. Perspiration. The squeaky ceiling fans spun lazily offering a stingy delivery of air at the occasional periods when there was power supply. Air was the blend of carbon dioxide, human stench and sometimes, insidious farts.

My first year in the university served me much disillusion-
ment. I was disappointed with the dearth of proper infrastructure, even as the inadequate facilities available suffered from the
pressure of a huge student population. The teaching method was
much less satisfactory. With little room for lecturer-student
interaction and a course system that lumped multiple courses
into the schedule of short semesters, students learnt nothing
other than the ability to cram and withstand pressure. Learning
became drudgery, rather than an enthusiastic experience, whose
reward was in the acquisition of high but meretricious grades
that did not reflect the accurate degree of refinement in the
individual.

I had come to learn so as to improve my self-value and capacity to positively affect society, not to partake in the social
fashion of being called a graduate. My personal credo was out of
sync with living life merely for the sake of convention. I did not
have to part with a third of my security job salary, pay huge sums
as school fees, read up bland books just to have my name on a
piece of paper that would exaggerate my worth. Cerberus had
insisted - that was the name I gave Moses, the operations
manager and chief guard of Noble Guards - Cerberus had
insisted on a third of my salary to grant me weekends as work-
free days for my schooling. Approaching him for that favour was
a herculean task given his usual unfriendly disposition but I
softened him.

"I'm really very grateful that you have kept me in this job
despite that I'm least qualified for your kindness, sir. Please
accept this bottle of wine and the token in the envelope. Like
Peter in the Bible, silver and gold have I not."

"But money is both silver and gold," said Cerberus, a repressed grin hovering over his face.

"Well the money in the envelope is far less in value than bronze, let alone silver. It must be like mere metal or even wood," I added, and Cerberus's grin grew broader.

I left his office after the gesture. That was about six months before I earned admission for a part-time study in the university. Each month that followed within the subsequent five months I gave him a fair chunk of my salary to water down his rigidity and bring him closer. It worked. The barking sessions ended, and a new amity was enacted between us. Severally he prodded me to ask for any favours, like redeployment to a more lucrative beat, elevation to the post of beat supervisor, etc. No sir. He became convinced that I was giving without any ulterior motive. The bond grew stronger and stronger, such that I even discussed personal issues with him, though without asking for anything from him. There was no compromising the chances of a bigger favour by earning the gratification of little ones.

But Cerberus was not a man to grant the kind of favour I wanted without monetary inducement. Friendship or not, he demanded a third of my monthly package.

"It's not for me, my brother. I've to settle your beat supervisor too.... You know how these things work", he said.

"It's ok sir."

No degree of shylock exaction was reason enough to forgo the chances of a university education.

That university education, however, turned out to be a disappointed expectation. The crunchiness of the chewed bitterkola did not reflect its taste. The rot of infrastructure was not bad enough. There was yet a bigger issue of students – youths – lacking the capacity for thought, the elementary brilliance to engage themselves intellectually. Only a minority seemed to have enrolled for schooling for the noble purpose of discovering self and impacting society. Most of them had no vision for the education they had come to acquire, apart from that nebulous ambition of graduating and getting a job in this or that firm, buying the latest car from the prospective famed emoluments, and indulging in other fatuous luxuries life can offer. I had thought that the university was a place where young minds would be honed to enable them think for themselves, discover a need in society and acquire character to fill that need. This one seemed like a travesty of that purpose, a process that looked exactly like those recitation sessions in primary school where a pupil could read out an entire poem, a national anthem or a religious creed without understanding the philosophy behind that undertaking. What was internalised were the words, not the thought behind them. University education was a mere consumption and regurgitation of processed garbage.

The lecturer's definitions must be relayed back to him verbatim in the exam, unless the student wanted to fail. Rather than set questions that should address real-life experiences and elicit solutions to real problems, the system set out seeking grand textbook definitions. List and define; mention this and that; draw and label Newcomb's Model of Communication, etc. As a publisher, how would you tackle the problem of the Brown Envelope Syndrome in your news medium? How do you deepen investigative journalism in a polity of corrupt politicians who can hack down the whistle-blowing reporter? As a business manager, design a sound blueprint for a small-scale business with a start-up capital of five hundred thousand naira? Such questions were hardly asked. Definitions. Dogma. Anachronistic academic conventions! A few students who had the ability to cram and vomit same on the answer sheet made fantastic grades. Ask them the same questions a week later and you'd be surprised at their ignorance. Some others who had a knack for personal reading and self-development acquired the real value of a university education. The rest came out either looking so alike in their conception of the realities in their fields, or as robotic recitation experts, with neither prospect for novelty nor a firm grasp of the status-quo. I wondered how the much-touted paradigm shift would materialise.

Many of the students did not deserve to be in senior secondary school, let alone occupy learning space in the university. I found them totally despicable. I was pissed off with fellow students who could not discuss any subject insightfully and constructively, who had as much intellectual ignorance as an average Alaba market trader.

Not that there were no exceptions. Their minority was just too alarming. I met one of such one day when I went to look up my score at the result board. The creature had a rich, dyed Afro haircut hewn to perfection. A well-ironed white short-sleeved shirt was received smoothly into the waistline of his black trousers, whose crisp line of ironing could possibly sever the throat of a fowl. Nails neatly pared, and the glow of a pair of black shoes meant the presence of a dandy. Tony was a perfectionist. Everything was in its technical position. The caps of a blue and a red pen peeped from a breast-pocket; books were properly arranged in a portable file strapped to the chest with the left hand. Steps landed so lightly on the sandy ground to restrict the influence of dust on those shoes. Even tracing his name on the board was a technical affair: a finger ran through the column for names, his file went up to meet the finger as a horizontal ruler, and his identity popped out: Abang Abang Anthony – 70.

I was impressed with this new man, much for his sense of hygiene as in the testimonies of that score. Only three people had A's in the course, the rest clustered around varying degrees of failure and mediocrity. Tony ran his eyes along the column for scores, and then stopped abruptly at a startling discovery. "Eighty-three! Oh my! Who's this Victor Ekwueme chap? He's always high up." "I'm here sir", I chipped in, in apparent self-congratulation. Banters. Further introductions. My excitement at this new meeting was obvious, for, I had finally found a very sound mind who might share my frustrations about the system, a friend who turned out to be far more intelligent that I had thought. We sat down for a chat.

"So what are you doing in school?" Tony asked.

"Here to find myself. But the system has nailed a box around me. It's a citadel of nailing."

He laughed. "I get you, the system does not recognise that we all must not all reason alike. Why must there be only one correct answer to every question? It's not always so in the real world."

"It baffles me, Tony. Everyone must think within the confines of a box. It's an academic custom. I failed the last assignment on Public Relations because I did not define the concepts like the textbooks did. The lecturer said I spoke too much English instead of putting it the way Sam Black did in his text."

"I'm learning the system - cramming. But it's like learning to be left-handed at old age. I went to a secondary school where students were allowed to think for themselves.... But how come you were able to score 83 in the displayed result if you are as frustrated with the system as you say?"

"I don't know, this Calabar man, hahaha! Anyway, have you ever thought about your final year project?"

"Na wa for you o, you wan choose topic in Year One?"

"Not really. I hear this school's been running for about 30 years now. Imagine the number of students that have graduated. We could have over 20,000 project works in different fields. Works gathering dust at dusty shelves! All in the name of tradition! Hardly does anyone read them after submission even if they have useful recommendations to solve real problems."

"Hmmm. Well you can refuse to write yours in your final year. You must be some fanciful idealist, the one to change the world."

"Tooony! By the way, how many schools make use of these research works? You are too intelligent to refuse to question unproductive traditions. If after five years one is not able to create value from one's education, not able to do something new about solving society's problems, the education has not been optimized. Education is limping if it's only academic; it must include intellectual and social development to guarantee a full baking of the individual."

"You did not add religious development. That, for me, is the crux of the whole matter. An intellectually sound, socially balanced, and academically groomed person would be a nuisance to society if he does not have the knowledge of God and morality", he proclaimed.

"Religion is not the only moral teacher, my friend. I know a lot of non-religionists and humanists who are moralists, but let's not veer off into the subject matter of faith yet."

"Ok. So back to the education issue, what will you do to change a culture put in place by learned men who have read more books than you have ever done?"

"I don't know, for now. See, we'll all graduate looking for the same jobs that do not exist, lacking the capacity to create wealth. Well, not like I'd employ any of these laggards if I were an employer."

He let out a guffaw. "You're right, most of them are laggards. You need to hear them speak English. Until WAEC and NECO are able to conduct transparent and cheating-free exams, we'll continue to have undergraduates with poor academic grounding," he added.

"It's not about the entrance exams. It starts from primary and secondary schools. Most of the teachers there are unqualified. How will they be when most of those who study courses in Education in the university are the dregs who could not earn admission to study 'better' courses? It's a cycle."

The discussion continued, moving from one subject to another. It was as if we had known each other for too long. Suddenly, Tony's face shrank, his eyes narrowing down to the many rashes on my arm. I understood the inquiries in those eyes and interrupted:

"I work as a night guard. Those are the imprints of mosquito bite. There at the beat, the sky is the roof."

His eyes widened at the bluntness of that revelation. He was surprised at how I was not ashamed to declare my 'despicable' livelihood.

"You must be a very honest chap, are you a Christian?"

"I'm not always honest. Sometimes one has to tell necessary lies, but not about one's status. The first condition towards personal freedom is living according to oneself, not according to others. To lie about yourself is to be a slave to others...Depends on how you define a Christian."

"A Christian is one who's Christ-like. But then politically speaking one could be a Christian without being Christ-like."

"Let's just say I believe in the Christian Faith, Tony. I attend no church though."

"You attend no churrrrch? How do you hear the Word?"

"I don't believe anymore in sermons. We've heard enough. Everywhere is littered with thieves, killers, and liars, yet everyone is godly! The same people that preach and listen to sermons! Preach by your deeds, finish!"

"You'll soon become an atheist with this kind of reasoning. You need the Word to sharpen your faith."

"See, religion is a very subjective thing. One shouldn't take it too seriously. You could have been a Hindu if you were born in India, and would consider Hinduism to be the ultimate Truth. And perhaps intercede that God should have mercy on Christians and the rest by bringing them to Truth; your Faith. You wouldn't be doing that out of mischief, but out of conviction."

"Wait a minute, I'm trying to understand you. What exactly is your basic philosophy?"

"I'm concerned about the human condition. I'm a weak moralist. Morality is a relative thing anyway. What is right in one place or religion could be condemned in another, so one who is a moralist is only relatively so, since there's no objective moral standard."

"So how do you go about the work of God if you do not take it 'too seriously', to quote you, if you are not passionate about it? You sound like a lukewarm, carnal Christian. Besides, there's an objective morality, and that is what God represents."

"I believe in God but I don't go about screaming it down people's ears. I hate loud-mouthed religion. I treat the next man in such a way that God will be happy with me – for me that's Godliness. It's not about trumpeting Bible quotations and attending church service while you serve your house-help sour meals."

"That's ok too. At least you look up to God as your ideal for moral actions. Doesn't that imply, somewhat, that His moral standards are objective, contrary to your claim of a lack of objective ethics?"

"Our conceptions of God differ: He represents different things to different religions, and even to different denominations within religions. For instance, one religion says He hates polygamy, another says He doesn't. One denomination says He hates women wearing trousers, another says He doesn't. And each of these claimants can find some verse in the Bible or in some other Holy Book to justify their position. So there might be an objective Divine ground-norm ideally, but we are not agreed on its contents."

"Victor the problem is that these are human doctrines. If you want to know the mind of God, you can reach Him genuinely and He will reveal Himself spiritually to you. You don't read His Word as if it were some textbook. Let the Holy Spirit guide you. Pray to God in your own way and ask Him to show you the true religion."

"You make me laugh. Each of the people making the divergent claims I talked about say the same Holy Spirit guided their beliefs! The Holy Spirits seem to be working at cross purposes. An Indian friend who was preaching to me about Krishna the other day said the same to me – pray to God in your own way and He'll prove the Krishna truth to you."

"Haha, you are mischievous! Ok, concerning morality, even if we don't have a consensus on the Mind of God, even if you can lie about the Holy Spirit and all, at least you can't lie to yourself. Your conscience will always tell you the home truth. The conscience is an impartial judge."

"Tony my brows are yet to return from the back of my head over your previous claim and you make another! The conscience is not often an impartial judge. It can tell you untrue things. It's even temperamental."

"You've come again! How on earth can your conscience lie to you?"

"The human conscience is a product of socialisation. It functions within the context of one's socio-cultural matrix. If you were born into a culture that sees twins as evil, you wouldn't feel guilty slitting their throats since you would think murdering them was a divine mandate. Just as Boko Haram elements would not feel guilty dispatching innocents since their ideology justifies the act as one divinely inspired."

"I'm tempted to believe you. But there are still acts that are bad for which the conscience would prick one, no matter one's socialisation or level of depravity."

"Of course there are exceptions. But let no one go hee-hawing about a completely impartial conscience."

"You also said the conscience is temperamental. How is that possible?"

"Tony have you ever been angry before, and you took actions that seemed right to you at that moment, only to regret when your anger was sated?"

"Oh yea!"

"That is the conscience playing its slippery and temperamental part."

Tony adjusted himself on the seat and cast a fixed gaze at me for some seconds, his left palm placed over his mouth from his jaw, squinting his eyes as if to unravel the mystery he found in my personality. He seemed to be in a hurry to understand me completely right away.

"You say you're a Christian...even if in an ambiguous sense," he said, "do you believe there's a Hell?"

"The idea of Hell runs contrary to my idea of a kind, merciful God. It is the devil that would do a thing like that, not God," I replied.

"Life would be meaningless without some sort of divine justice hereafter, on how men have lived their lives on earth," he added, soberly.

"That is a curious argument. Now, let's say a young man dies at 25, after a very righteous life, tainted only by a little lying just before he dies. So he is to be roasted forever, not even for 25 years, or say, for a commensurate number of years - is that your idea of justice? And God would be happy with the overkill?"

"Well the ways of God are not our ways, Victor. It's not for us to determine for Him how to punish sinners."

"There's even a flip-side. Another man lives his life entirely by rape, robbery, murder and whatever evil that tickles his fancy. And just before he dies, he shows quite some genuine remorse and is forgiven by God. On the account of that eleventh-hour repentance he earns for himself an entire booty of heavenly bliss, forever! Is that justice?"

"I already told you that God has His ways. So you think there's no form of divine justice over there for the life we live here, we just die and it all ends?"

"I don't know, I'm only thinking aloud. And then one has to be very wicked, full of religious sadism and lacking in empathy, to hope to sit cross-legged lounging in heaven, larded in a clean-white robe and a bristling crown, perhaps mowing angelic meals, yet knowing that perhaps his father or mother, best friend, sibling, children, etc., are singeing away in Hell."

"Viiiictor! In the hereafter there'll be no family. Everyone's on their own."

"Ah, are we not assured in the Bible that we'd see our long-dead relatives and reunite with them, that parents will give account of how they raised their children, what are you talking about, Mr Tony Abang?"

"When you die you'll find out, young man."

"But the Bible says the dead are conscious of nothing, so why do you think I'll find out? Anyway, I'm in support of living a good life, for me, the life dictated by Christ, doing good to fellow men because I share in their humanity, because it validates my essence as a loving soul; doing my best for a better world. I'm not driven by the hope for a luxurious hereafter. It is too selfish, and reflects a deficit in human reasoning to do good only when threatened with eternal evil, or promised some celestial largesse. And life is long enough to end at death."

Debates. Unending inquiries for Truth. We met as frequently as possible to discuss whatever subject that caught our fancy. Schooling became very exciting as the bonds of our friendship grew firmer, rendering the many inhibitions in the school system ineffectual. Friendship had never been so soothing.

It went beyond the circus of school-life argumentations and the barter of vicarious assistance. Home visits, constructive quarrels, all. Granted, friendship has always been a selfish agenda, a social design for the mutual gratification of interests. The best of friends lose commitment the moment the service of favour becomes one-sided, when one party feels short-changed in the reception of benefits. Friendship is such a self-oriented social business, so inferior to humanity, that virtuous enterprise imbued with a sense of service to the next man without necessarily seeking to advance self. Humanity does not covet gratitude or direct personal reward from the discharge of a certain office; it derives fulfilment in the intrinsic honour of having helped a fellow man, a distant yet close member of the existential community. What lived between me and Tony was a friendship bordering on humanity.

The relationship performed its mandate when trouble showed up for me at Podrecca Nigeria Limited. A Lebanese accountant had helped himself to the contents of the company's till and taken to his heels. The exact sum that left with him was unknown to outsiders. Grapevine circular bandied about different figures: 'N200 million; no N300 million; not at all, nothing was stolen, it's all rumour'. Company drivers, expatriates' cooks, security guards, and all other members of the gossip department continued to reproduce fables of the theft. Confirmation soon came by way of corporate insolvency. For six months no vendor had been paid. Gradually life began to leave the activities in the company premises. Vendors wrote letter after letter, demanding payment of overdue invoices. No response. Finally, skeletal services. I was back to square one, my entire business fund had been trapped.

The relapse to acute poverty was immediate. The Cerberus effect on my monthly salary pushed me further down the abyss, coupled with the new responsibilities from schooling and personal accommodation. Persistent scouting for contracts in other firms yielded nothing. I had become learned enough to despise the harassment of poverty, showing neither worry nor hope. I held hope in high suspicion, and embraced indifference. For me, hope was not only a slippery fellow but also a manifestation of a lack of strength to face an ugly reality. There was this stunning neutrality in my own affairs, one that however, justified affirmative efforts. Work must go on. But to interpret events and actions in the course of work as signposts of some imminent positivity was not my business. Indifference was safety. What often matters most is not the trouble one encounters, but one's construction of that trouble in the mind, and the reaction towards it.

Tony helped as much as he could but it was dangerous, if not silly, to trust charity for too long. A sense of pride compelled me to feign a positive state of affairs sometimes, to reassure him that all was well. A victim must not always own both pity and misery. He became more in need of consolation than I.

Nothing strengthens a suffering man like meeting another whose condition is worse off, such that belittles his own hell. Within the period I stumbled on Kachi, a secondary school classmate, now an operator of a manual pepper mill in Boundary Market in Ajegunle. I did not believe my eyes when I saw a bare-chested man with Kachi's facial identity vigorously spinning the handle of a mill, the ground ingredient squashing into a plastic bowl. The sweaty Kachi was unaware of my presence. He was rather lost in the euphoria of ribald jokes from his market women neighbours, responding to one remark here, another there, happily. I called up a flashback of those days all the way from primary school.

Kachi lived with foster parents who forced him to hawk for them while they forbade him from schooling. He loved education, and defied the constant beatings that attended his being spotted in school by the foster devils. He always wore his school uniform beneath the tattered mufti clothing meant for his hawking itineration, often taken off halfway to attend classes. Twice a week was commendable attendance. Reliance was mainly on notes from fellow pupils, yet no one ever beat him to the first position in class every term. Secondary school was a miracle. He left his foster home for the thatched hut of his late parents when maltreatment got to a level that could make hell jealous. Livelihood was the sale of firewood hacked from thick village bushes. He remained the best student every term also. Soon the community banned the business of firewood since it threatened the availability of shrubs in the farm. His schooling was consequently affected. Teachers got tired of sacking him over school fees and at form four, he quit, and left for Lagos. In Lagos, one ugly incident led to another and he finally gave up on his ambition. One of the many cases of the under-utilization of self.

For me, Kachi's degeneration was not a warning on why I should keep my head up. I was already fully self-motivated and did not need further lessons on the dangers of resignation. What I found was some form of inner strength from experiential brotherhood. Creating an additional source of income became, once again, a new headache. I needed some casual earnings to help dislodge my bills.

The headache was palliated with Sandra's incursion into my life. I had become quite popular in class with much female attention. I anchored extramural classes for fellow course-mates, did assignments for many for a fee. A swarm of girls. Caution. I knew my weakness with women. Sandra seemed to have a business mission, no strings. "Do all my assignments, and I'll pay handsomely." A most sophisticated lady on campus known for high-end fashion and make-up, she was a brazen adult truant. Nothing was left undone in her creation. One had to be very stupid to ignore her physical appeal. She was an object of endless lascivious hunt by men in intimidating cars on campus. I took the offer. She paid bounteously being impressed with her high scores engineered by a rented hand. Extrapolating a romance between us seemed illogical; the social gap was too wide.

But between men and women, possibilities are infinite. It began with sensuous hugs whenever we met. Soon her text messages acquired a permanent suggestive ending: "Loads of hugs sweetie." I did not have to assume anything, sweetie had generally become a word of casual semantics. Gifts, and more gifts, from her. "Guy you won't even let me know where you live?" Sure! Sunday evening, a visit. It was the most seductive day on earth. Her curves were flattered by a skirt that was no more than four handkerchiefs sewn together. Fragrance was sexy, it alerted all stakeholders in my system. She sat on the bed, very close to me so that the gum she chewed noisily echoed inside my ear walls. A wet tongue was flicked as she chewed and spoke. Exaggerated laughter threw her onto my body. I was

close to implosion, clenched my equipment between my thighs
to suppress the growth I felt. She must have understood the
willingness and lust that enveloped me. She drew closer breath-
ing harder and I gave in, suddenly thrust my lips into hers. Our
teeth knocked but it was okay, the passion knew no pain and we
soon got very busy. Pleasure was given a whole new meaning:
Sandra had truly been around in the business.

Sex became the new currency for compensation; money
ceased. Her visits became too regular in the quest to douse
nymphomaniac hormones. I choked from the strangulation of
her academic workload. But a greater danger lurked in the
jealous temperament of one old man, a lecturer. She had been
playing too many pranks with the man, denying his groins the
aerobics they sought. Twice, a hotel room had been booked,
expectation and some randy nerves must have probably played
their part in stimulating madness in the flabby organ, but lady
failed to turn up. She balked at the imagination of his senile
touch and clumsy pulsations. And he was a dirty man that
always harboured dirt in his nails. The man began to probe into
the whys and wherefores of his privation, and finally drew a
conclusion: the young chap that was always by her side must be
the distraction, the factor behind this whole shenanigan. That
was how I became the object of a vindictive rage. The man
taught my class Psychology that particular semester, and persecution was fully activated: missing test scripts, dubious failures in
assignments, embarrassing put-downs during interactive sessions
in class, etc. I knew the cause of this hounding – this scape-
goating of innocence – and begged Sandra to end what she

started with the old thorn, however she would do it. She would not.

The gods waded in by suspending her interest in the whole project of schooling. Finally, she dropped out in second year and I was relieved, both from burdensome class-work undertaking and from the seething jealousy of a deprived lecturer. And of course there was also freedom from Sandra's oppressive sex. Different strokes: one man was frowning over sexual inundation; another, over its deprivation.

But the lecturer's politics of sex got me wondering how that little piece of exercise could make a whole lot of difference between peace and sheer evil. A man can easily concede his material possessions to another, can tolerate emotional cheating – that occasional pastime of his wife crushing on other men, say, celebrities. To spare that little piece of meat, even for his best friend, never! Long friendships, peace and love can vanish at the mere appropriation of sex, even as such encroachment reduces neither the proportions nor the pleasure quality of the very asset!

The three years that followed presented the most turbulent experience in hardship. My salary had been marginally increased, but with the gruelling tithe that went to Cerberus, I felt no improvement in my condition with the residue. No one could live the semblance of a normal human life in Lagos in 2007 with a monthly take-home package of seven thousand naira. I couldn't afford new clothes. Collars that lost their colours were chopped off and replaced with suitable material from the tailor's off-cuts. The same tailor, my neighbour whose workshop was a corner of a small room, had an amazing intelligence for clothe repairs. No matter the degree of depreciation, every piece of clothing had a chance of life beneath Taye's needle.

I managed to wobble to my final year. Final exams were around the corner and I needed to pay up all my debts in school to be qualified to sit for them. Podrecca had now owed for three years. Promises of payment were extended as soon as they elapsed, for the umpteenth time. No opening at the other firms where proposals were submitted, still. If I was unable to write the exams, my Grade Point Average would be adversely affected, and all the previous efforts that yielded superlative grades would come to nought given the implication of carry-overs. Much as I did not believe in grades, I felt obliged to obtain a merit so deserving, having worked so hard to trounce my demons. Fifteen thousand naira stood between me and the exams. Tony had been so helpful all along so when he said he had no money on him for assistance, there was no basis for any scepticism. For once in a very long while, I became very anxious. My indifference failed. Neighbours, relatives, none had money to lend me. Tales of excuses tumbled over one another. The first paper in the exam was three days away. All that had been laboured for in the past four and a half years was at the verge of crumbling. The last hope was Chima, that short kind man that bailed me out of the woods when Okey failed to help execute Luigi's first order. Chima should not just fail me.

He did, unfortunately. Stories. All were credible.

The only option left to me was to beg the director of students' affairs in school. The man had an erratic mood, wore the same clothes everyday, and soliloquized a lot. He alone could issue a clearance to enable me write the exam. I had openly challenged him one day over an issue of school conventions. A mutual hatred was alive between us. There was no point trying.

Two days to the exam I called a friend in Podrecca, the young man that ushered me into Luigi's office on that very first day. Maybe he could help me talk to whoever currently pulled the strings in the accounts department to see if any little sum could be paid to help solve the problem at hand. No way. The company had been emptied of cash, and even of personnel. All the expatriates who held strategic positions had either left the country or gained employment elsewhere. The remaining personnel were mostly those who saw no future outside, who clung so tenaciously to the hope of resuscitation for lack of choice. The company owed me well over N300,000 yet I lived as a pauper. Money held in bad debts equates to that child-like pastime of claiming ownership of sleek cars and mansions on the streets, possessions whose utility ended in zones of the imagination.

My phone discussion with the friend at Podrecca scoured off all vestiges of hope for payment. More revelations showed that financial haemorrhage had set in. But there was something very auspicious about this corporate collapse: Roberto, one of the Italians who worked there had pulled out and set up his own construction firm.

"Maybe you should come to the office here to see him, he still comes around very often. He needs a contractor to work with", said the friend on the other side of the call.

"I'll be there tomorrow morning, and wait till he shows up whenever he will," I chirped.

By 8 o'clock the next morning, I was already at Podrecca. As I was exchanging greetings with my friend within the company premises, Roberto drove in. I approached him as soon as he got off his car. He was a man sprung by a demonic sense of haste. He walked with a briskness that seemed like he was being perpetually pushed forward at the back of his head by an unseen hand. I introduced myself, my business and all. A few questions and then, "Come to my site tomorrow morning, Sipco Oil's premises at dockyard, Apapa."

The Sipco site was a three-thousand square-metre loading base under construction. The rhythm and boisterousness of work filled the air with prospects of contractual engagement. The buzz of the compactor on its suppressive tread; the stationary chug of the cement mixer as it emptied mortar into headpans carried by dust-suffused labourers mandated to fill up spaces for casting; the whine of a Bosch grinding machine on that tedious task of cutting several millimetre ranges of reinforcement bars; the fall of carpenter hammers on wooden frameworks; the rise and fall of the excavator's fang chewing holes in the ground... Roberto propelled himself around from one work spot to the other supervising, shouting at some incompetence here, commending a piece of good job there, cigarette in hand. A young man in his mid-twenties, he was filled with that enthusiastic energy of a goal-driven entrepreneur. He had just set up Rontech Nigeria Limited with the supervisory assistance of his father Enrico, who had lived and worked in Nigeria for over forty years. Roberto sighted me walking up to him over mounds of granite and laterite. He drew a long inhalation from his smouldering cigarette, puffed a linear smoke over his nose, threw it down, stepped on it, and walked hastily forward to meet me up on the way.

"My friend! You don come already? Very good! Very good."

"Morning sir, such a big site", I remarked.

"Yes! This is our first job, we're new in the business."

"Yes I know sir, I knew you back then at Podrecca, I know that Rontech just came on board."

"Podrecca is a closed chapter now," he said ruefully. "Your people were thiefing all the money when a black man became the general manager in the Lagos branch... All of Podrecca's big projects in Lagos .... The estates at Lekki and Victoria Island, you people thief all the money with Lebanese man..."

He was already getting angry, gradually, judging by the look on his face. I was not about to let a nostalgia I knew nothing about get in the way of the chances of that meeting.

"Well I was only a vendor in Podrecca sir. All my money is stuck in the whole mess even."

"Anyway, I need three rolls of 20kg binding wire urgently. Can you supply now now?" he asked.

"Sure sir!"

I left, happy yet troubled. There was now a new opening, yes, but there was no money to either fulfil the requirement of that opening or pay up my debts in school. The exam would start the next day. That I had not been reading for the exam was not within the scope of my worries. I needed to execute this current little job from Roberto to earn my place, a prime position, in this new company. There was no one to go to, no hope from anywhere. I shed tears as I left the site. I remembered I had not prayed in a long time. "Father please see me through, amen."

I hated long prayers, no matter the severity of a problem. I did not believe God to be so hardhearted that one has to suffer oneself to be able to impress Him. Communing with God, I felt, was primarily an act in silent psychology, featuring a consciousness of the divine ownership of life and everything in it. On the few occasions I went to church ever since I began reading quite extensively, I always dismissed my own service before the pastor did, whenever matters got to repeated prayer points amid the commotion of spiritual chants.

"God already knows whether He'll answer your prayer or not. Is He not omniscient?" I'd often tell Tony whenever the issue of casual praying came up. "See, everything is already predetermined, Tony, forget those lofty arguments by the Existentialists. We only have to pray and act since we do not know what is in the frameworks of our destiny, still matters have already been decided."

I left the site without knowing what to do, where to go. There was little money left on me so I decided to trek all the way from Apapa to Ijora, a forty-five minute journey by foot, to see Chima. Though Chima said he was broke, there was no harm in sharing the Rontech news with him. Again Chima, incarnation of the spirit of that Biblical Samaritan, picked up the gauntlet. He lent me money for my school debt and for the execution of the little order! I hurriedly picked okada to hasten delivery of the binding wire, after which I practically slung myself down to the designated bank to pay up the school debt. Roberto was impressed. "Come to this site every morning to pick orders, you're fast on delivery." There was joy in heaven over the happiness of one man on earth - my excitement had reached there.

The final exams lasted for over one month - part-time exams were scheduled to take that long. Within the period, I went to the site to pick orders every morning, mainly supply orders, most of which were sponsored free of interest by Chima. Profits were fair, but not as much as I would have liked. Roberto paid upon delivery and that made a lot of difference. He even made advance payments for orders that involved fairly larger sums. Little by little I began to build up capital from this string of daily small earnings. On the last day of exam, I shared my testimonies with Tony.

"I've been thinking, everyone had to disappoint me when I wanted to borrow money to pay up my school debt, such that I was pushed by desperation to call my friend at Podrecca, who gave me the information about Roberto and his new firm.... Doesn't that tell you something about destiny?"

"Those were blessed disappointments," Tony responded. "Do you know I had some money I could've lent you, but I had a burden not to help? And if you hadn't called your friend at Podrecca, you wouldn't have seen this new opening."

"Chima my friend said a similar thing too, that he forgot he had some savings somewhere."

Tony was silent, appeared to be munching over a thought in his mind. A stare into the void and suddenly he jerked up.

"Does that mean God prevented us from giving at that time so you could find your destiny?"

"Perhaps! It appears the path to destiny is a pre-determined one. The individual is only being tossed about by events within the contemplation of fate."

"Hmmm! So personal efforts do not change anything?" he queried.

"Maybe they 'change' only what was pre-destined to be changed. To us, there's a change but to destiny, everything is the same as pre-ordained."

"That's wrong, Victor. You tend to suggest that one cannot kill one's destiny by laziness, or find it by conscious effort."

"I think your destiny finds you, not the other way round. The efforts you made were part of the plot of the drama. That's why it's ridiculous to allege that destiny can be delayed and not denied."

"How?"

"See, if there's anything like destiny it is something no one has control over. Destiny is the overall circumstances of one's life as determined by fate. What you call 'delay' is already envisaged in the whole script. Like, you were scripted to get rich at 28, and at 25 you got so close to it but it slipped, and you go about alleging delay."

"Viiictor! So the people that say your destiny has been diabolically tied down don't know what they're talking about?"

"Well you said so. Destiny is not necessarily positive remember. Christians merely redefined it to fit into a perpetually positive slant to suit the Biblical quote that 'His thoughts for us are thoughts of good and not of evil.' Christ was meant to die so we could live, so says the Bible. Doesn't that tell you that someone had already been prenatally nominated by Fate for the task of betrayal?" I asked.

"Your philosophy is capable of making people lazy and justified in not accepting responsibility for their actions. But then do you think a just God would lodge evil on someone arbitrarily?"

"Tony it depends on what you call 'evil'. For instance, if the wellbeing or safety of millions of people depends of the death of one man, would you call the machination that led to such death 'evil' since it serves a just cause? Men define evil in very shallow terms."

"I don't understand where this argument is going since you always confuse matters more than you clarify them."

"I'm only thinking aloud, I hardly draw conclusions on knowledge. I know things I held so passionately to be true some years ago, defending them wherever. Now I look at them and shudder at the arrogance of my ignorance in arguing for such knowledge."

Like one of our many debates this one raged on from one topic to the other, back and forth until some extraneous event intruded and wound up the intellectual pastime. This was to be the last in school. We were now graduates, at least in the hope that there wouldn't be any carry-overs. Tony was to pursue a career in journalism, make some money and pursue further degrees, after marriage. A girlfriend was already waiting in the wings for this twenty-five year old man who was so honest he never cheated on the lady throughout his undergraduate years. I wouldn't want to work for anyone. An entrepreneur, I would make money from Rontech, set up more businesses in construction solutions and possibly also, set up an advertising agency.

Supply orders from Rontech became a daily affair. Sipco Oil, owner of the loading base being constructed by Rontech at Dockyard, Apapa, later reviewed its contract with the construction firm to include the construction of a five-storey office block. This increased the demand for cement. As a clear-eyed entrepreneur, Roberto knew the advantages of buying the product directly from Flour Mills Ltd; a first-rate cement-importing firm with huge economies of scale, rather than from middlemen and cement dealers. He had sent a couple of e-mails to the firm without any response. He approached me.

"You're a Nigerian, maybe you could have a way around it. I don tire."

"Will try my best sir," I intoned.

He often code-switched. I offered to help. But the first and second time I went to Flour Mills, overzealous security men turned me back when I said there was no previous appointment with the director of cement operations. The third trial and I was able to gain entrance. At first the director was supercilious, softening when I spoke fairly eloquently.

"We don't sell cement to every lame-duck company. Our product could be adulterated and resold," he bragged.

"We're lucky then since ours is not a lame-duck sir. This is a construction firm building a 50,000 tonnage capacity loading base for Sipco Oil, one of Nigeria's foremost players in the downstream oil industry."

I exaggerated, but it worked.

"Very well then. Let me see your company profile and I'll see what I can do."

My course of study encompassed training in Advertising and Public Relations. That training was brought to bear on the conceptualization and design of the company profile. Rontech was a three-month old firm, so it was difficult projecting any

unique selling proposition. I had to dwell on the pedigree of the
two owners of the company, Roberto and his father Enrico,
especially as the latter had worked in the construction industry
for about forty years, starting from Italy. I also thrived on
illustrations: several angles and views of high-definition shots of
the Sipco site, equally focusing on strategic pieces of work, were
featured. A ten-page spiral-bound corporate profile with an
introduction written in elegant prose interspersed with eloquent
pictures did a lot of convincing. Roberto saw it and smiled
contentedly. Upon submission the Flour Mills director only
nodded, took off his huge eye-glasses and slammed a stamp on
the first page and minuted on it. Rontech could now pay directly
into F.M's account and get a 7% rebate per bag. With an esti-
mated need of 20,000 bags, the cost-saving implication could
only be imagined. There was also no imagining Roberto's
excitement. His respect for, and admiration of me, grew tremen-
dously.

Christo La Madonna

Rontech Nigeria Limited carved a niche for itself with the deployment of superb Italian building technology in the Sipco contract. Sipco's internal technical auditors and supervising engineers as well as discerning visitors praised the quality and speed of job. One of such visitors was a certain oil magnate, owner of a prosperous chain of oil and gas service firms across the West-African sub-region. He needed to construct a 50,000 tonnage capacity loading base for his numerous trucks at his private oil jetty in Lagos in addition to three multi-storey office blocks within the jetty. Construction of an underground palatial residence on a five-plot piece of land in Ikoyi and that of three other housing units in Banana Island were also open for bidding. As soon as Roberto accepted the condition of ceding 40% of Rontech's equity to this magnate, the deals were closed. Rontech won all the contracts, the total of which was in the neighbourhood of five billion naira. A new chapter was opened for anyone who had anything reasonable to do with the company.

Upon the reception of the mobilization fee, Roberto imported some Italian civil engineers to man strategic operations, rented a befitting corporate office in high-brow Ikoyi, and bought some necessary equipment and vehicles for take-off. For the residential houses in Ikoyi, the client imported most of the building materials and accessories out of a flamboyant passion for post-modern structural aesthetics. But there was still some-

thing substantial left for the likes of my small firm, Famalec, in
the small-scale category of supplies, especially at the loading base
site. I stood a better chance of winning any local supply order in
the face of competition from prospective entrants; Roberto had
come to like me a lot after the Flour Mills cement feat. Enrico,
now technical director of Rontech, wanted a bidding system that
would award orders to the cheapest vendor across board. With
the new string of contracts, he had to resign his position in a
notable Italian construction firm in Lagos to fully join his son in
building a new company. But his son wanted to reward me for
engineering the Flour Mills price advantage in cement purchase,
especially now that the demand for the product given the new
jobs had multiplied over and over. Accruals from the rebates
given were just too impressive.

For Enrico, a man in his late sixties, business was to remain
devoid of sentiments. More suppliers were trooping into the
sites offering to supply materials at ridiculously cheap rates. The
general business scheme was always to penetrate a new company
even at the expense of profit or by forfeiting part of invested
capital. There would always be other means to recoup later.
Enrico was a real Machiavellian known for crude tactics and a
penchant for violence despite his age. He was also a twin brother
to Luigi in the art of shouting though his own eardrums were yet
intact.

But generally speaking, shouting has always been Italian.

At the time, Rontech had no definite organisational structure. Both Roberto, the managing director, and Enrico could
place orders, especially with the fact that most of the materials

were always urgently needed. So whoever was around between them could give approval, but most of the time it was Roberto.

The first set of orders went to me, from Roberto. Good profit. Roberto advised that I should expand the vista of business by learning at least the rudiments of other areas of technical support: tiling, roofing, epoxy screeding, blanding, grouting, Plaster of Paris, painting, specific technical installations, etc. I did. More and more orders came tumbling in. At a point I was obviously under-equipped, technically and otherwise, to handle all. Delays. Roberto tolerated it all, resisting the urge to revoke some orders and re-award to intrusive vendors. Enrico was the man of the site, the other, an office man. The old man wanted requested materials supplied on time to speed up the job; he wanted indentured jobs executed within the stipulated time. Sentiments would not let those happen.

Soon tempers flared between father and son, between reason and sentiments. The old man visited one of the sites to see how I was faring with the acoustics in one of the special rooms in the Gym at the Ikoyi residence. A disappointed Enrico pranced angrily about, took off his eyeglasses and smashed them on the wall, screaming and throwing up his hands: "Christo la Madonna! Christo la Madonna! You no sabi work! You delay too much! Christo la Madonna! Deo kani! Contractor la melda! Christo la Madonna!" A phone was prised out of his trouser pocket, numbers punched, and it went to fill up a scaly earlobe. Roberto was at the other end. The harangue was conducted in tensed Italian language, in pitches that yo-yoed between calm and aggravation. 'Christo la Madonna' was the most assertive phrase, repetitive in its vent of foreign frustration. Finally, call was dropped. "Stop work! Come to the office tomorrow morning. We have cancelled the order!"

The mood at the office the following morning was unnerving. I sat at the reception. Roberto walked in and out of his office a couple of times through the reception, pretending not to have seen me. Greeting was ignored. I rehearsed my speech, panting nervously.   I had wanted to consolidate the opportunity in Rontech towards the attainment of other dreams to disappoint poverty finally. If another vendor should be given a chance to clamber onto the scene on account of this flop, things would never be the same again. I knew this, and it bothered me. I wondered why Sod's Law always manifested against me - why things would always go wrong whenever I thought I had reached stability. While I was brooding over the situation, Roberto called me into his office.

The Italian in him took over: the shouting was savage. "Go away! You delay my work! I no want you again, finito!" It went on and on, both hands slammed vehemently on the table, shaking some stationery out of position. Anger exaggerates offence. There was no space for my speech given the pre-eminence of his howling. There was equally no point sitting down there like a frightened pupil, taking in roared vilifications from a white lad. The anger was righteous, I acknowledged. But the dimensions of its expression and the arbitrariness in the halt of a signed contract challenged my own sense of rebellion. I equally acknowledged that any confrontation with him over the manner of this abrupt revocation might restore the job to me, but there would be no second chance after that. Right from my childhood there had always been this visceral hatred of subjugation, the hatred of being treated like an inferior person. It was this hatred that propelled me to stand up to Ekwueme after the separation from Mother; that edged me towards juvenile deviance in secondary school. The same spirit that weaned me from general conformity to illogical convention in school, that placed me at loggerheads with Cerberus. My study of philosophy had helped me eschew my main hubris of anger to a large extent.

I left Roberto's office in silence, angry. Or rather, sad. Nothing could be more ennobling than silence in the face of provocation. First, it keeps the other man off-balance, leaves him guessing at the quality and nature of retaliation. It also saves the silent man the danger of giving himself away in rash skirmishes, saves him from the latter charge of foul language. More importantly, it exalts him above the depravity and childishness of insolence. Yes, anger enables one to speak pent-up, bitter truths to others, but spoken truths lose nobility when encased with vituperations. The silent man is almost always the winner. I won, by silence.

Hardly had I got to CMS from Ikoyi when Roberto called me back. A second meeting, same office. A fluttered white man was the image, flouncing from one corner of the office to another, smoking but not smoking: the cigarette smouldered between fingers, the ash coming off on its own. Pure theatrics. A stare on the floor, on the ceiling, in the void. A scratch in the furry hair as if to scratch out decisions. A deep breath, followed by a humane question.

"Victor, do you know why I'm giving you all the jobs?"

"I know sir."

"So why can't you do your part well? My father is bringing another vendor to replace you; you failed me with unnecessary delay."

"I feel so bad for disappointing the expectations of a man who wants the best for me. No excuse can justify that sir. Can't say much, please give me a last chance. I'll round off all my jobs within five days. It's a promise."

"So after five days I can cancel the orders if you fail?"

"Exactly sir."

Roberto's brows were raised. He shook his head and brought out his cheque booklet from the drawer.

"I'm going to pay you everything in full. I hope you won't run away with the money. If you fail this time, there won't be another chance. You need money to push the jobs."

He flipped through the contract papers, punched numbers on the calculator to put the figures together, and scribbled stuff on the cheque leaf. A customised Zenith Bank envelope emerged from the drawer and the cheque was slipped into it and handed to me: Three million Naira Only. Happiness was a lesser word for what I felt when I left Roberto's office and opened the envelope. It was the value of all the jobs I had at hand. I had never owned such money all my life. The net profit was about half of the paid sum. Work was intensified to ensure completion within five days: a standby okada was on a daily hire to take me round the sites from Apapa to Ikoyi as often as was necessary, and to wherever I needed to go in the course of work. Also, a generator was rented to facilitate night work. Ultimately, I delivered. An excellent quality of work was it, a befitting compensation for the delay, one that impressed fastidious Enrico.

Roberto felt vindicated in the presence of his father, as I took them round for inspection.

Meanwhile, another juicy order was already sleeping in a requisition file at the corporate office in Ikoyi. The inspection ended at one of the residential sites in Ikoyi, and the team, comprising the Italian duo, a driver and I, headed back for the office in a double-cabin Toyota Hilux. A happy Enrico was locked in an Italian chat with his son at the back of the car. I was strapped to the passenger seat at the front. He had replaced his smashed eyeglasses with very dark ones that suited his ruffian mien. Old yet young in his workaholic energy, he often took ill whenever he could find no work to do, and would soon recover when plonked on the site for some new task. Most site supervisors would merely supervise work and hurriedly seek comfort in some air-conditioned office or car. Not Enrico. A man with a very curious constitution that performed better with age, he hated the sight of both conventional and make-shift seats on the site - he never sat down, and no one should. He would walk the length and breadth of the site inspecting some ongoing task here, another there, cracking jokes in Pidgin English. Sometimes the perambulation was for the fun of it, or a facilitation of the mental voyage for solutions to work palaver, if not a mechanism to cushion the bite of unending phone calls. No, the calls always ended, but either in the fatal dismembering of the phone from being smashed or in the ear-splitting pitch of shouted Italian insults. The regular hurling of phones on the nearest barrier in the height of anger necessitated purchase of very cheap models, those whose imminent crash would be of easy toleration.

But he was also a very humorous man. There was always a
taunt for everyone: the short man he'd playfully chide for being
too far from the reach of grown men; the tall one needed
calibration for site measurement needs. And don't ever tell
Enrico that you forgot to do a job he assigned to you. Else he
would go, "Christo la Madonna! Every time forget! Every time
forget! One day you will forget your penis between a woman's
legs!" He lived his life one moment in anger, the next in joy, as if
by compensation.

From the back of the car he threw a sudden question at me.

"How old are you?"

"Twenty-eight sir."

He mumbled something to his son in Italian, apparently ex-
pressing surprise that I was a year older than he, Roberto.

"Which state are you from?"

"Imo, sir."

"I know Imo. I don work for Awomamma before when I
was with Cappa and Dalberto. From there I go Aba and Uyo....
You do face like beta person. If you can do your job well, I don't
have a problem with you."

"I'll do my best sir."

"Only say you never get experience, you just dey learn, dey
hire technicians up and down," he whined.

"Baba give me a chance. The job is like sex: it's learnt in the
very act."

Laughter. Both of them were very fond of lewd jokes. All
the while Roberto had been silent in the car, only laughing
occasionally.

"Anyway," said Enrico, "I'm making you an offer: if you can give us good prices and discounts for all supplies and contracts, we'll give you all the work. No need inviting quotations from new suppliers."

I looked back to face them, smiling. Enrico's toothy smile showed off the wealth of yellow cream over his aged teeth, a decay that looked like a natural costume to blend with his skin tone.

"That is not a problem sir. What is important to me is the turnover, not the size of mark-up per unit," I stated.

"Very good! Very good!" said Roberto. "Keep your promise and we'll keep ours. We no be Lebanese, we no be China or India, we're Europeans. Be a good man and you'll make money from us; we'll make you rich."

That sounded a bit boastful but the gentleman was not out to flatter himself. He meant every word he said, Enrico too, and I recognised that the door had been opened for greater exploits. I was pleased with the cordiality that had just been established.

Manifestation of that European pledge did not take long. I added little value as mark-up in every quotation, but it did not matter since orders were a daily manna and payment was very prompt. Testimonies in the sterling quality of Rontech's jobs soon raked in a couple of new clients. The coast broadened, especially for my Famalec, whose capital base had grown astronomically within a space of eight months. Notable physical changes swirled all around me: a fresher skin, exquisite fashion and some other signatures of contented, improved living. Soon I realised, as if suddenly, that my one-room apartment was such a demeaning rabbit hole. A new, decent flat was rented and furnished modestly but impressively. With the new state of affairs, I decided to resign from the security job. I had even been too lackadaisical in that job since the new realities showed up at Rontech. It was time to bid farewell to a seven-year old slavery and chart a new course. Apart from the Rontech bounties, the feeling of being a competent graduate enlivened the thought that I had already been bred for greater things through education. To remain in the job was to accept a lesser definition of myself, to bless my own humiliation. Cerberus pretended that he would miss my services, as if it was not obvious that what would be missed was the monthly exaction that saved weekends from the abetting of slavery. I had continued to remit the corruption to him even after graduation, so I could enjoy weekends like every other normal person.

The new apartment had much sapping effect on my finances. But it took only a few months to refill my pocket given that Rontech kept me busy with many contractual offers. Work had become too demanding, more elevated, such that public transportation could no longer offer the needed convenience. I would have liked to be patient till I could afford a brand-new car, but that would be a long wait considering that my income was yet not big enough. A tokunbo car would be just fine in the meantime. I got one.

It was now one year since I left school. The result was out, my performance was outstanding. I needed to visit the campus to do my clearance and collect my result so as to commence my post-graduate studies immediately. The plan was to pursue my second and doctorate degrees seamlessly in preparation for a latter aspiration of being a university lecturer on a part-time basis to contribute in correcting some of the anomalies in the system hands-on. Visiting the campus for clearance was an opportunity to meet Tony again and review the events in our lives. The Calabar man had become a senior state-house correspondent in a national newspaper. He had been working in the medium all the while we were in school. In the past year, we had merely maintained telephone conversations, and had been too busy to honour a meeting.

Tony was impressed with the transformations that had taken place in my life. Together we recollected the destitution of the past, tooting triumph in repeated guffaws.

"It shall be permanent my brother, provided you continue to pray to God. There's nothing like prayer."

Again and again Tony hooted this conviction until I cut in, and another round of debate ensued.

"You talk as if prayer were a cure-all formula," I noted.

"Yes it is! There's nothing prayer cannot do."

"Tony, prayer is over-hyped. I know a lot of people who are successful without being too prayerful. The black man is too superstitious, so he thinks little and prays more."

"Listen, one can never be too prayerful: You don't read your Bible, it says pray without ceasing."

All the while the argument was taking place in the car. Tony spoke casually as he was busy checking out the beautiful features of the car, opening and closing compartments, admiring the digital display of the stereo, feeling the texture of the leather seats, etc. I drove off towards a snack kiosk. Soon we were munching away gala sausage rolls, sipping the yellow soft drink.

"You see," I began, "We pray about everything in this country. We pray to earn admission, to pass exams, to graduate, to get jobs. We do nothing about our school system that churns out unemployable graduates; do nothing serious about our economy while progressive less-praying nations are thinking and creating value-driven products and services, bolstering up their economies. We'll turn around to use their products, like BlackBerry phones and Facebook, to broadcast silly messages warning ourselves about killer phone numbers. Our major industries are religion and politics."

"Hahaha, see as you just serious dey talk the matter. But seriously we need prayers to turn things around in this country, to get God-fearing people into government."

"There he goes again!"

"Mr Man, without God, we're nothing! No human endeavour or government can succeed without Him."

"Listen Tony, God asked a white man and an African man to close their eyes while they were praying in His presence. The African man shut his eyes firmly, while the white man opened his a little and was able to catch a glimpse of what God was doing while the praying was on. God was doing something on technology and development, and this white chap grabbed the knowledge instantly from the view of an open eye! Today his society is better for it. This explains the First-world-Third-world dichotomy."

"Hahaha, that's a hilarious joke! I get the allegory but I don't know how we can survive the current socio-political stalemate without constant prayer," Tony submitted.

"I'm not writing off prayers in the scheme of things, I'm only complaining that we pray when we should think. Our prayers are even too selfish: personal aggrandizement. According to Elnathan John, that Nigerian satirist, you attend a political meeting where people have come to discuss how to steal government money, they start with prayer. Boko Haram kills 50 people in Borno, we pray that God should shield us and our relatives from the attacks, as if those others that die are not His."

"Baffles me that in a post-millennial 2011 someone is willing to kill 'for God'. But don't you think if all of us as lovers of peace can fervently pour out our hearts to God this terrorism will stop? God has the hearts of men in His hands."

"Hmmm! We need to remind God to save His children, otherwise He wont? We can as well pray to God to forgive and change Satan like He changed Saul, so we can all have peace on earth!"

Tony was not in the mood for another round of discourse. He gave up and we went to the offices that would issue the clearance. Soon we left, promising to deepen our friendship with regular communication and visits, and share ideas on personal and career development.

For me, life had just begun. Proceeds from my current business would be ploughed back into other lucrative businesses to create multiple streams of income which would in turn be reinvested for positive multiplier effects. The current business was merely a tool for the huge task ahead: the task of creating sustainable wealth to enable me help others. There was a need to change the social status of my family by making sure my younger siblings had quality education; a need to help the poor and leave a permanent legacy in society; a need to champion socio-political re-engineering through youth empowerment.

Taking a wise, bold step in the whole process of berthing my dreams meant making informed investment decisions. I did not want to deal in goods merchandising. I felt it was too pedestrian, had too many risks around it, and demanded too much of a hands-on involvement. Preference was for career investment, for skills acquisition and development, one that required rendering of services rather than sale of goods. There appeared to be more economic security in skills and service-related businesses. There was a plan to set up one or two businesses dealing in tangible goods but a stronger passion was for the lofty idea of conceptu-alizing and selling television and radio programming content. My post-graduate study was in the spirit of learning innovations in television and radio programming, and in the quest to meet field persons who could contribute meaningfully to my idea.

But my flair for charity did not have to wait until I had sav-ings in millions. The posh car and a grand duplex in Lekki would not be threatened by a little grant to an indigent soul. I had a longing for modest material comfort, with a world-view that knew where to draw the line between comfort and ostentation. The argument that comfort is as good as showiness is lame. A sense of genuine comfort does not primarily seek to wow the onlooker by the sheer glory of a possession's grandeur; it seeks to satisfy personal longings for convenience and art, without regard to a flattering external opinion. Ostentation is the exact opposite, and can even be personally inconvenient. The only convenience to self is in the fatuous pleasure of an inflated ego, in people who derive their worth from the estimation of external opinion. I had a silent mandate of committing a part of my earnings to anonymous charity, no matter how little.

Human desires have a tendency of promising what they cannot do. I knew this, and knew that man lacks the capacity for a perfect, enduring happiness on earth. I knew that the red Ferrari that blazed so much excitement to its owner would soon turn monotonous; the new, coveted degree would soon become part of the accomplishments of the pauper's studious son; in ten years the exotic building would lose its cynosure appeal. Man can acquire new ones, yes, but has he saved himself from the budding cancer? Does his high residential fence follow him about to insulate him from the predations of the suicide bomber? Even death, that arrogant reality that does not necessarily need the assistance of a terminal ailment to assert authority, has not been settled. Man's life is an elusive quest for perfect happiness; the moment he attains a desire that promised that happiness, if some new trouble does not reduce the glow of that feeling, the feeling itself would naturally fade away. Happiness would be sought in yet another desire. Again and again the shadow-chasing persists till death. The individual who has cognition of these truths would be less swayed by material blandishments, and would do his part in the present to help fellow humans, to impact society with the little he has. He must not let desires stop him.

The real reward of charity is not in the reception of gratitude or in the prospects of divine benevolence. It is in the noble, privileged opportunity of playing the divine role to a fellow man.

But one must practise charity within rationality. Humans have a notorious tendency of wanting to receive perpetually for free. The benefactor must develop the character to say no to certain demands, even at the risk of losing his regard or incurring enmity. For, to grant people's endless requests at the expense of self is slavery, not charity. Part of the problem with generosity is the fact that the individual asking for some "little help" from another does not so easily recognise that he might be the tenth person on the queue. "I ask for just a little sum and he claims he has no money, how much is this little sum worth to him?" he reasons, faultily. He does not know that he has nine other colleagues making the same "little" demand, all seemingly genuine and life-threatening demands, the aggregate value of which is someone else's annual salary.

But I later identified how dangerous it could be to render help from a lack of relative security. I had to put charity on hold and build funds first. Later, I set up a retail outlet dealing in construction and engineering hardware. With proceeds from Rontech, I was able to raise part of the high capital demand for such a venture. I had to improvise, and in a few months, the outlet started operations with only three members of staff, including me. With proper management and periodic injection of capital, the outlet would, much later in the future, turn out to be another success story.

Sentenced for Nothing

The Peugeot 504 saloon car purred smoothly down the smooth Umuege road of red earth flanked by a withering farm of cassava and yam. It was harmattan. The trail of kinetic dust caught up with the haze, forming a thick whirl that blurred visibility behind. The wind wrought a beautiful uniformity with palm trees whose fronds were brushed to a side like women's hair. A patina of dust was encrusted on nearby leaves and on the lids and hairs of okada riders. An entire log of chewing-stick squirmed at a corner of the driver's mouth as he hummed the rhythm of Aka Nchawa. A man in his fifties clad in a sweater turned brown by dirt, he indiscriminately spat out the chewed essence of the stick from his side of the window. The wind pushed the matter back to the car where it came from, for the umpteenth time. I recoiled, noticing the act perhaps for the first time, having been lost in the thrill of the nostalgia I felt. I was not given to taking the owner's seat, but the taxi driver's mouth odour when we bargained the fare before taking off was sufficient warning against further proximity. I cautioned the driver, asked him to slow down since we had now reached Umuege. My return evoked mixed feelings. I was happy that my fortunes had fairly improved, but Nne was not alive to welcome me.

It was now six years since she died. When the car drove into Ekwueme's compound, I saw her grave and my eyes felt heavy. I could not attend the burial because I had neither money nor

Cerberus' permission to do so. Nne lay beneath that finite rectangular bed with edges hedged with bricks. Death had never felt so final. I wept like a child, unmoved by the jubilation my return had generated. The epitaph formed itself in my mind:

There lies a heroine, whom the world could not honour for lack of fitting words; who put poverty to shame by dying rich at heart...

Nothing much had changed in the village. A few brick houses had sprung up but acute poverty still had a firm grip around. There were stacks of blocks bearing layers of green fungus signposting unrealised building projects.

Some young men came to greet me. They looked unappealing from an apparent lack of vitality. I offered them a bottle of tonic wine but they laughed noisily, mockingly.

"This one is water mixed with colouring and sugar! It can cause diarrhea. Or even diabetes," one of them sneered, the rest chuckling annoyingly.

"So what do I offer you?" I said smiling, but feeling a bit slighted.

"Gin!" they chorused. "This is harmattan. We need warmth. And we need to rinse our mouths."

"But I don't have any alcohol here, my brothers. The bachelor, who climbed an oha tree to pluck its leaves and make a soup for his guest, would serve the guest a ready-made soup if he had any."

"No problem," another replied, "And the Dibia who demanded an ant's heart for a charm knows that money can replace it."

We all laughed. "But don't you think tonic wine is more nutritious?" I asked.

"Who's looking for nutrition? Look at this one here," another said, pointing at his colleague, "He has just fathered the seventh child. Can one who lacks nutrition perform such a feat in just a space of twelve years?"

"I'm not even done yet," father-of-seven boasted.

"What do you need seven children for, mister man? You want to form a complete fence with their sheer number?" I asked, my eyes popping in surprise.

"Onye nwere mmadu kariri onye nwere ego – he who has people is richer than he who has money," father-of-seven rationalised.

"Very well then," I surrendered, "If you're curing a man with a swollen penis and he's still having erection, then it's better to allow him to go have sex with the dead woman he's lusting for."

I gave them some money to go buy ogogoro. The money was more than sufficient for them, and they fetched as many bottles as possible. They went hilarious as soon as the one who went to get the liquor came back. The oldest among them insisted on having the foretaste. He poured himself a short, planted the tiny cup on his mouth and gulped, sucking the mouth of the cup deliberately to produce a funny sucking sound, one that testified to the superb quality of the gin. "Aaah! This is it!" he confirmed, wincing as he put the cup down, adding, "Nwa-Akpa will make heaven – she doesn't ever adulterate her gin!"

I left them and went into my room, as they jested with one another, quaffing the alcohol excitedly.

Later, I went round compounds to greet people. My heart
bled with the degree of hardship I saw. One particular household was a heart-wrenching encounter.

I shouted my greeting in front of a tacky house owned by a
man who once lived abroad. A voice asked me to come over to
the backyard and I went. The man was eating. His right hand
would yank a fistful from the mound of fufu onto the other
hand, and both hands would cooperate to squeeze the white
matter thoroughly. He would scoop water occasionally from the
bowl by his side onto the fufu to let it attain the right consisten-
cy. Then both hands again would roll the fufu into a handy
cylinder from which he would cut little portions from either end,
and mould smaller balls at the wrist part of his palm. What stood
for soup lacked definition. It was supposed to be an egusi soup,
that often scrumptious thick cuisine made from ground melon
seed. That one was a mere sprinkling of grain in the midst of
grey water, with one or two strands of vegetable. No meat or
fish. Two of his six children sat at a corner mewing over the
insufficiency of soup in their own plate. His wife ignored them,
claiming she had already given them two rations. "They lick too
much soup," she told me when I asked her to grant their request. "I keep telling them, they don't necessarily have to drown
the ball of fufu wholly in the soup. Just an arc of it in the soup
and it'll still roll well down the throat."

The man was deported from Europe in the 80s for reasons
no one but him knew. No doubt a very brilliant man, he was in
Britain for fifteen years where he read criminology and nuclear
physics. After deportation he moved from Lagos to Port Harcourt and finally to the village when hardship got to a head. A

wasted life. Either out of shame or foolish desperation to redeem ego, he peddled a fictional script of the life he lived abroad: how he got so educated in Europe that the white man could no longer employ him, for his worth was far above what any firm could afford – and since the white man had no place for him, how would he get a job in a less-vibrant place like Nigeria? Asked why he did not stay back for a more tolerable poverty in Europe, he claimed he returned at the instance of Yakubu Gowon, a former Nigerian Military Head of State, who begged him to come back home and dedicate himself to the enormous challenge of nation-building; the nation needed people like him. Everyone in the village believed him. Lack of exposure often results in a sweeping sense of credulity. He spoke English like the white man, and deliberately mispronounced Igbo words to project a noble displacement from local life. He ultimately got tired of his affectations and mixed with the local crowd, more foolish and miserable.

But his assimilation into local life was complete with some additional excesses. In the evening of the same day that I visited his household, disquiet broke out between him and his wife. Those who gathered inquired from the man what the contention was all about. He referred them to his wife, who referred them back to the man. A discerning adult among the crowd smiled and left; he knew the agitation was about sex. The wife did not want any more children and, given the couple's lack of where-withal for proper contraceptive medication, she recommended abstinence but the man would have none of that. "I suspect she's seeing another man," he whispered to yet another adult in the fold. "Must she slam a total ban on the exercise? With proper timing, can't we determine when the threat of a baby is lurking in her waist and hold our peace?"

I moved from one household to another on courtesy calls, swarmed by little children who called me Dede, asking for one childish favour after another – I loved children. I heard my own story told in glorious fictions, tried to debunk them but the people that spewed those stories thought I was being too modest. "Don't be scared to admit how rich you are, we've heard it all. We're not asking for part of the money, just be grateful to God and be honest enough to admit His work," they'd say.

"It's for lack of talk that we say the tortoise has grown too tall," I'd reply.

Ekwueme was behind such stories. He went about boasting of an illustrious son, the one that he had been praying for all along. He even claimed the credit for my younger brother being in the university.

He had just relocated finally to the village having lost his job in Port Harcourt. Niger Delta militants would not stop kidnapping the expatriates in the company where he worked until the endangered whites fled the country and the firm collapsed.

When I got back to the house, I noted that a particular child among the children that followed me about refused to go, when his peers had all left. I needed to rest, but the little child was all over me, even though he had never seen me before. I gave him some money, and pleaded with him to go home and come back to play with me in the evening.

"Thank you, Dede," he said, Botu ngaa wu na nke anyi." – I'm from this house.

"Who's your mother?" I asked.

"Auntie Ebere."

I felt remorseful. And wicked. Ever since I came in that day I had not even asked of my only sister. I was still angry with her over how she disappointed me by getting pregnant again and again. I knew she was ill, but I didn't know it was as bad as I later saw –she was now terminally ill. The little boy's innocence was too cruel in indicting my aloofness to her plight. Ebere lay on a mattress that was too hard to distinguish from her body which had become flabby flesh stretched over a bag of bones. The room stank terribly yet I could not leave. She looked at me and saw the tears in my eyes. She made a sound that showed that she wanted to cry too, but there was no single strength left in her to express that emotion. She hummed the cry within. It was not bad enough that she was dying; she also could not cry about it.

Ebere's predicament had a long history. While I was still in Umuege before migrating to Lagos, she had dropped out of secondary school in form two when no one could beat her to the last position in class every term. She took after Ekwueme's erratic nature right from childhood, exhibited traits that qualified her for the tag of a demon-possessed child: she could take seriously ill in the morning only to jump around in sprightly health at noon without any medication; she couldn't tolerate passing through an entire day without a single quarrel out of a so-called demonic thirst for fighting. And none of her peers, not even the male ones, could ever throw her down during a fight. Hers was a physical strength that was incredibly unusual of a female teenager, which gave her undue leverage to trounce adults too, thus reinforcing that calculation of spiritual influence.

Back then, suspicions of her spiritual whatever-it-was got further validation when she came back from the farm one afternoon and fell down, convulsing. After about a minute she got up uttering meaningless things, soon regained normality but everyone was worried about the strangeness of the incident. There was no idea what led to the spasms, no idea what to do to avert a recurrence. Prayer was that it shouldn't happen again. It did. Exactly the same pattern. It soon became more frequent, and Ekwueme had to come to the village to take her to his spiritual church in Port Harcourt and the ailment stopped. But she was a mysterious child who would introduce the family to a new trouble to replace the one that had just been tackled.

Barely six months after I left Umuege on that first trip to Lagos after secondary school, I got reports from Nne that Ebere had immersed herself completely in deviant behaviour. "She'll soon get pregnant", Nne pointed out. That was in 2000 when mobile telephony still had elite exclusivity, so I could only write her counselling letters to preclude any embarrassment to the family. I begged her to realise that she was expected to provide leadership in the house since I was no longer around, begged to remember that I was in the city to pluck our own share of the world's wealth; that she should not disappoint me. I knew her delinquency was partly due to the absence of parental responsibility – Nne was too superannuated to wield authority over a girl of twenty.

In no time, Nne's prediction came to pass. I was extremely enraged at the news. Worse still, Ebere would not mention who was responsible for the pregnancy. She later had her baby and everyone thought she had learnt her lessons. How wrong they were! She got pregnant the second time six months after delivery. I moved from anger to indifference to the point that when one daring young man later came to marry her – daring by the sheer effrontery of that marital quest – I refused to be involved. I felt she would not cope with marriage. The man loved her, curiously so, despite her being troublesome. She had a child for him, her third, which she later abandoned and disappeared. Soon news reached her husband that she had instituted a case against him in a very notorious shrine in a nearby town, a shrine whose deity had gluttony for human sacrifice: it could kill an accused for contempt of injunction, or a complainant over failure to give thanks after justice. Problem was that she was still missing.

Months later, she was found wandering far away, pregnant yet again, though she later lost the baby. But that was not even the problem. She was now virtually mad. I got out of my indifference mode, spawned by a sense of embarrassment, and sent money across to Ekwueme for her psychiatric medication. The female psychiatrist turned fraudster, staging one episode after another of medical extortion. A second psychiatrist, a third and it was confirmed through experience that the extortion virus ran in the profession. It had now become a full-blown insanity with nothing to show for the astronomical charges of the psychiatrists. I was tired of spending money for nothing, but consanguinity propelled my resilience in trying to find a solution to a sister's ailment. She soon escaped from the last psychiatric home and went back to Umuege, virulent. Her extra-ordinary physical strength had been amplified beyond human regimentation to the point that no rope was strong enough to curb her violence.

Locking her up in a room was a waste of time; by God-knows-how means she would loosen the rope and break the door.

Ekwueme's relocation to the village was just some months old then. He told me how he went to the notorious shrine and performed some prescribed rituals in the fear that she might have incurred the deity's wrath by her frivolity. She didn't get better, got even more violent. He and some able-bodied young men in the village subdued and handcuffed her. She pulled at the manacles fiercely, dead to the pains of the incisions they bore in her wrist. Blood flowed, wrist-bones became visible by the sheer vehemence of her pulling but she would not let the chain be, and persisted in her tugging at the cost of her flesh. Within months the injuries worsened, stinky from suppuration yet she would not stop. Out of pity Ekwueme unhooked the handcuffs one day and the entire neighbourhood would not have peace. Sedatives couldn't work and she was handcuffed again. Clipping the hands became the only painful option. She felt no restriction if her legs were chained: her frog-jumping was faster than the run of most adults. Her power was in her single-boned hands.

Soon gangrene set in. Antibiotics were a waste of time, and the psychiatrist I had contracted to administer out-patient medication threw up his hands.

Details of her deterioration were not very clear to me until that moment I stood watching her struggle to cry. I felt my anger had carried me too far in judging her, that I could have possibly done something, earlier, to save her other than just send money across for her medication. If I had been involved, I would have known better how to handle schizophrenia. I cried, held her palms ignoring the stench in the room, and said sorry. Then I prayed for her. That moment it dawned on me that I had not begun my charity where it mattered most.

That night I could not sleep. Memory is a heavy burden when it carries guilt. The situation united me and Ekwueme. It was very painful watching her inch away helplessly.

How I embraced Ekwueme without squabble and placed him on a monthly grant surprised Chima, that benefactor that helped with Luigi's orders and those first orders from Rontech. Chima also hailed from Umuege and was equally home for Christmas.

"I'm really amazed at how you put aside all what your father did to you. Now you treat him so well," he said.

"I treat him so well because he did me a huge favour."

He looked even more surprised. He did not understand how a man who abandoned his children when they were yet tender granted them a favour by so doing.

"He pushed me to self-discovery, to my destiny," I explained, "If he had taken me to Port Harcourt and trained me as a mechanic as he had suggested, I don't know if I would have turned out well. He helped me by default. If you do not forgive those who denied you favour, those whose hostility catalysed your growth, you are being ungrateful."

"Hahaha. You and your funny principles. Anyway I'm very happy about this. Please don't ever stop being nice to him....Meanwhile, are you coming for the occasion holding today at the Town Hall?"

"What occasion?"

"You never heard? Emeka, the rich businessman from the neighbouring village is to be honoured with a chieftaincy title today. He's being crowned the Omereoha 1 of Igboland. Every who-is-who in all the bordering villages and communities will be there. All his big-boy friends will spray money today like they pluck it from trees."

"Lucky him. So what am I supposed to be doing there since I don't have money to spray anyone?" I inquired.

"Don't be stingy mister! It is in things like this that you establish your social status and prestige and let people know you've arrived."

"I do not have a problem with self-esteem, nor do I need to prove anything to anybody. I haven't even arrived in the sense you mean."

"You may not have arrived, but you are better than most of the people who spray money in occasions like this."

"Even if I need to give money to someone in a ceremony like this, I don't have to throw it in the air in single notes so that the crowd can cheer and rate me a rich man."

Chima counteracted, "Well we came for Christmas. It's all part of the fun. Don't be too hard on yourself. When sleep becomes too enjoyable, one should start snoring."

I turned over my palms in apathy. I detested that culture of neo-elitism in Igboland expressed in the blatant idolisation of wealth in gaudy celebrations. Some rich men and women afflicted with a mirror-licking sense of self and cynosure mentality would pay community leaders staggering sums of money to be conferred with high-sounding chieftaincy titles – titles that are sometimes, deceit attires covering criminal livelihoods and hollowness in values. Often, the braggart-oriented appellations ended with that numerical primacy "1", to assert the title holder's premier status.

The following day after my return, I went to Mbaise my maternal home to see my mother Nwugo. She was overjoyed. But I was not impressed with her appearance. She had grown too lean, not from a lack of proper nutrition, but from the tyranny of divorce stigma. Marriage, to the native Igbo woman, is thought to be either stoic toleration or sybaritic pleasure, summed up in that pair of marital motto: Di bu ndidi and Oriaku. In the first, husband is patience; in the latter, it is an invitation to a perpetual feast – both depending on the content of the man. The Igbo culture has structures for patriarchal impunity, by which the woman is often deemed the guilty party in divorce; she is expected to tolerate every piece of marital nonsense dished out by her husband. So when she is divorced notwithstanding the reason, she is silently socially ridiculed and stigmatized.

Meanwhile, Mother had been saving all the money I sent her rather than use it to buy better food and clothes. And she still believed Ebere could be cured, so she spent much of her savings on native medicine for her.

As she bounced all around me, embracing me repeatedly in sheer rapture, I smelt the whiff of dirt in her hair and clothes. Her hand stank of fermented cassava, that raw stuff for fufu, which she was sieving and later abandoned when I came. Her beauty was still intact.

But nothing could so easily repress the love of one's mother, not an obsessive sense of hygiene or the righteous anger over a mother's self-neglect. I held her firmly onto my chest and felt a pulse of emotions that ejected a few tears. I wiped them. She disengaged from my hold, looked at me again with unspeakable joy as if to be sure of my identity, to be sure that it was not a dream, and hugged me again. The second hug took longer than the first, her head buried beneath my arms. Suddenly, I felt some dampness around my chest retained by my light-tissue polo shirt - her tears of joy in reminiscence of an ugly past that seemed like it was never going to end. Her neighbours clustered around the two of us, complimenting what they called my rapid maturity. Shortly after the hugs and banters, she ushered me into a room for a private chat.

"Lagos water has shown all over you my son, eeh! You're welcome."

"Mama, which one is Lagos water again? Hahaha, I'm very happy to see you after all these years."

"Ehen now! Lagos water is different from the water we drink here. I'm very happy you're back. That's why I told you on phone the other day you called that it's not about sending money to me. Just seeing you can cure me of this rheumatism."

"Ah, you have rheumatism?"

"Hmmm, does your mother ever sleep at night? The pain struts from the back of the head through the spine, down to the pelvis. Then in the morning, it strolls all the way down to the knees and ankles and remains there till night again."

"So why didn't you tell me on the phone the other day, eeh? Have you taken medication?"

"My son, the palm-wine tapper doesn't tell everything he sees from the altitude. I've been taking Nkwocha's mixture. The ori has finished, but the other mixture for drinking is still available."

"That's good. But are you getting any better?"

She sighed. "It's no longer like the Nkwocha's mixture I used to know. When a medicine man begins to do evil, taking people's wives and lands, his powers are diminished."

I smiled. "So have you tried another medicine man?" I asked.

"There's no other in the whole of Ubahi-Mbaise. Everyone is now chasing ego bekee in the city. The chemist shop at the junction is useless; the man is now selling chalk, not drugs. You take them and it seems as if the ailment were revived afresh."

My eyes were fixed on her dirty clothes, then down to her interlocked fingers that still dripped water from the fermented cassava she was sieving. I felt embarrassed by her look, angry that she was not taking proper care of herself.

"But Mama, what have you been doing with all the money I'd been sending you every month? You look too hungry, too unkempt! Obviously you're not eating good food!"

"Don't be angry, please. I've been saving everything; I need to start a new business...."

"Oh my God! You mean you leave everything in your bank account? Please and please, use up whatever I send you, eat well, dress well. Whatever I send you is from the business I opened for you in Lagos. You don't need to open another business. Now dress up, we're going to Owerri; you need some new clothes and medical care."

She smiled and disappeared. I left the house to greet my maternal uncles and was held up for not more than an hour, within which time Mother had already quickly made an oha soup, my favourite.

"You're still not ready, Mama," I said when I got back to the house, as if I were not excited about the treat set before me.

"No, my son. God forbid that you come all the way from Lagos after so many years and I cannot serve you fresh oha soup."

The aroma flirted in the air from an oku, that black clay-plate of ages which was said to contribute deliciousness to soups, flanked by a similar plate bearing pure-white fufu that was smoothed into an arc. In the cream beauty of the soup I saw juicy pieces of stockfish and mangala, that smoked black fish of head-scratching taste. Mother made the soup just the way I liked it: neither too thick nor too watery. It was the highlight of my homecoming. I smiled and began the demolition, and in a short while the entire mound of fufu was relocated to my belly, but a small pool of soup was left in the oku. It seemed like wasteful-ness to leave out that residue to be washed away, and I simply lifted the oku, planted its edge in-between my lips and drank the remains.

On our way to Owerri we discussed every other important issue. She wanted me to begin thinking of marriage. I urged patience, claiming it was too early. She blew up the moment I told her my plans of bringing her and Ekwueme together.

"Never! I'll never live in that house anymore with that man who brought me out in the public and stripped me naked."

I was stunned that the wound was yet fresh in her mind giv-en the vehemence of her reaction. I placated her at the back of the taxi where we sat, whispered to her not to let the driver hear the discussion.

"Mama you often say that the child who talks too much will unknowingly greet corpse bearers."

"Allow me to talk, please!" she stressed loudly.

I kept quiet for some minutes to allow her gain some emotional stability before I spoke:

"But I never said I was going to bring you to his house. I'll build a house for you; that's one of the reasons I came back. I had wanted to renovate Father's house and create more rooms to accommodate you but I changed my mind."

She was happy with the plan and gave her blessings. I tried my best to pep her up a little and give her new orientation to life.

The new house was to be a modest but beautiful four-bedroom structure. The architectural plan was drawn by an Italian friend at Rontech. It reflected some trends in a postmodern building approach. As soon as Ekwueme allotted a land for the project, I contracted a builder and work began in full swing. The speed of work further buoyed my estimation by the villagers, who were used to seeing piecemeal, slow-paced work in similar projects. Before I later left for Lagos, the work had gone considerably far. Though there were a few decent structures around, houses built at such speed no matter the size still earned their owners undue flattery. I hated such elevation, for, it had the likelihood of placing one on a higher social pedestal, which could invite envy. Those who had self-conceit would find such idolisation very appealing. I wouldn't.

It was out of my distaste for materialistic flaunting and glory that I tried as much as possible to make my charity donations anonymous. But not every of such gestures could be perfectly shrouded in anonymity. I visited some poor widows in the village and some other persons to whom the receipt of Christmas goodies was a mere wishful thinking, and gave them whatever little sums I could afford. There was a general notion that prevented people from giving monetary charity: that witches used such money as a point of contact to destroy the giver's livelihood supernaturally. I did not bother about that, in my disdain for whatever looked like superstition. I, however, ran into another aspect of the charity problem.

It happened that some of those who received money from me felt convinced within themselves that I had much more to give. They made financial demands which, if not gratified, rendered the previous gestures invalid. They would define me by the present refusal, not the past giving. It had to do with that human nature in greed. All that did not bother me. I was not interested in their rating of my person, but rather, in my own intrinsic thrill at playing a humanistic role in another being. Close relatives who did not receive any gestures from me were angry, as if I owed them a responsibility in the first place. Some others who got sums below their expectation felt underpaid! No one understood that my giving was from my own insufficiency, that I just wanted to play a part in people's lives no matter how little.

As the New Year celebration approached, I left for Lagos. Roberto had called earlier inviting me to an Italian year-end party slated for the eve of December 31, the same day I left. After boarding at the Owerri Airport, the flight would not take off. Due to the scramble for air tickets during festive seasons, it was always difficult getting economy-class seats. I grudgingly had to fly first-class. Ten minutes after all necessary announcements the plane was still stationary. People grumbled, no one knew what was wrong. The flight attendants disappeared for lack of answers to passengers' queries. I was engrossed in reading Marcus Aurelius' Meditations. I often read it whenever I was aboard a plane, especially the pages that had to do with the need for a phlegmatic resolve in the face of death. I had no phobia for flying, no. I loved it even. Only a sense of death, especially given Nigeria's chequered aviation history. At a point I looked up, cast glances around the plane, and for the first time realised that the seat beside me was vacant. Only that seat was empty.

Shortly a young man with elitist airs got into the plane sweating profusely, quickly traced his seat number and sank into the vacancy beside me. In less than a minute the plane began to taxi. That was the God-knows-whom VIP that kept everyone waiting, whose fragrance smelt pleasantly feminine. There seemed to be an obsession with the Gucci brand, from wristwatch to shirt, down to his belt and shoes. I scanned him in curiosity through covert glances. Most air passengers are often too snobbish; one could fly for hours without a casual chat with a neighbouring passenger. This latecomer courted the impression of a self-conscious person, but he wasn't.

"I'm Jerry. Jerry Ohanekwe. How do you do?" he greeted smiling, offering a handshake.

"And I'm Victor Ekwueme, how do you do too? You kept everyone waiting sir. Money calls the shot," I remarked jokingly.

"Money ke? I'm just an ordinary Nigerian. I had an engagement with the governor. I think his protocol officers were responsible for delaying the flight since they caused my delay in the first place. They have their way around such things."

I smirked, asking: "And what manner of an ordinary Nigerian has an appointment with the governor of a state?"

"It's a media-related kind of appointment, my guy."

I became even more curious. I often had this kindred feeling
towards anyone who had anything to do with the media, having
majored in broadcast journalism in my study of Public Relations.

"Oh, you work in a media organisation?" I asked.

"Yea. I'm the general manager of TLT Limited."

"Haven't heard of that before."

"Many don't know about the name, they only know our
news outlets. TLT stands for Three-Lane Traffic. We own a
print medium, a radio and a television station, all headquartered
in Lagos."

"Now I understand. A media consortium kind of."

"Yes. Each of them has some autonomy in management yet
under the bigger umbrella of TLT, which plays supervisory
roles."

Jerry looked too young to occupy such a position in con-
temporary Nigeria. He exuded so much humility. We went silent
for some minutes after talking about his job, and I had to change
the topic.

"Ever read a philosophy book?" I quizzed.

"Yea. I read some during my degree programme in Law. I
hated them, they were too abstract and complex."

"You're not alone; a lot of people hate philosophy. It partly
has to do with that general notion of confusing it with atheism,
and also because most people feel it doesn't put food on the
table, that it only plays word games and makes men lazy."

"Haha, every profession has some form of societal denigration. We lawyers are said to be liars."

"And arrogant too," I chipped in, mischievously.

"You can't be serious! And you, what did you study, philosophy?" he asked.

"I just got back into school for my Master's in Broadcasting. I study philosophy as a vocation, in my quest for Truth."

"Nice. You work in a media outfit?" he asked me.

"No. I'm into construction business. But I have some aspirations that motivated my current academic pursuit....But if I may ask, is Law that relevant to management in the capacity you're in?"

"Well if you're a good graduate you can fit in anywhere. Besides I hold two Master's, in Company Law and in Management respectively, from Emory and Yale Universities. I left the US finally for Nigeria a year ago."

Not long the flight landed in Lagos; it was 8pm. We exchanged business cards, promising to keep in touch.

The Italian year-end party to which Roberto invited me was to hold that same day that I arrived, at night. I had just a potable hand luggage, having refused to take Mother's parcels of garri, vegetables and palm oil. Given the convenience of the hand luggage, I declined going home straight from the airport, and rather took a taxi to Roberto's house in Ikoyi.

By 9pm when I arrived there the party was already at its hedonistic best with the superfluity of alcoholic drinks. There were a dozen drunk, luscious Nigerian and Italian ladies. Roberto's living room, venue of the sybaritic banquet fumed with clouds of cigarette smoke whose bite was not cushioned by air-conditioning. Italian music rent the air as Roberto and his countrymen danced, amid shouts of joy. He was only too happy that I made it.

"Victor! Very good. Very good, you're here," he chirped, champagne in hand.

"Yea, I just came, sir."

"You can see everyone is happy, a lot of fun. Unfortunately you don't drink, you don't smoke. I don't know what kind of man you are. At least you go fuck,abi?"

"Haha, not today sir," I replied.

"So what will you be doing, you'll just sit here looking at us?"

"I'll take soft drink, and I like the smell of grilled meat that I perceive around."

"Pauuul! Serve Victor!", he ordered his cook.

"While he gets the meat ready, let me show you something at the garage," Roberto added, and I followed him to the front of the house.

"That's my new ride," he declared, pointing at a brand-new Wrangler jeep that squatted beside his two other jeeps.

"Wow! This is rugged! Good for our roads....And beautiful too," I complimented.

"And this is for you, this black jeep. It has a minor fault – overheating. You like it?"

"Sure! My car is too low for our roads; this is so useful, wow! I'm grateful sir!"

He threw the key at me and I started the car, revved it a little, and inspected the interior. I had an addiction with feel-good, cosy car interiors. "The interior of a car is the car owner's own reward," I often tooted. That jeep Roberto just gave out was his first after the Sipco Oil contract. The mileage was still very low. Our relationship straddled serious business and playful life. We were both in our late twenties, liked each other well enough to quarrel at the office over some work issue in the morning and get on the phone in the evening to talk about sex-capades and fashion. We had the same passion for Italian fashion. Roberto always didn't want the social angle of our relationship to befuddle the fact that he was the rich young millionaire boss who called the shots between my Famalec and his Rontech. Nor did he want too much formality between two 'happening' dudes.

I was full of smiles as we walked back to the party spot.

"I think I'd rather take the meat home, let Paul make it takeaway. I'll drive home in the jeep, my house will be best-suited for the feeling I have now."

"You're free, Victor. Drive carefully, eeh?"

"I will sir. Once again, I'm so grateful."

In the comfort of the jeep on my way home, my mind raced through so many issues in my life that had not been settled: I needed to create a political reality TV show for youths, one that would identify and honour brilliant young Nigerians across the nation, to be later extended to the West-African sub-region; I needed to establish two other private businesses to help firm up the future, one of which would be an advertising agency; and there was equally a need to institutionalise my charity endeavours. There wasn't that much money for everything, and my bread-winner status in the family further impacted negatively on my finances. With work demands at Rontech, coupled with my Master's programme, time was also a problem.

Each of the aspirations had a defined purpose: the proposed private businesses were to further strengthen my economic security and guarantee sustenance in the evening of my life. I knew that the law of diminishing returns applies to everything: that there often comes a time in one's life when things will take a nosedive, when progress is either stagnated or diminished; when the individual's glow is a bit dimmed. It must not necessarily translate to economic retrogression. For the politician, it might come in the form of reduced political successes and recession from limelight; for a show-business celebrity, the evening might come as diminished public charm; for the businessman, as lower fortunes. That evening is often there, and safer are they who see it in their daytime and prepare for it.

The youth and charity programmes were to be my legacies for society. Private wealth is nothing if the individual has not, by a dint of altruistic resolve, earned for himself some little positive place in human history, I reasoned. The mansions, fat bank accounts and biological posterity are too banal and primitive as one's only legacies in a world that created the arena for the expression of one's talents. The individual must force himself into the memory of the world by positively coveting a space on the earth's horizon for his eternal sign-off.

Part of my overall business diversification plan involved opening more vistas for contracts and supplies other than Rontech. I identified with a firm in the Victoria Island area of Lagos, Nanshet Limited, which was saddled with procurement functions for Oceanic Bank. Nanshet's manager was a very kind man who gave me a few contract offers. But before long a new governor took over leadership at the Central Bank of Nigeria, and sacked the managing director of Oceanic Bank over gross misconduct. The new management that was thrown into Oceanic cut off relations with Nanshet. I was adversely affected by the whole shuffle: Nanshet owed me approximately half a million naira and its manager had closed shop and absconded to the US in escape of the EFCC's manhunt for him. There were heavy allegations of graft purportedly involving the sacked Oceanic MD and Nanshet, for the latter was touted as a proxy of corruption. I was plunged into yet another loss, just as was the case in Podrecca.

The new Oceanic management, however, opened the door for independent vendors to come in and register with the bank, through a process of scrutiny. Vendors were asked to submit their companies' profiles, and come in person on a slated date for final, oral interview. On the interview day, the reception hall was filled with the fake glory of desperate-to-impress entrepreneurs, who decked themselves with grand designer shirts and suits, pruned their beards and hairs, plus other costumes of exaggerated personae. It had to do with that hypocrisy culture in interviews. Various brands of perfume merged to form a riot of scented air, such that relegated my Encre Noire to the status of talcum powder. I viewed the gathering without any loss of confidence. I loved simple high-end jeans trousers, and I wouldn't hesitate to wear such to any occasion if it pleased me no matter the level of formality demanded. That day, I wore a sleek pair of off-blue jeans, a striped Italian short-sleeved shirt with a white background, and a pair of suitable sneakers. My rather long goatee was a personality signature I acquired back in the university.

I was the last to be called into the room where four inter-
viewers sat around an arc-shaped table. The only female among
them was the anchor, a woman that looked sixty-something. As
soon as I entered the room, she withdrew the smile that tickled
her fat face, a smile created by whatever jest she made with her
colleagues before I entered. I had hardly sat down before she cut
in:

"Excuse me! Excuse me! Are you for this interview?"

"Yes ma."

"And you're dressed so casually like this? What's your company's name?"

"Famalec Limited ma."

She ploughed through the heap of bound company profiles
on the table and brought out the one for Famalec, skimmed for
some seconds and looked up.

"You're mainly into technical hardware and office equipment."

"Yes ma. I have some references at the back page."

"You don't tell me where to look at, young man, I know my
job! By the way why are you not responsibly dressed? This is a
corporate environment, you don't come here for this type of
interview with this kind of Osama bin Laden beard."

"I appreciate your observation ma, I'm sorry I couldn't edit
my personality for the sake of corporate pageantry. I thought
what was important was efficiency, not stage-craft. But I've
learnt now."

Laughter. There seemed to be an unspoken consensus that
there was no further need for more interview questions.

"Well I only made my observation as a mother would to her son, not in my official capacity. As you may know this whole process is to select only three vendors that will satisfy our procurement needs competitively. You'll hear from us soon, congratulations!" she said, wearing a conciliatory smile.

"Thank you very much ma, and sirs, I'm grateful."

I was very delighted that another auspicious opening had been created. But my enchantment was deflated as I drove out of the bank's premises. My phone rang. Ekwueme had bad news: Ebere had just died. I drove straight away from Ozumba Mba-diwe to Bar-Beach, both in Victoria Island. I needed a quiet time at the beach to cry privately a little, and think. I thought I was well prepared for that news having seen her when I travelled for Christmas. But I wasn't. I was devastated.

Her death unveiled the mask of envy and hypocrisy in Umuege. Just a week of mourning and I got wind of the rumour making the rounds that I used her for money-making rituals! The hearsay raged across nearby communities, a case-study of excellent percolation in the faceless act of rumour evangelism. Authors of the rumour, hard-working in their supposed ano-nymity, were extended family members who had come to receive money from me during my Christmas visit. There was no accurate word to encapsulate the emotion I felt: rage, sorrow, self-pity, hatred. My new emotion heightened when Mother called, tearful, recounting encounters of being embarrassingly looked at in local markets and gatherings. I had bought her a scooter, for which she was being silently stigmatised as one who was basking in the comfort of her son's 'blood money.' Not that she in the least believed the rumour.

Umuege was not the only poor village in the many communities that made up Ngor-Okpala in Imo State. But it was about
the lowest in education rating and socio-political exposure. Poor
village gossips had a story for everyone that was rich – and being
rich consisted merely in the ownership of a third-class tokunbo
car. Accomplishment of any ordinary monetary feat was often
suspicious to most villagers. The village gossips would commis-
sion envy-driven inquiries into the nature of past deaths in your
family at the news of your purchase of a 1982 Honda Accord -
all in their desperation to establish that your 'wealth' was acquired through money rituals. If they found nothing validly fishy
about such deaths, they would seek culpability in your personal
eccentricities, like your frequent wearing of a red shirt in your
red car, and your goatee must be a mark of occult membership.

In the throes of my grief, I visited Chima one evening to
share news of the grapevine circular of ritual wealth. I made it
clear to him how badly I was betrayed by a people I loved,
vowing not to attend any village gatherings again – those gatherings where indigenes discuss the progress of their communities.

"I don't want to contaminate them with my blood money.
Of course I'll pay any general levy, but that is the most I can
ever do. That passion for seeing our people grow out of the
present economic quagmire is gone forever," I whined.

"Oh no, you don't have to go that far. Not everyone in the
village is spreading the rumour. You say you believe in justice, is
that justice to impose on everyone the guilt of character assassi-
nation?", Chima asked.

"It will be difficult to identify the people fuelling this rumour, Chima. But it's only when you 'punish' everyone that this

issue of ascribing every little success to ritual killing can be brought to the level of community discussion. But hey, it's not as if they need me in the first place, so I'm not trying to sound important. It's a personal decision that'll have no impact on them."

"So what will you have achieved if you shun village meetings and refuse to play your own little extra part in bringing development to our people?"

"Well, I cannot sit in a meeting discussing progress with people who do not genuinely believe in that concept; who inwardly feel unhappy when progress comes in the life of a fellow kinsman; who lack the moral capacity to engage that topic by the contradiction between their acts and thoughts."

"Victor you're blowing this out of proportion."

"No! You're the one trivializing it. You don't know what it means to be accused of murder, let alone murder of one's own blood sister for money. It's very insulting because when they say I acquired money by black magic, they imply that I'm so stupid I couldn't have made it by legitimate means. You don't know how it feels to be sentenced for nothing. Chima just pray to God that if He's about to bless you, He should please hold His peace if someone is about to die in your family before or after that blessing."

Chima forced out a wry smile. He was genuinely disappointed in the rumour, having played a fundamental role in my little growth. He was just trying to minimize the agony felt by a kinsman.

"My brother you know the level of illiteracy and poverty in the village. You ought to treat them with forbearance because you know better. By any standards are you even a rich man?" he questioned.

"But it's not only the villagers that are hawking this rumour. It's also being spewed by some of our people here in Lagos; the people you'd think had been exposed to civilisation," I said.

"That would be very wicked of any Umuege man here in Lagos to peddle such nonsense in the village. Who among them doesn't know what you do for a living?"

"It's not for lack of such knowledge. You know some of them have been in Lagos for over two decades with nothing to show for it. They'd have to defend, or rather justify their failure to their parents at home that Lagos is such a hard place to make it; that this Victor guy must have done something supernatural to break even in less than a decade. Not that they believe themselves."

"Human beings!" Chima shrugged forcefully, his two shoulders literally touching his chin. I shook my head and said, "Most of the people who wish you success do not really mean it. They know that many human wishes do not come to pass and they inwardly pray that theirs for you would be one of such".

I later put the whole drama behind me. Ekwueme offered me much emotional support in the face of this evil rumour. There was that father-son relationship and it further cleaned out whatever was left of the unwholesome past between us. Whether his readjustment to fatherly responsibility had to do with the change of regime in the family's economics was not important. I wondered: Was his action in the past influenced by some personal factors that were not properly managed? He seemed to still have a heart. Family was born afresh.

But I recognised that generally speaking, rumours and such demonisation of success are not particularly a function of rural ignorance, nor are they always born of the undue awe by which pedestrian achievements are deemed great due to a lack of exposure to higher ideals. In developed cities across the world, especially in show-business, there has been an avalanche of reports accusing sterling musicians and performers of occult connections. People do not understand why a select few soar far higher than a teeming majority in a field of endeavour where the majority seem to have been around for ages, with lesser exploits to show. Lazy losers and haters circumvent proofs of an achiever's personal sacrifices, and replace these with one-eyed interpretations of the achiever's unique persona. Signatures like dress codes, gestures, and mannerisms, so long as they are unconventional, are seen as evidences of Illuminati or satanic links. The occult could possibly influence success, but this thorough-going attempt to invent or impose guilt on people's achievements is proof of man's arguably natural discomfort at the triumph of his own kind. Man is a hater of success in another – individual difference is only a matter of degree. In those intra and inter-family disputes, religious rivalries, and political differences among nations, there is often that underbelly of fear – the fear of domination from the success of another.

My discussions with Chima that evening concerning the rumour, and Ekwueme's fatherly support, had a cathartic effect on me. I simply resolved to continue to pursue my dreams: the aspiration to expand my business, leave a legacy through a youth-empowering reality TV show, and organise my charity programme, one which would specifically target poor children.

As I drove home that night from Chima's place after our meeting, I felt rejuvenated with Eminem's I'm Not Afraid wafting from the car stereo placed on repeat mode. I often found solace in books and rap music, and this time the music therapy was just at the right moment. I was so ecstatic that I did not bother to look at the text messages being buzzed into my phone, as I would have ordinarily done even while driving. Nothing else mattered but the elation of the moment expressed in vigorous nodding to Slim Shady's lyrical alliterations. I got home and slotted in yet another Eminem CD and set the volume high so I could hear the song from the bathroom. The text messages had still not been read. I needed to freshen up, lie on the bed and read them leisurely.

When I finally picked up my phone to read them, I saw that they were debit alerts from my bank. The first read "Three hundred thousand naira debited for POS transaction." I didn't understand the message since I did no such transaction. The second message was a fifty thousand naira debit alert. The third had a lower volume, all of which approximated half a million naira. I read the three messages again word after word, cross-checked the account details; they were mine. I started panting, seeing that a new account balance had just reflected. A hand reached for the remote control and paused the music, then reached for my wallet and confirmed that my ATM card was still there. Disorientation. A call was made to my account officer narrating what had just happened.

"Oh my God! Hackers have accessed your account", she screeched.

"Wait, wait, wait, you mean the money has left my account just like that?"

"It haaaaas, oh God! I need to call head office right away so that they can block your ATM PIN to prevent further access, though obviously the hackers have reached the PoS and ATM withdrawal limits for the day."

I was dumbfounded. The account officer later called back.

"Come to the branch office tomorrow morning with a complaint letter so we can commence investigation", she stammered.

"So you've confirmed the money has actually left my account?"

"Unfortunately it has, Victor. So sorry about that."

"God! But my ATM card is right here in my wallet!"

"Hackers don't need your card to do that, they have their way around it. Just come to the office first thing tomorrow morning. The bank will find out what really happened."

The next morning at the Creek Road branch of Zenith Bank I was ushered into the operations manager's office. The man's lack of empathy struck me.

"Just drop the letter and go, we'll look into the matter. But I'm sure you must have compromised your PIN," the manager pronounced irreverently without even looking up from his computer screen.

"You've not investigated and you've already drawn a conclusion, is that how you work here?" I snarled.

"Well that's always the case – PIN disclosure to a third party. I'm just saying, anyway."

He stood up from his swivel chair, picked a document from a printer tray and walked towards the door leaving his office.

"Are you leaving or what sir?" I asked.

"I've already told you we'll investigate. Come back in a week."

"Can you imagine! You don't even have customer empathy."

The man ignored me and disappeared, leaving me extremely enraged. I found wisdom in keeping my anger under control until the investigation report was out.

Exactly a week after, I went back to the insensitive manager.

"Here's the report," he said, without sparing any emotion. The report claimed "PIN was compromised", citing also a certain central bank regulation that absolves banks of liability from fraud in all "switching services."

"This is crap!," I snorted, "What makes it an investigation report, just because it carries your bank's letterhead?"

"If only you'll calm down and listen. You're not the only one affected by this wave of fraud. Go home and ask your spouse or the people living with you, they could have seen your PIN where you wrote it down. Once anyone sees your PIN they can clone your card."

"Of course they saw it written in my brain! I live alone! You run a system in which the fraudsters are smarter than you, the operators. You must refund my money!"

"This is an office sir, you're shouting. If you don't feel comfortable with the report there are legitimate means to contest it."

"Exactly! You'll hear from my lawyer."

I charged out of the office and headed back for my house to write an article stating everything that transpired, titled: "Open Letter to Zenith Bank and Interswitch." I e-mailed the letter to four major newspapers through my journalist friends in those outfits. None ever published the story, for fear of losing advertising patronage from the bank and Interswitch. Even my friend Tony, who had become a business editor in a newspaper company, could not get the letter published. I was frustrated. I then remembered Jerry Ohanekwe, the young man I met on the plane, general manager of TLT Ltd., a media consortium. I called Jerry and booked an appointment.

Jerry was very happy to see me again, and promised to ensure that the open letter was published in the newspaper outlet of TLT. It was, and I felt exultant. I was no longer driven by the urge for refund, but by a sense of justice to expose the institutional porosity that had left many at the mercy of sniffing hackers. News coverage of such cases of fraud was very low, even sketchy whenever there was one. No news medium was ready to lose advertising revenue from blue-chip finance firms for the sheer glory of journalistic responsibility. There was a silent corporate conspiracy that created a preference to watch people lose money rather than watch a firm lose image. And with the long litigation processes in the courts and the slippery nature of law, court action seemed futile. The money was never refunded and the matter died a natural death.

After the publication of the open letter, I called Jerry again for another appointment to discuss the proposed reality TV show. I had earlier done a draft proposal explaining shooting and administration frameworks. We met at a club in Ikeja, one Friday night. Jerry pored through the proposal occasionally smiling, raising his brows or nodding.

"Great job!" he exclaimed, patting me on the shoulder. It was the VIP section of the club. The lights were dim and he lit the pages with the torchlight functionality of his smartphone. The acoustics were not excellent, so the music from the dance hall still buzzed around our ears.

"You think it'll fly?" I asked.

"Sure it will. It's something out-of-the-box, away from all the deafening razzmatazz of singing, dancing, or fun-seeking youths in the reality TV shows that we have."

"The idea came during my first year in the university, and was heightened by my observations on Facebook and other social media platforms. I was struck by the poor quality of thought exhibited by the average Nigerian youth on national and global issues. By this I intend to raise a platform for socio-political debate. Their hatred of intellectual discourse contrasts with their empty quest for fun and materialism."

"You're right, Victor. Even the so-called educated ones are intellectually illiterate. They are always the first to send you BlackBerry messages warning you not to wear red clothes today or tomorrow otherwise you'll die."

"Haha, but the problem is whether our youths will watch a programme that'll be too serious like the one I'm proposing," I noted thoughtfully.

"They will, if properly packaged. See what you'll do, integrate music and dance in the whole package; let it have 'swag'. Don't worry, I'll get the sponsors that'll turn it all around, that'll stake the prize money so high and make crazy media noise about it to generate attention. If you leave it at only politics, economy and international relations, the youths won't be interested. They need to be literally lured."

"Yea, I see your point," I acknowledged, "The idea is to groom youths for political leadership. If we believe they're the leaders of tomorrow and there's no mentorship programme of any sort to prepare them for that task, I think we're not being proactive."

"It's a great idea, my brother. Repackage it in slides with graphics, do the copyright and come back, I'll take it up from there. Then we'll later discuss how to share the millions."

I laughed. "I just pray it scales through. I'm more motivated by the legacy perspective than by monetary returns," I stated.

"Oh c'mon Victor, we'll achieve both. You don't know how much money this idea is worth. You're a great guy, very brilliant."

"Great and brilliant you say, but I hope you don't expect me to thank you for that because I owe no gratitude for compliments that are above my merit, just as I do not get angry over insults that do not reflect my person."

Jerry smiled. It was already past 1:00 am and he needed to go. He drank up the residue of the Cognac in the bottle and stood up.

"It's high time I left, Victor."

"So soon? Oh I see, madam is at home," I jested.

"No madam, I'm divorced."

"Sorry about that."

"Sorry for what? I'm ok man," he cut in.

"So you're going back home on a Friday night all alone? There are beautiful ladies everywhere around the club...."

"Noo, I don't do chicks," he interrupted.

"Nice guy, I like that. I do chicks sometimes though....Anyway I'm leaving too."

"Why leave now, you don't wanna stay back and have fun?"

"I hardly club because I neither drink nor smoke, and I don't know how to dance. I like music, but not when it's too loud, hence clubbing is not that much fun to me. So which way are you taking?"

"I live in Ikeja GRA, not far from here. You didn't come in your car?" he asked.

"I didn't. I couldn't get petrol due to the current scarcity. And I couldn't do all that wahala at the filling station."

"And where do you live?" he asked again.

"FESTAC."

"Quite far. I'll drop you at Ikeja bus stop. There are cab drivers there, always. But you can actually put up in my crib till tomorrow, can't you?" he asked.

"Hmmm, I would rather you dropped me off at the bus stop. But let's leave first, I may change my mind on the way and go with you to your house."

"Hope you ain't picking any whore?" he quizzed with pretended disgust.

My eyes popped out: "Whore? That's a harsh word. Well when I say I do chicks, I don't mean sex workers."

We left for the car park. It was a sparkling BMW X6.

"Nice car. Crazy interior," I sang, as I sank into the front passenger seat.

"Thanks man. I love machines," he admitted.

"Jerry everyone no matter how modest, has at least one fantasy or vanity. For me, it's simple but exotic structures with a lot of green, or a car with a comfortable interior and mad engine power."

Jerry wore a grin instantly as he put the car on reverse.

"We share a lot in common," he said, "I can't drive a six-cylinder ride because when I'm on the highway I do up to 200. You need a V8 engine for such sport else your car somersaults."

"Two hundreeed? I run fast but not that much, abeg o," I screeched in surprise.

The jeep was already gliding down a dark, lonely road in Ikeja. The chat went on and on, dwelling mainly on cars: BMW has the most fantastic engine. No it's Mercedez. It's not Mercedez, Mercedez is just about Formica interior and powerful suspension for negotiating bends, not a speed car....The argument rolled on amid guffaws. Jerry's right hand occasionally landed in gesticulation on my left thigh. I observed that it was getting too frequent and that it was partly brushing my crotch, deliberately. I moved a bit further but the hand kept coming. Soon the hand was left hanging between my thighs as he continued talking, gently scratching a thigh in the effort. I went mute as a way of ending the chat so the encroaching hand would leave my thigh. He seemed to be enjoying the monologue, and the hand was becoming too amorously inclined as it began to feel the size of my manhood. We were now at Ikeja bus stop close to a taxi park. He pulled over, looked straight into my eyes with a silly beam on his face, one that contrasted with my unappealing countenance.

"Are you still going back to FESTAC this night? C'mon come chill out in my crib."

"So you'll sleep with me right?" I asked with a straight face.

"Wow, you understood! Can anything be better than making love to a handsome man like Victor Ekwueme on a Friday night?"

"Sorry I'm not gay. The very thought of it makes me wanna puke."

"You're not gay, but you don't sound seriously anti-gay. I had expected you to flare up all the while we talked on our way here but you didn't. Free your mind man. I can see you have a gay nature, don't suppress it."

"You see what you wanna see. I'm just open-minded. I tolerate contrary worldviews," I replied, smiling.

"Sorry to embarrass you then," he pleaded, "I had studied you for some time now and noted that you're a non-conformist. I thought that meant you'd be gay-oriented."

"I'm naturally uncomfortable with blind, irrational convention, but the gay thing seems to me quite untenable. The whole argument based on human rights and freedom of choice doesn't hold water at all, else fathers should equally be free to marry their daughters so long as there's freedom. Bigamy should no longer be an offence. People can even make out in public; those who do not like the scene should just turn their eyes away," I said.

"I don't know about that," he stated, "but who has the right to determine how others should live their lives? Sin is sin – that's if homosexuality is actually a sin. Besides, not everyone believes in God, duuh. And why is no one screaming against fornication and the other sins? People should let God judge matters Himself."

"The problem with liberalism is that it doesn't often recognise where to draw the line. Not everyone can handle freedom sensibly. If we grant all freedoms and let God judge later by Himself as you say, we're gonna lose the last vestiges of morality that we ever had. Man is a moral animal; it is primarily a sense of morality that sets us apart from the other animals."

"I thought Aristotle said we were political animals, now you've changed it to another. We'll hear more," he said.

Not too far from us were some cab drivers under the bridge at the bus stop. They sat on their cab bonnets chatting away, probably also wondering what a BMW jeep was doing there by the roadside at that time of the night, its occupants feeling at home in the midst of some passionate chat. It was one of those moments when one could forget one's immediate environment, and get carried away by some impromptu distraction. The chat had gone intellectual, and being intellectual was something I could afford at any given time.

"Jerry, Aristotle probably forgot that some other animals have a capacity for society and hierarchy, and that is politics. Look at ants and bees. You think without communication and authority they'll live as they do? Moral values are all we've got my brother," I stressed.

"First, I don't agree with you that liberals don't know where to draw the line. If it were so, then liberalism would also mean anarchism – but of course it's not. Liberals are of the view that freedom is paramount in everything, except the freedom to harm another. It is a basic tenet that since man is an animal with dignity, the liberty to act within his conscience ought to be guaranteed. I don't see how homosexuality harms those not involved in it," he espoused.

"Homosexuality offends conventional morality, simple! It harms the conscience of others who have a stake in society and cannot keep quiet and watch a weird minority destroy societal values."

"I don't know who is offended in this case now. The rationale behind liberalism is the hatred of the suffocation of man throughout history by autocratic conservatism. The kind of conservatism that cannot stand to be questioned, criticized or improved upon. The kind that stifles every luxurious instinct in man; that proclaims itself God, and man, slave. Laws are made for man, not man for laws. Talking of morality, who even defines it for the rest of us? You don't have the right to force me into your own construct of morality. I have my free will. For me, morals do not imprison a man, they set him free," Jerry affirmed, looking a bit worked up.

"Oh please, don't tell me you're angry over this. We can still be friends."

"Sure we still are friends," Jerry said, forcing out a smile from his smooth face.

"Now considering the fact that you're gay, and given your position as the GM of TLT Ltd., couldn't you have influenced some pro-gay editorials during the deliberation of the anti-homosexuality bill in the National Assembly?"

"You know our society is deeply religious. No news medium here would be bold enough to do that at the expense of losing public goodwill. At the most you can only write pro-gay articles with fictitious names. And believe me, there could be some pro-gay National Assembly lawmakers who couldn't have voted against the bill during the deliberations. They could be mobbed."

"Interesting.... So did you divorce your wife due to your sexual orientation?"

"Not necessarily. But naturally I don't feel shit for women. I can't easily sleep with a woman without condom because I can't imagine the moisture touching my organ."

"Guy you're really deep in this stuff, gosh! Anyway, I think I'll be leaving now."

"No problem, my brother. Call me when the graphics are ready. Don't forget to make the changes we discussed, please."

As I opened the door to leave and consequently got the car brightly lit, Jerry saw two buds of rash that sprouted at the back of my neck.

"Wait o, what kind of rashes are these?"

"Rashes, where?" I asked.

"Your neck."

"Oh, I felt them yesterday while I was having my shower. I haven't really examined them in the mirror since I can't see them."

"They're too big! It's like you need antibiotics. Go see a pharmacist please, you may have an infection."

"I will," I replied, feeling a bit embarrassed.

We parted. In less than a week I effected all the changes in the proposal as discussed, but Jerry Ohanekwe had already walked out on the project. Calls were no longer picked, text messages were never replied. When I visited his office, access was denied. Either out of a sense of shame or a hatred for contrary sexuality, Jerry reneged on his promises. But there was no giving up the dream.

Meanwhile, the rashes had become more pervasive. Feverish feelings, particularly weakness, followed. I didn't consider them that serious for proper medication in the hospital, and chose rather to visit a pharmacy shop down my street. And that turned out to be a costly mistake.

The pharmacist was not in, the day I visited, but there was an assistant who didn't seem like he knew his job given his poor professional comportment. I showed him the rashes and demanded to see the owner of the shop.

"I'm here sir, I can attend to you," he boasted.

"Are you a professional pharmacist?" I interrogated.

"Them no dey write am for face sir."

"Very well then, I need antibiotics to deal with these rashes. I know I should have gone for medical test to ascertain things but I guess it's not that much of an issue, though I feel feverish...."

"You don't even need to waste money on test, this is Chicken-Pox. The medicine dey here," he interrupted.

"Jeez! I only read about it in primary school books! Must be some serious disease. That means I need to go to the hospital."

"E no serious anything, na im dey reign now. But you know naa, una wey be big men dey like to throw-way money for everything."

I felt convinced that there was no need for proper tests and medication in a hospital.

"If you say so. Bring the drugs then."

The quack cast glances around the drug shelves, picking one container after the other. Soon he arranged them on the counter....

"Take this three times a day. This one, once every evening only, for three days. This liquid one is the main thing, drink it like six times a day. Na im go purshue the rashes come outside, them still dey inside your body. If them no come outside na that one fit kill person."

"Ah, kill person? So this disease can kill?" I wondered.

"Nothing go do you, oga. Big men, una too fear to die."

I was a bit pissed about the 'big men' tag but chose to ignore the ever sheepishly-smiling young man. That evening, I took the drugs as specified. I had this habit of burying my drugs in balls of eba to keep sourness out of the tongue's jurisdiction. The so-called all-important syrup had earlier been taken four times. The next morning, I noticed that the rashes had become more ubiquitous, especially on my face. I felt more feverish. Every Nigerian neighbour is a potential doctor. My neighbour saw me and reinforced the theory that the more the rashes grew on the skin, the better for the patient. Survival must be at the cost of a supple skin.

"As the drug don chase them come outside like this, e go soon go. The thing don do me before, na Calamine lotion save me," noted the neighbour, who gave me more free counsel on what lotions to buy, what soap, and so on.

By the second morning of the medication, matters had reached a head. The fever had intensified and my whole body had become a luxuriant plantation of rashes. Even unusual parts of the body had more than adequate representation: the scalp, tongue, palms, genitals, buttocks. Sitting down was to burst the prickles, painfully, worsen the itching and increase water secretion. Standing meant thrusting my entire weight on the fleshy spikes under my feet – the pain was unbearable. I looked at the mirror and almost ran away from myself: inside the nose and ears, my eyelids, temple, and lips looked totally jagged like the creation of some devil-may-damn horror-film costumier.

When I plunged into my car to drive to a hospital, my doctor-from-hell neighbour was taken aback at the sight of a young man wearing what looked like a skin of thorns, but the sight still didn't stop the useless advice:

"Na God dey save person o. Maybe if not for that syrup wey purshue these rashes come outside like this you for no survive this disease. The thing plenty for inside your body, kai, keep taking it," he counselled.

"I see. Now that there's no more vacancy on my skin, if I continue taking the freaky syrup the rashes may as well begin to burst inside for lack of space," I countered in soft anger, started the car and drove off.

The traffic jam on the road that led to the hospital at Surulere was quite killing. It was the last Saturday of the month, the customary date for a monthly sanitation exercise in Lagos that normally took place between seven and ten o'clock in the morning. Lagosians, notorious for a perennial haste disorder and God-knows-what hustle and bustle, would troop out like a herd at the tick of ten. That often resulted in a total traffic paralysis: at some foot bridges at bus stops, pedestrians would queue behind one another to put down raised feet in the slowed motion of human traffic; motorcycles and tricycles would knock each other down in the fierce contestation for marginal and walkway spaces, often pushing down one or two walkers in the course of their frenzy, scampering away in mobile triumph;   vehicles snailed forward one minute per cycle of wheel, bumper-to-bumper, amid the blare of ear-splitting horns that   warned the driver ahead against laziness, or against the perceived time-wasting charity of letting other cars join the lane. Everyone was often angry in the situation. Carbon monoxide emission, the clash of honks and other noises, and the clumsiness of the movement created an open asylum for the practice of lunacy. A car would scratch another and their drivers would be sprung out to verbally pound each other and further enhance the stagnation of life. I hated going out on any sanitation day.

In the midst of the traffic, my car started over-heating. The air-conditioner was immediately turned off to cushion the speedy rise of the engine temperature so that I could pull over and find a solution. Window glasses were wound down as a result to allow air soothe the itchy rashes. But there was no air in circulation, not in that stationary traffic: what blazed forth was an elemental mixture of engine smoke, noise and dust, all of which lacked the tranquillity of humane air. There was no room to steer off the lane and pull over, when every road space suffered the occupation of either human feet or frenzied tyres. I got increasingly worried; my car would soon pack up in the middle of the road and place me at the mercy of disgruntled motorists' verbal missiles. That was even the lesser concern. My major concern was the shame of having to get off the car and bare the misery of my jagged, unsightly skin to the mockery or shaming curiosity of the traffic community. The car started giving off smoke from the engine when temperature reached a danger zone, and I switched off the engine. I ignored the arrows of stare shot by a colony of eyes around and approached some Area Boys a few yards away to help me create space and push the car off the road, for a fee. I later got an auto-electrician to fix the problem.

The auto-electrician was bold enough to ask questions.

"Oga wetin do you for body?"

"Do your job Mr man let me leave here!"

The electrician apologised, raised the bonnet and fiddled with the engine.

"Oga your fan relay no good. I go need to change am and I never sure say parts sellers don open shop by now, today na environmental, they open well well from 11 or 12."

"So I have to stand here waiting for about two more hours?"

"Na so sir."

A young, very dark man in his late twenties, the electrician was discerning enough to know how badly I needed obscurity from public viewership of the forestation of rashes. He took me to his nearby shop, a shack of tarpaulin stretched from a brick fence over four wooden stands, cascading down to the ground. I raised the sprawling tarpaulin and crawled in. I was so angry about the spate of my frustrations in recent times. Soon the electrician got other hands and the car was pushed close to to his shop. From the shop I watched as he did the job with calm and joy, despite apparent poverty: his fingers, roughened by hard work, ploughed through the engine, occasionally scouring off grease stains on his scalp. A pair of overalls whose thread lining at the buttocks had weakened revealed a nursery of anal hair each time he bent down in the course of the repair; a little child of about ten, obviously his son, given the resemblance in meaty ears and huge eyes, helped bring one item after another, for daddy. I was touched by the little boy's enthusiastic agility and smartness in correctly interpreting his father's gestured requests for work tools. My love for children was often spurred by such little things. After paying for the work, I offered to pay the boy's school fees for as long as I could afford and arrangements were made to that effect.

At the hospital I was the most consequential object of attention and shame, worst-case specimen of Chicken-Pox pathology. Doctors dug studious gazes at me, one wanted to photograph me but I declined, much to my humiliation. I was placed on admission and subjected to a barrage of injections, as fever reached alarming proportions. Lungs seemed to have broken down momentarily on two occasions leaving me gasping for breath. A week later I was discharged, or rather released, from the trenches of death. But a permanent history of that experience was preserved in a few scars that refused to submit to the dermatological ministrations that I later adopted.

By the time I resumed at Rontech after recovery, a lot of damage had been done. Earlier I had submitted some quotations and approvals were given for supply during my absence. Enrico was allergic to any form of delay. Whatever patience he had could not last for a whole week to enable me get back to the site and make procurement. He worked on his son Roberto to withdraw the approval and make alternative arrangements for the materials ordered for. Roberto had to first, get in touch with me to ascertain the state of affairs with the request, to know if any efforts were in progress for the supply. It happened that my employee saddled with the supply task goofed twice on specification, and the supplied material was rejected. By then Enrico had moved from impatience to desperation, and sent one new Rontech staff to go scouting for the material. The new man, who had become a pest to me in recent times with his endless requests for money, was out to impress his boss. He had access to my rates and all he had to do was lower his a little. He had no material investment in the transaction. Enrico gave him a vehicle, a driver and the money for the purchase. Smart guy, he returned the savings to his boss and earned a pat on the back. He did not need money anymore. He was preparing his way for greater things. Two other requests were given the same treatment, at which time new man suggested to Enrico that he could be made an official purchaser for the company for more savings. Enrico, being a typical capitalist, welcomed the idea and my relevance in Rontech became redundant.

At that point it did not matter to Enrico anymore that the relationship between me and Rontech was beyond business. On three occasions I had wired a total of about thirty million naira to Italy for Roberto and his father, through my dollar account. The transfers seemed illegal and even technically difficult for the Italians to make without breaking money-laundering laws, and given that a Nigerian now had equity in Rontech, it was unethical and questionable for them to do so. Audit reports included scrutiny of personal accounts of board members. They could open independent bank accounts and wire the money themselves leisurely but they had this awe for the oil tycoon co-owner of Rontech, whose connections in the corporate firmament of the country were extensive. They reasoned that he could find out. I was trusted, and it made more sense operating through me. That way, their tracks would be effectively covered and the risk of the offence would be dispelled from around them. At first I struggled with the moral quandary of such assistive role in a dubious deal, but the prospect that it would strengthen my bond and opportunities with the company made a realistic sense to me. Economic survival and ethical morality contested for my soul. The former won – it always did. And there was this opportunistic justification that whether I played the part or not, the Italian duo would effect the transaction nonetheless. They were determined to repatriate funds to their country. Enrico threw away all these considerations of past favours in the short-term gains of precarious savings. Precarious in the sense that the new staff might disappear one day with any money entrusted to him for the purchases. Besides, companies do not engage vendors out of charity. There is often a sense of safety in pushing to another party the risks of logistics in procurement, together with the administrative convenience in credit buying.

For me, upon a latter soul-searching over the Enrico betrayal, there was a tinge of retribution for my facilitation of that Italian heist. I was endlessly haunted by contrition and shame for compromising my integrity. I felt used and dumped at the instance of what seemed like an imperial conspiracy that had no regard for the sanctity of relationship. It took long before I could forgive myself. I was deeply wounded by the development. At the time, my new outpost dealing in construction hardware was just a month old. I had little money left in my account, having spent a lot on the new outlet and on the building project in the village. I feared a recession to poverty and a loss of wherewithal for my heavy responsibilities in the family and for my proposed charity plans. I did not want to incubate any financial hope on the TV programme, for, it arose primarily out of a passion to play a little humanistic role in my country's scheme of evolution. The Rontech offers were the springboard for my other aspirations. The suddenness of the turn of events threw me off balance and edged me towards extremities I could never have imagined.

On the night I got the news that a new work order had set in at Rontech, I drove to Obalende. In one of those dark corners there at the bus stop was a thriving market for marijuana, run singly by a young man simply called G. Short and dark, G. had a very mean look tempered a bit by his frequent grin. His large lips were darker than himself, roasted to that specification by ganja smoking. Black crusts of plaque made egregious fences between one tooth and another. I was there to buy ganja. In that area, it was not unusual to see people smoking ganja openly, especially in the evening. I was extremely worried about life, about how my dreams were beginning to hop on one leg. My psychological situation at that time bordered on an insanity that could justify suicide. I could not go to church to find solace and Divine guidance since I was not a member of any church. For me, churches wasted a lot of time singing and re-singing, praying and re-praying. And it seemed to me as silly hypocrisy to instantly embrace fervent faith only out of misery. There was no one to talk to. My mission in that weird location was just to distract myself with some novel adventure.

The moment G. saw me, he gave me a long scrutiny. I cornered him and told him my mission.

"Wetin? We no dey sell that kain thing for here. Oga comot for here abeg," he barked, frowning.

I gave assurances the much I could but he ignored me. I went a few metres away for some minutes and later went back to him.

"Wetin dey worry this man? Who tell am say them dey sell ganja for here? You dey craze?" he growled.

The people around were alerted by his loud voice. I didn't care. I understood the situation and decided to change my approach.

"Brother take am easy! All of us dey together for here. I no be ajebutter! Na only you no know me. See my ID card, you see Olopa for there?"

He looked at my identity card and compared the image with my face. I knew he was not still convinced.

"Wait I dey come," I told him, as I went to my truck and brought out a file folder. I showed him documents – invoices, letterheads, business cards, etc., proofs that I was not an enemy. Soon G. wrapped the nonsense, about the size of his index finger, lit it, and handed it over to his new pupil. "I never smoke ganja before, broda," I muttered. He collected it back from me, drew a long oral breath through it and blew the smoke over his nose, in demonstration. New pupil could not still find the nerve to try. Instead I asked G. whether I could run mad in the process and G. said no, and promised to give me a befitting slap to restore sanity just in case. We both smiled. I took the smoldering menace back from my tutor, recoiling at the disgust of its smell.

"No, I no fit." G. shrugged in indifference and gladly took the stick from me and enjoyed it in glamorized panache. I moved away and sat at a corner, head in hands. "Wetin dey worry u, oga, them don bilala your wife?" he inquired. I ignored him.

Shortly, a Toyota Corolla with the emblem of a bank pulled up. G. knew the car and the exact volume its owner often purchased. So he prepared the consignment and took it to the car owner seated at the back. "Shon ma!," he saluted, taking possession of crisp notes from manicured fingers. I was stunned at the gender and quality of his clientele.

He returned to his usual spot and opened a covered plastic plate. A mound of amala shared habitation with a pool of stew in the plastic bowl, made visible by a lit bulb draping from the spine of an overhead bridge. He did not wash his hands. With fingers he would prise out a portion of amala, soak it in the stew, and send it where it should belong. A customer would come and he would drop the food, render service, and return to his swallowing. It was past 10:00 pm. He did not have to bother about late-eating and its potential for grooming potbelly – his whole life was already one whole stretch of an exercise. He had no worries over some grandiose television programme, over that affliction called humanism, by which an individual would lose sleep in the pursuit of a thankless concern for others. G. had no worries over a threatened livelihood, no worries about house rent, car maintenance, marriage, and did not give a damn about earning a space in history. As I sat brooding over my tedious search for definition, I envied his mindless ownership of a huge portion of the peace I lacked. A man in his late thirties, he was far happier than I, apparently. In him there was this vindication that bliss lay in innocence and ignorance, exemplified by his enviable peace, one that made a life beleaguered with ambitions seem like an encumbrance. We later got talking about some personal issues. He was not very sure of the number of children he had sired outside wedlock by so many women, nor did he particularly care. Of his many children he singled out only one to be trained in school, hopefully to a tertiary level. Asked why he cared less about the rest, he said he had to be truthful to himself: that there was no way all of his children would be useful in life; that by foresight he identified the sensible one. The rest were abandoned to succeed or fail.

He walked me down to my rickety truck and saluted, baring his familiar dental rot. "Twale!" he shouted, stamping a foot on the ground, and a few naira notes left me for him. As I drove home, I pondered over my discovery of yet another paradox: that if happiness is the ultimate standard to measure life, it appears that one is closer to it the more detached one is from conventional aspirations. But I had already lost my chances at that brand of peace and happiness the moment I began pursuit of lofty ambitions. I was now at the point of no return. I marveled at how I could not summon a measure of will and aplomb within me in a time like that, despite my fair exposure to knowledge from motivational reading. There was this realization that men are better counselors to others than to themselves, that the theorist and the sideline spectator are sages whose endowment with wisdom often evaporates as soon as the hand is on the plough. But lessons were drawn from the whole experience.

I learnt never ever to embark on projects of little commercial value until there were alternative income sources. The building project in the village should have waited until after a successful diversification of income. To build a house when one has not yet strengthened one's income base is to prepare to be a poor landlord. And I relied too heavily on Rontech, in the assurances of the intimacy of the relationship between me and the Italians. No level of security offers complete protection indefinitely. There will always arise some lapses, or the need to strengthen the fortress. Gradually, friends began to withdraw from me. My little savings were getting depleted in basic expenditures and nothing was coming in, not even from my new outlet. It became more difficult coping at that level than before, since my present status had a whole lot of baggage.

Pioneering Change

Tony's new roles as the business editor and chief political correspondent in the newspaper where he worked offered a lot of travel opportunities. When the paper came under a new management, the organisation downsized as a means of cutting down on overheads. In some cases, two or three positions were placed under the responsibility of a single editor. Tony did not complain. The overseas travels, mostly at the behest of the United Nations' world programmes office, spun dollar payments and other perks. And as a business editor, he was able to get advertising revenue for his organisation and enjoy fat commissions. With a First-class Honours degree in Public Relations and an excellent grasp of media work, his rise was expected. He was also very smart. He knew which politician would lose the next election, and why. There was no faulting his political permutations, and he would beforehand, identify with a winner and build a relationship. With the busy schedule and financial bounties, however, came a lot of burden.

He had no time for himself. Relationships were built mainly on phone and e-mails. No, not phone calls – he hardly ever picked his calls. Text-messaging, mainly. For those who did not understand his work troubles, his success was "making his head swell." Part of the burden also was that of bias. Once he liked a politician for whatever reason, he would never see reasons to criticize the person no matter how valid the evidence for criticism. I called it intellectual treachery. We always argued about that. Our friendship since after graduation suffered due to work demands from both of us.

From the back of the car seated beside his wife Mimi, he kept singing praises for Babatunde Fashola, Governor of Lagos State. I had just picked them up at the airport.

"You need to see the developments in The Gambia. I don't regret it one bit that I chose to holiday in West-Africa and not in Europe," he bragged.

"I'm happy you guys followed my counsel to that effect. I really have to be persuaded to holiday outside Africa. Tourism is not just about development sights anyway. It's also about having to see my African experiences duplicated in our brothers in other African countries. Like, visiting some villages in rural Kenya," I said.

"We visited some Gambian villages too. But by and large modern development is at the centre of tourism. That's why I'm so ecstatic about Fashola's work in current Lagos. The State is inching towards a tourist status. The APC is the party to usher in the change we've been yearning for in this country."

Mimi had been quiet all along, only smiling endlessly. Unlike most young ladies, she was politically aware. Just like her husband, she had sympathies for the All Progressive Congress, Nigeria's major opposition party.

"The APC is ideologically different from the PDP. The party is the incarnation of Awolowo's political legacy in the South-West, and Buhari's political legacy of integrity. The PDP is People Deceiving People. Them no get agenda for the masses abeg. For fourteen years now, they've been in power at the presidency and there's nothing to show for it," she groused.

Laughter. It was the first time I heard the coinage People Deceiving People in the place of Peoples Democratic Party.

"Mimi that's a funny name," I said, "For me, both parties are two sides of a coin. I do not see any divisions in our polity in terms of ethnicity, political bloc, or religion."

"That's funny!" Tony interjected, laughing derisively. "How can anyone deny tribalism and partisan discrepancies in our politics? Unless you don't live in this country...."

"If only you'll let me explain," I cut in: "Ethnicity, religion and cries of marginalisation are all phantom creations of the politician, all in his slyness to bamboozle and divide the credulous masses. If a Yoruba man is president, how does that confer some special benefits to one Taiwo in Ajegunle? The North has ruled Nigeria longer than any other ethnic group has ever done. How come we still have more Hausa beggars but more prosperous Igbo merchants? We only have two fundamental divisions: the political elite and the masses. Every other division is a smokescreen."

"Ok, if the political elite are all the same in one category and the rest of us are in another, as you claim, what choices do we then have in an election?" he asked.

"We have a choice of bigger or lesser evils," I replied.

"And how do you distinguish between bad and worse evils?" he asked again.

"Naturally, choices in life are preferences of certain evils over others. I don't know what parameters you'd use to make distinctions....Now consider this, our lawmakers increased their salaries and other emoluments. During the deliberations in the House, did you hear any dissenting voice shouting APC or PDP or Islam or Christianity or Yoruba or Igbo? All voices, previously antagonistic to one another, were instantly united. They had a common goal, a shared elite interest. There was a lucrative lack of opposition."

Mimi chuckled. "Politics is like that everywhere. It's full of intrigues and manipulations," she noted, "Even in Obama's America during the last presidential election, didn't you notice the malicious use of propaganda by both sides? Didn't you notice the resurrection of the Obama birth scandal? Romney's 47 % middle-class flop? There was even desperation by both men to lay claims to poor backgrounds, to please the average American voter. Didn't you observe the racist war? Didn't you see how the Republicans took over some news media to red-hot Obama's weaknesses? Politicians are very unscrupulous characters; they must be the ones the devil helped in creating while he was still an angel in heaven."

"You mentioned the media, well the media have never appealed to me as an objective institution of truth, especially in Nigeria," I affirmed, "They're all owned by the politicians, and used as tools to push forward political agendas. Those not owned by politicians are owned by private business people who need advertising revenues from blue-chip firms owned by the same politicians! So there's political loyalty. The situation leads to the practice of what I call power-bloc journalism, with little room for objectivity and truth. Look at the media coverage of the Obama-Romney campaign, for instance. Fox News was the propaganda medium for Romney. Even when he was obviously losing the election the report was that he was winning! Today's media truth is daubed in the colour of the party flag."

"You're always against everything anyway, without proffering alternatives. Since you've painted this ugly picture of vested interests and falsehood in the media, what do you suggest we do about it?" Tony questioned.

"I'm only thinking aloud. I stand in the middle, raising what I consider to be relevant questions, to disabuse the minds of fellow youths who may have settled into unexamined facts. But honestly I thought our youths were not very politically conscious till I saw their passionate involvement in the Ojota Anti-Subsidy Protest led by the Occupy Nigeria movement. We need to sustain this momentum of political participation through television programmes that'll sharpen their knowledge of politics," I explained.

"Just that the Ojota Protest was still a far cry from my idea of mass rebellion. We could not persist long enough in our demands, if only to shame the politicians who say the Arab Spring experience cannot be replicated in Nigeria. They mock at our lack of populist cohesion which they plant in our ranks through divisive sentiments like tribalism and religion, as you said before. Our disunity is their strength," Tony added.

"You guys actually think our youths are sufficiently interested in governance?" Mimi asked, shrinking her face in doubt. "Many female Nigerian youths are keener on make-up, celebrity gossip and fashion than on how much was budgeted for recurrent expenditure in the current national budget. Just as many of our young men are more interested in D'Banj's new release, the

Premier League and how much Van Persie is earning, than in matters of the state," she added.

"Do you blame them? The art of governance in this part of the world is so uninspiring. This political apathy is borne out of patriotic anger," Tony rationalised.

"Nothing justifies this lack of political interest by a generation whose future is being mortgaged by today's hawks-in-power. Such deliberate nonchalance merely assists the mission of the thieves in power positions. Look at the protests against president Morsi of Egypt over his arrogation of sweeping new powers to himself. The protesters were mostly youths – students, office workers, artisans, the unemployed, name it! Such an issue would not generate populist frown here in Nigeria. Even if it does, the reaction won't go beyond the launch of verbal missiles on the social media. The irony is that we've had democracy for decades yet we as youths don't know what to do with, while the Egyptians who have tasted it for barely a year are putting it to proper use – well they are beginning to abuse it now anyway," I stated.

Mimi had a way of steering political discussions towards international politics, her field of study. She charged into the Arab Spring topic:

"The Arab Spring is a dangerous dimension to mass revolt. Look at the escalation of suicide bombing in post-Gadaffi Libya, and the lack of peace in post-Mubarak Egypt. Masterminds of this suicide warfare are loyalists of the old regime, who see the anti-Gadaffi movement as an American project, and by extension, as anti-Islam. So the suicide bomber is on a religious mission."

"The suicide bomber has reduced the concept of Super-power Nations to the rubble. As a so-called super-nation, you cannot invade a terrorist nation and go to sleep. Bombs will start going off in your embassies, around your nationals, and even in your country if possible. If the terrorist nation does not use suicide bombing against you, it could deploy nuclear power. There's an ugly balance of power in world politics," Tony supported.

"You guys are right," I agreed, "This is the reason America cannot so easily champion the ousting of Bashir Al-Assad of Syria. Americans are tired of making more enemies through such interventions. And with China and Russia staunchly in support of the Assad regime in furtherance of their national interests, the matter has become more complicated. A third world war may not be too far from now. The UN is even more divided than I thought. It has failed the Syrian people, and has failed humanity by playing international politics with human lives."

"Enough of this gloomy discussion," said Tony, "That reminds me Victor, what's the position of things with the reality TV show you once told me about?"

"Bimpe is trying to push the proposal through in the advertising agency where she works. The agency would help link us with possible sponsors. She has even made some professional input. She says her agency is having some challenges winning over some brand managers, who want to be convinced that they can reach their target audience through the show."

"Let me have a soft copy of the proposal. I can talk to some brand managers who place adverts in our newspaper. And since Mimi here works in the corporate affairs department of a manufacturing firm, she could also do something about it," he assured.

Mimi wore a grin like someone who was excited about some secret thought.

"And who's Bimpe?" she asked, rolling her eyes.

"A friend in my M.Sc class," I replied curtly.

"So is she the one to come or do we expect another? She must be very close and trusted to be given such a classified document to work on," she added.

"Oh yes she's a close business friend."

"But Bros when are you getting married?" she probed further.

"For now I don't know whether I can handle marriage. I love my space. And I'm not sure I'm ready to afflict some innocent woman with the complexities of my person."

"Complexities kwa, na waa o. So it's easier to cope without a wife?" Tony asked.

"Whether you get married or not you'll suffer for it," I answered. "I'd been in love in the past," I continued, "and I've recently searched for a soul mate. Love is such a miserable thing: if you don't have it you'll strain to have it; if you have it you'll fear to lose it. I doubt if I have the emotional muscularity to weather the storm."

I represented a very difficult challenge in romantic relationships. In the past years, I had had stints with a number of ladies. The affairs all crashed due to my fastidiousness, fickleness, or lack of romantic emotion. My sense of hygiene bordered on a kind of psychological disorder. Little things like mouth odour, smelly hair, dirty nails, etc turned me off permanently. Once, I lost interest in a lady just because I found her walking barefoot in my balcony. I was very erratic, the kind of man that could wake up one morning and quit a relationship. I knew I had a problem with relationships and it bothered me. Tony thought something was wrong with me. The last lady I broke up with was quite an interesting experience.

She had just spent a weekend in my house. No quarrels, nothing. We cooked and ate together, made love severally, played, and laughed. Monday morning, I was set to leave for the day's hunt. I woke her up, made a long speech about how we did not share values, how she deserved a better man, how I wouldn't want to waste her time, and so on. She listened, silently. Her eyes were wet as she sat cross-legged on the bed, clutching a pillow. Soon her head was buried in the pillow. Tears. I hugged and pecked her on the forehead, and left. I didn't want to see her cry, somehow it hurt me. She would leave before my return from work in the evening.

By the time I returned in the evening, she was already gone. I observed that my room stank terribly, of faeces. I turned on the light bulb and found no shit on the bed or floor, but the stench was persistent in its nasal assault. I then realised that the putrid vibes emitted from my bedroom toilet. I switched on the light bulb in the toilet and found the mayhem: a huge mound of shit, disgusting in its marshy presence, was lounging in the toilet bowl. I wondered, could she have forgotten to flush the matter in the absent-mindedness of heartbreak? Or was that rather a deliberate vindictive souvenir to protest the heartbreak?

I thought that would be my last love affair. I resolved to be alone and let Nature have its way. But when I saw Bimpe's performance on a day of presentation in class, something clicked in me. I decided to ask her out. I had this obsession with fair-skinned women, but she was dark and not quite pretty. It didn't matter to me – her complexion and unimpressive looks – since she had already adequately compensated for those with her massive breasts. I liked busty women. In bed, a woman's curves are more important than her intelligence.

Bimpe was a hard nut to crack. She hated men – or rather, she didn't give a hoot about them. It mainly had to do with her background. Born into a broken home, raised by a foster father who sexually abused her, and dated by a guy who would often beat her up, she turned out to be an extreme feminist. She went to school from the proceeds of very demeaning but legitimate livelihoods. With a good job and a phenomenal intelligence, she championed her feminist cause through writing and by financial-ly empowering poor, abused women. I wooed her for over six months yet she wouldn't budge. I soon found out what she so admired: poems. I wrote her one.

A week after I sent her the poem, we ran into each other in an empty class in school where she had gone to read before the start of the evening lecture. On sighting me, she smiled and called me lover-boy. I smiled back, hugged her as we sat down for a chat.

"When are we gonna start making babies? I passed my fertili-ty test yesterday," I jested.

"Lucky you," she answered, laughing, "But sorry, I won't be an accomplice in bringing more children into this hell-of-a-world. It's so unfair. I'm a just woman."

"And what just woman would leave a man's heart dangling from her butt for six months?"

"That would indeed be a very lenient thing to do to men, if only they had hearts. Unfortunately they don't have hearts. Whoever made them – and it's not God – whoever made them forgot to affix hearts before they hurriedly bludgeoned their way into the world, in their usual haste."

"Well my manliness rests only on two zones: my waist and my head. I own a feminine heart."

She smiled and said: "I have to be very careful, mister. The man whose father died by the fall of a coconut would use metal to sew his cap."

We went on and on, till we got into personal details, and found out how we were bound in past experiences. There was a mutual feeling of oneness. That was the start of the most fulfilling relationship I ever had. We shared a lot in common. I had a deep respect for her, for her cause and her dedication to it. She was my idea of a woman, one who was interested in tackling the human condition. But we differed remarkably in religion: I was lukewarm; she was a Christian fanatic. She objected to pre-marital sex out of her Christian persuasion and I respected her wishes. It took time before she could understand my religious views. She initially thought I was an atheist, given my many arguments and questions about religion.

I had earlier chosen Christianity over the other religions not due to any perceived inferiority in those others, but because I found in it sufficient matter for a good life if practised with good sense. There was an obvious element of bias in that choice: I had been a Christian all along, and since my inquiries into all the religions I studied, including Christianity, revealed questionable ideals, it was only better to go back to source. My Christianity recognised the validity of contrary religious and non-religious views, as kindred thoughts among the same humanity sprung by a thirst for Truth. Out of the over 7 billion humans that afflict the Earth, Christians are about 2.6 billion. I could not accept how the rest would rot in hell on account of a belief system – religion – that was mainly sociological.

Meanwhile, God would understand that the genuine Muslim, in his love of God, thinks all Christians are wasting their time; the Hindu thinks the same of Christians, Muslims and others; even the Deeper-Life Church member thinks the Catholic is hell-bound. And each of these people thinks this way not out of mischief, but of innocent conviction, sometimes out of a sincere love of God. The major problem with religion is branding: if the early teachers of each had instilled in their followers the thinking to concede validity to the others, recognising the relativism of spiritual knowledge, there would be no Jihads or Inquisitions.

I could not find how a belief in God detracted from my human essence, or how it made me more stupid than I already was, given that both faith and the lack of it could provably be conditions of utter brainwashing. Man can overcome ignorance, but not foolishness, that gland for the perpetration of gaffes. Let him be as learned as possible, he will still be driven by certain strains of irrationality. And foolishness being also a relative thing proves even more difficult to objectively overcome: for the opinionated atheist, all theists are silly; and vice versa.

But even with Bimpe's knowledge of my idea about religion, it did not still sit well with her how a man could be a Christian but refuse to go to church. We quarrelled a lot over my refusal to identify with a "Bible-believing church." I did not have to be too rigid; I loved her, and was willing to make sacrifices for the relationship. She wanted the best for me, and believed that dedication to church things – or if you like, Godly things – was capable of changing my declining economic fortunes. I still stuck to The Lord's Prayer no matter the turbulence around me. But one day, I decided to follow her to church.

That day, when we got to the gate of the church, I stopped. It caught my eye, a billboard bearing the picture of the general overseer of the church and his hat-wearing wife. I stood there looking at the billboard till she came and pulled me away.

"It smacks of proprietary arrogance," I voiced with unnecessary resentment.

"This is no time to speak grammar. Close your eyes to the faults but open them to Godly knowledge," she retorted, virtually dragging me into the church.

The church building was filled to the brim with a sea of religious humanity, as worship songs tore through the air. It was a waiting game: the pastor was yet to arrive. Suddenly a procession of exquisite cars forcefully thrust into the church premises, with armed policemen ejecting themselves from security vehicles in military theatrics to usher in an elegant figure cocooned in a jeep with tinted glasses. Could that be one of those people plagued by the convoy mentality, those polling-booth personages called politicians? They it was who owned this brand of traffic hooliganism and cynosure-minded choreography. Has this one come here yet again to appropriate divine blessings that have hardly reached everyone in the congregation in the first place? Is he not blessed enough by the political inertia of the Nigerian populace, by our collective resignation to the fate of bad governance? He's already well-protected by fellow masses, these Krovo policemen who have been armed and mandated by law to secure their own oppressors. Whoever said law was not an elitist creation! Or is he here just to have his sins washed away so he could further his corruption on a brand-new slate?

My speculations ran to a halt with the general reaction of people towards this man, a very charming, gorgeously dressed man whose entry instantly decorated the ambience with a pulsating charismatic aura. "God bless you! God bless you! God bless you...." he chorused smiling, distributing oral blessings to ushers and some other church members who greeted him. So that was the pastor! I was not comfortable with his entire package, but apparently the congregation was.

Soon he mounted the pulpit, preached a few lines about wealth-making and divine blessings, and then called for donations for a certain church project. He pegged the donation sum at a hundred thousand naira for each donor. Those who made pledges were asked to troop to the altar where they were prayed for and "anointed for favour and breakthrough" with a certain oil. Then he lowered the peg to eighty thousand naira, then fifty, twenty and all the way down. He repeated a dozen times, the story of a certain woman who testified to the breakthrough of ten million naira two weeks after sowing a seed of five hundred thousand naira, during his last ministration in Port Harcourt. Another, he said, was blessed with two million naira after a far lower investment in seed-sowing. The crowd cheered. They were reminded repeatedly that no one would be poor in that church that year, and that no one would die among them too. There was apparent brand advertising, an implication that Christians in other churches were less fortunate. After he had called for hundred naira donations, he said: "Today is a happy day and we don't have to discriminate. Let everyone come to the altar, money or no money, and get anointed for favour." Everyone but I went to the altar. I was a lone figure in the midst of empty seats in that large hall. The pastor saw me and shouted, "I say everybody, even if you don't have money, come forward!" Ushers came to me, asking me to join the crowd. No, thanks, I'm okay sirs. Bimpe was angry. From the altar crowd she saw me, and wondered what I was up to.

"Please!" I pleaded with one of the ushers, "Can I get a blank sheet of paper and a pen?"

The items were provided. I wrote:

"Dear pastor, you made mention of about four people who sowed seeds in your Port Harcourt service last month, who testified to being generously blessed by God in return. What of the thousands in that same service that equally sowed seeds but got nothing in return, did they also testify? You sounded too absolute in your motivations; you made it seem as if you were very sure of God's automatic reimbursement. I think God blesses people as He deems fit, and not necessarily due to the obesity, or even thinness, of donations. I don't think He's some spiritual merchant or money-doubler. Methinks this psychological bullying to elicit donations is unfair. Thanks, sir."

I appended my name and phone number, dropped the piece of paper in the offering box, and left for home. For me the service was over. Later at home, Bimpe and I argued about the matter. I told her I would not attend that church again. I subsequently either held Sunday devotions all by myself at home, or strolled into the service of any nearby church.

From then, our relationship merely tottered along. We, however, managed to keep it in place, and unconsciously chose not to talk about church matters again. But inwardly, Bimpe was not happy. She wanted a good man: one who would be blindly dedicated to the catechisms of religious worship, not one who asked too many questions and found only faults. One who would sharpen her Christian life, wake up every morning and lead the morning devotion; guide the prospective kids in the ways of the Lord, not a philosopher! When I finally proposed to her, she asked for time to allow her ponder over the issue. She was to give me an answer the following weekend.

At that time I was practically jobless. In Oceanic Bank, my other source of contracts, yet another corporate shake-up had taken place following allegations of a fatal loss of liquidity. Another bank acquired the institution completely and the new procurement system shut out all previous vendors. My newly established outlet for construction and engineering hardware was stagnant then. Worse still, my personal upkeep was funded by a daily subtraction from that outlet's running capital.

It no longer bothered me, the gradual slide towards poverty. In life, one must not anchor one's happiness mainly on material possessions and things external. The individual must find within himself an Identity, an independent, firm source of joy, one not too subject to the world's troubles. After wealth is lost or shaken; when death snatches a loved one; when evil attacks things that make life beautiful, one must fall back to oneself – to one's Identity – that somewhat permanent asset which only death or extreme infirmity can take away. That Identity is what is entirely our own of all things, namely, a strong, impenetrable will; a belief in self – a belief that one still has the spirit and resource to re-establish oneself; a disdain for material things and the possession of a soul firmed up in learning and wisdom; a certain great passion for the soul, like love for the arts or something abstract; and for theists, a belief in God. Without Identity, the individual is to be pitied at the strike of misfortune, since his happiness is hinged on his material fortunes. My Identity was my flare for Godly humanism and philosophy, and my love for the written word.

I had extensively been prospecting for new clients, and hope was that one of my proposals would be honoured someday soon. But that would not happen.

Given that going out every day for marketing and contract sourcing meant incurring extra costs to fuel and maintain my two cars, among other things, I resorted to working from home, most of the time. Over fifty proposals had been sent out, mainly to construction and engineering companies in Lagos. Follow-up was by phone calls and e-mails. That reduced cost, though occasionally too there was need for physical visits to such firms.

Working from home was a sort of social predicament. Neighbours! "Bros you dey on leave? I dey see your car for house everyday nowadays....You no go work today, hope say you no sick abi?" The sheer frequency and monotony of such questions were an additional persecution to the plight of unemployment, one that made a certain jobless fellow, sometime in the past, leave home every morning fully dressed like a worker, to return in the evening like other useful human beings. The fellow's dignity somewhat depended on that pretence. Neighbours! Forget the worry on their faces when you tell them you have lost your job. Most times such news is a gladdening piece of knowledge to them, one that makes them psychologically punch the air in jubilation. No, neighbours are not necessarily sadists. It has to do with that tussle of social rivalry that creates a cold-war situation among them. There is a constant quest to outdo one another and oppress. Acquiring possessions like cars, house furniture and others is not often decided upon without regard to an air of superiority to surpass a neighbour, especially in Nigeria. Even the choice of school for your children is determined, most times, not intrinsically by what a school stands for, but by its elite appeal in contrast to your neighbour's own choice.

The Nigerian variant of this neighbour rivalry has actually gone beyond pretence, technically speaking. Given the nation's epileptic power supply history, everyone has become their own local government. Citizens have since assumed responsibility for the provision of certain basic amenities like water, electricity, and security. But then discharging these imposed duties depends on income. In middle-class areas, your access to borehole or well water, the sound of your generator, and the availability or lack of a security post in your compound, are all powerful social statements. The higher your perimeter fence, the higher your status. Generator sounds often reflect their size or make – they tell whether they are made in China, that profitable source for

Nigerian importers of substandard goods, or made in Europe or America.

In slums and some other low-class areas, generators are generators. They are mostly pint-sized, funny-looking, smoke-emitting, potentially fire-causing contraptions. Cheap China toys. But even with their low cost, they are status markers. One needs them, particularly at night, to prolong life contrary to the wishes of heat. A neighbour in such deplorable neighbourhoods wins instant elevation at the purchase of one of such mechanical urchins. But alas he also wins instant jealousy or hatred. Days after the purchase of your little machine, you'll start receiving petitions. "The exhaust of your gen is directly facing my window; my lungs must have, by now, totally turned black from the fume." Yet there is no safe place to place the generator, when the landlord has filled up the whole space with a circle of ramshackle structures. Perhaps the only safe direction for your generator's exhaust pipe is your room. Let the exhaust pipe face your room, power your ceiling and standing fans against heat, and die from carbon monoxide poisoning. Choose one death over the other. You reap what you sow!

Recently, however, an ingenious fellow invented a commonsense technology to remedy the China manufacturers' lack of neighbour-friendly intelligence. Nowadays all you need do is buy a long hose and cock it to your generator's exhaust pipe, to guide the smoke all the way beyond the habitat of human noses. Let them talk to the marines – those people screaming about a depleting ozone layer and climate change. Would they rather you depleted your lungs?

Meanwhile your long smoke-discharging hose has solved only a part of the problem. Your generator will soon have crankshaft problems and become an implacable noisemaker. And your oppressed neighbour will come back to you.

"My little baby could not sleep at night. Abeg make you dey off your gen on time." If you don't heed her advice she'll soon secretly remind your landlord how a house in the next street was razed by a generator-induced fire. Given your 'higher' status in the compound your landlord may agree with you that your neighbours are just being envious; that their babies sleep like logs of wood at night, otherwise the couple that just had a new baby a year after their older baby was born wouldn't have had time for sex. You'll have your way ultimately, people should just buy earmuffs. Or they can use cotton-wool. No wonder this little, troublesome machine is christened I pass my neighbour.

For me, neighbours' inquiries about my staying at home during work hours meant no bother. "I no get work. No money also. Tell the other neighbour so he doesn't come asking me too, I hate repetitions," I told two of my neighbours, smiling to make it seem like I was not pissed at their queries.

Bimpe was deeply concerned about my economic status and wondered why I would propose marriage in the circumstance. Yes, our master's degree programme was over, but then the programme was never an impediment to my getting married in the first place.

The awaited weekend finally came for her to give a reply to my proposal and she visited. She was full of life and gave the unspoken impression of a positive response. It was a cool Friday evening. While we had dinner I fed her frequently amid hearty chuckles. I fed her rice with my own spoon, and fed her meat with my tongue or fingers. Once with our teeth we held a piece of meat between us, cut it and chewed separately, only to kiss with mouthfuls of the matter, exchanging the pulp of our mastication. From the dining table we went straight to the bathroom, had shower together and made love for the first time, right in the bathroom. We later got to the bed and repeated the act, more passionately. I asked her twice in the course of the event whether she would marry me. She did not answer but rather continued moaning. When we were done I brought up the issue again.

"You ignored my question twice," I said, looking a bit serious. I pulled her close to myself, our faces facing each other, as we lay sideways on the bed.

"You don't ask someone for a favour when the person is drunk," she replied, grinning. "By the way you are very good. Very good, gosh! I broke my no-sex covenant with God today all for you, and it was worth it," she added.

I beamed. "Now that you're no longer drunk...will you do me the favour of...of being my wife, please? You have taught me how to love, how to live. You have brought me closer to a future that seemed so far away. We should not deny the world the opportunity of a beautiful example of marriage."

"It depends...!" she responded, with a deep sigh.

"Depends on what?" I asked, looking anxious.

"Depends on certain things. But...You lied to me! Why would you test me by claiming you had no job anymore? It's so childish! I'm totally disappointed in you. You think I'm with you for money? I'm not a hungry woman and you should know that.

Besides I'm disappointed that you don't still know me well enough to understand that I'm not moved by money...."

"Are you really talking to me? Because I have no idea what you're talking about."

"You'll get me angry if you pretend, pleeeaaase!"

I was silent. She moved away from me, her face locked in anger. I gently pulled her to myself again, and said:

"I want you to please calm down and talk to me. Why do you think I'm lying to you about my loss of Rontech and Oceanic prospects?"

She didn't seem to have an answer to that and so remained mute, avoiding eye contact with me by staring at the wall. I repeated the question and she snapped:

"The question should be directed to you! Answer: why would you test me like that?"

"Ok, I'll answer. I wouldn't test you like that because I'm yet to become so stupid to assume that a woman who has paid her dues should not aspire for a moderate measure of material comfort."

"Meaning?"

"Meaning that in the first place I see nothing wrong in your having to give a hoot about whether or not your man has the capability to take care of your material needs. You've worked hard in life so you deserve some comfort. It would only be wrong to aspire for that same comfort if you were a lazy, good-for-nothing lady looking for some rich man from the blues to take care of you and your family."

"That doesn't prove anything, does it?"

"Well I have nothing to prove to you, you can believe whatever you like," I retorted. "In any case it doesn't even make sense to test you or anyone else for that matter. How can I test a human being – a dynamic creature – in that regard? That someone is not materialistic today does not mean he won't become so in the future. Situations, friendships, anything can make a person change. So the result of any such assessment may not really take care of the future. The idea of conscientiously testing and over-assessing a partner in courtships doesn't appeal to me because most times the finding is relative."

I left her in the bedroom and went to my study room, wanting to replace my mind's preoccupation with something else. Shortly she was there in the study room looking so innocent like nothing had just happened between us.

"But you're too arrogant, Victor. So full of yourself! You can't even pet a woman! Who do you think you are?"

"Google me!" I sneered.

"Sometimes I wonder what I'm doing with a guy so stiff, who thinks he knows better than anyone else."

"You're trying too hard to get angry. Don't force it. Let it come naturally, that way you'll enjoy it! Wait...why am I even giving you free anger tips?"

She laughed. "You're crazy! You're not romantic. Too selfish yet I don't know how you manage to keep me stuck to you. Well, maybe because you're very handsome and intelligent."

"You can't even be creative with your flattery and insults: you're telling me things I already know."

She threw a mock punch on my chest and I caught the fist, drew her closer and kissed her.

"I love you dearly, Bimpe. I may not know how to dramatize love but I sure know how lucky I am to belong to you."

She smiled, her hand placed over her mouth.

"Why will you be reading this kind of book?" she said, snatching the book from me. The cover read The Pessimist's Handbook: A Companion To Despair by Niall Edworthy and Petra Cramsie. She desperately wanted to create a cordial atmosphere. Her hand went to the shelf and plucked Onyeka Nwelue's The Abyssinian Boy and dropped it on my laps.

"Read this one, it's a humorous book, you don't need despair. And it's too late already, come to bed."

"Thanks. But I read everything, both what I like and what I hate," I countered feigning woodenness, as I pushed the book off my thighs and left for the bedroom.

"Hope you're not going to the bedroom for another round of love-making, otherwise you can as well stay back and read, I don't wanna go home limping," she jested, trailing me.

I tried to hold back a smile. Soon we were back on the bed again and continued the discussion from where we left off.

"I'm sorry," she said softly, "I was just confused. Your finances have been very poor lately and the Victor I know ordinarily wouldn't propose to a woman in this state of affairs. So I thought you were up to something. You know, you're capable of so much drama. It's always difficult taking your words and actions at their face value."

We laughed and embraced. I had all along proven myself as a self-reliant man and a man with dignity, not one that would depend on a wife to run his home. So she was perplexed, wondering if I was claiming lack of job to test her faith in me and to gauge her sense of materialism. She was just being tactical in cross-examining me before giving me her response to the proposal.

"So tell me, why propose now when we're in a financial mess?"

"Proposal happens when a man is genuinely in love and is so sure about his choice of a partner. It has little to do with money."

"But money is an indispensable thing in the project of marriage."

"Yes I know. It's not as if we're going to the altar right away from here, if you say yes to me. I just want us to be fully committed to each other and work together for our mutual growth. I'm working on a lot of things at the moment; very soon I'll be back to my glory. At least I need money for my charity project for children."

"Talking about the altar, which one are we gonna wed in, should I grant you this favour you seek? You know you don't like my church and you don't attend any either." She stressed 'this favour' with smiles.

"Do we really need an altar to get married?"

"Helloooo! I can't skip the church wedding! I'm a worker in the church."

"No one is asking you to skip the church wedding."

"So what are you insinuating?"

"I'd wed. But not the conventional church wedding. I'm yet to understand its significance. And I hate waste and stress."

"So what kind of wedding would you want?"

"A proper traditional wedding. Very modest but culturally rich and simple. Then court wedding, after which you and I as well as a small number of guests would go to our choice, quiet resort for the reception. Preferably during the week. On Sunday we could go to church for thanksgiving, that's all."

"God forbid! That can't be my wedding," she barked, flicking her fingers.

"God forbid? What's wrong with that kind of wedding?"

"Nothing is wrong with it, it's ok, but not for me. I don't see the hand of God through a priest, in the joining. Why do you hate the church so much?"

"I don't hate the church; I just talked about Sunday thanksgiving."

"Thanksgiving as the last thing, to make it appear consecrated?"

"I don't know your understanding of Godly involvement. Both the traditional and court sessions commence and end with prayers. If you like we could even invite the Pope to seal the prayers for us and hand them straight to God to avoid traffic. And the thanksgiving is in the house of God too. What could be better than that?"

"Victor I'm not arguing with you, you're very correct. Church wedding has no significance but I'd want it. And my husband would want it too."

"The only significance I see is probably the social grandeur," I asserted, "It's just a mere convention and does not add or remove God from the union, nor does it guarantee its success or failure. I don't see how it adds value, unless to those who see it from the commercial angle. Or those whose social ego depends on their ability to gratify the wishes of a party-thirsty crowd. And what do you mean by your husband would want it too?"

"Is it not obvious? If you cannot consent to a proper wedding I don't see how we can get along. A wedding is the pride and glory of every woman."

She left for the bathroom for another shower. Her face was frosty. We ignored each other when she came back to the bed after having her bath, and she switched off the light. No one raised the matter again till we slept.

The next morning, she left for her home. From that moment life left the relationship. I raised the issue three times at different occasions but she had already begun acting like the matter went beyond a disagreement over our wedding. Later she confessed to her loss of interest in the relationship. That, apart from the sin of fornication which she committed for my sake, she had also realised how far away she had moved from God in the course of our relationship. She eventually stopped visiting. I was deeply hurt, wondering if I could ever again find another lady with her kind of charm. At twenty-seven, three years younger than I, Bimpe had all the qualities of the wife I wanted. Just a difference in our way of worshipping and seeing God caused a breakdown. She reminded me, the last time we spoke on phone, how I spurned her many appeals to me to visit a man of God for deliverance from my economic misfortunes. She believed my woes were spiritual but I would not buy that. As far as she was concerned, our differences were more complicated that I thought. I did not struggle to love her; it came naturally. It didn't take long before she stopped picking my calls. I moved on, vowing never to bother myself about marriage anymore. From then whenever Mother called reminding me of marriage, I would tell her that it was too late. She would protest that only less than two years earlier I had told her it was too early!

It was double tragedy for me to cope with heartbreak and dwindling economic realities. There was no willing sponsor to berth the reality TV idea, and no positive response from any of the construction firms to which proposals had been sent. My construction hardware outlet was on a progressive decline. Everything seemed cursed. Again the suspicion of spiritual undertones began to seep into my mind in the light of statements to that effect by Bimpe and Ekwueme. I shut down the thought categorically. It was hypocrisy, not Godliness, to instantly apply myself to the emotionality of praying and fasting, visiting the house of God only because I was in trouble. There was no giving in to such hysteria. One must show fidelity to time-tested principles and not jump around blowing hot and cold in reaction to the temperature of one's fortunes, I mulled. The Lord's Prayer was still enough.

Ekwueme, again, played the father that he never was as the storm prevailed. I had shared the story with him and he took it upon himself to camp in his spiritual church, fasting and praying for his son. He did not tell me about "the battle he was fighting" because he felt I would not believe him concerning any spiritual revelation made. So he went about the "warfare" quietly, and I only got to know much later. I was deeply moved by the act despite my doubts about the spiritual manipulation theory. It did not matter, for, Ekwueme played that part out of a genuine thirst for solution. From then the bond between us grew stronger, so much that I considered that gesture as a sufficient compensation for the deficits of the past. From then I began to address him as Father.

Within the period, Tony called. Mimi's boss was interested in the sponsorship of the reality TV show, but wanted to be properly educated on how it would benefit the manufacturing firm. A meeting was scheduled between me and the Indian brand-manager boss of the firm, Mr Vinay Jha.

As soon as I pulled up into a parking space outside the fence of the company that Tuesday morning, a stern-looking security guard charged towards me. I smiled at the guard, instantly recollecting how I had belonged in that constituency.

"Officer how work?" I greeted, as I got off the wheels.

The guard, shoed like a horse, looked indifferent, and literally threw the compliment back to where it came from.

"So anywhere wey you see space, you go jus' chuke head abi? This space wey you come park na MD parking space. You go go find another place."

"Sorry about that, my brother. But where I fit park now? No more parking space around."

"Wetin come concern me inside? See o, go find space now, na me go show you?"

"Guy no be quarrel, you jus' dey provoke!" I said, trying to pacify him.

"I quarrel with you? Where you dey go sef?"

My anger had shot up. I despised the needless overzealousness with which he discharged a duty that reduced his own humanity.

"I come see your brand manager, he's expecting me," I replied flippantly, scowling at him as I walked into the company premises.

"Oga you jus' dey waka dey enter, you no go come comot your motor for here?"

"Next time, if you want to reserve a space, put a no-parking sign there. Or you stand permanently in the space and stretch your hands sideways."

I ignored his noisy carping and went into the reception, sorted myself out there and got into the Indian man's office.

Mr. Jha was one of those Indians in Nigeria whose skin colour lacked specific definition. He was not dark enough to be black, or fair enough to be white. His black, flourishing moustache seemed like the legs of a millipede clustered above a pair of pink lips. With his smallish stature, he looked like a bearded child who had lost his way in that oblong office of files that circled a long, vertical desk, and then a chair that would not blink to support his weight. A tiny hand was stretched towards me and I shook it, carefully.

"Siddan Mr. Victor, you're quite on time."

His accent was very Indian, that somewhat threnodic articulation that often realised consonant sounds in words with a tinge of haste. 'Sit down' was compressed into siddan.

"I've seen the textual and graphical proposals for your reality TV show. They look good on paper. But what's in it for us? That's what will determine whether we can be part of it or not."

I did not understand "what's in it for us?" due to accent challenge, as Mr. Jha's tongue rattled in the vocal haste of Indian speech. I asked for clarification and Mr. Jha gave it.

"I mean, what does our company stand to gain by sponsoring the programme?"

"A lot," I enthused, "Most of your products are for the youths. I can assure you 80 percent of the youths of this country are politically aware and patriotic, and have been waiting for this kind of motivation. They'll watch the programme and you'll have the rewarding opportunity of reaching out to your target audience. On your part, it's also a mark of corporate social responsibility to identify with the political development of this country...."

"How did you get the statistics of 80 percent, you conducted a research?"

I had exaggerated. I had to lie to cover up.

"Yes we did a research. When next I come I'll show you the research findings."

The we in "we did a research" was also another lie in packaging.

"Good. But we don't need your programme to be able to do our CSR or reach out to our target audience. We have our own in-house programmes for such. If we have to sponsor yours, there has to be a way we can make some direct money from it, apart from the expected sales boom."

"You'll make some money after you've invested a little, first. We have to make a lot of noise in the media to generate attention and interest in the programme. That's the first step. People would respond to be part of the programme, by activating a designated short-code at the cost of one hundred naira. That's a whole lot of money if we have 100,000 activations in a week in the whole country – and trust me it'll be much more than that.

Whatever we generate can be used to administer the shooting and other things."

The mention of figures was deliberate. Mr. Jha looked a bit convinced but suddenly, like a squirrel, he cocked his head to one side, then to the other side:

"You have a strong appeal, Victor. But start first. Go and start the programme, if it's successful we'll join in the sponsorship. I don't think the management of this company will be willing to kick-start a programme that has not been tried before. Go and start."

I breathed out heavily, waited for some passing seconds, took a valedictory handshake and left.

Two days later, a call came in from Roberto, who had just got back to Nigeria from a three-month rest in Italy. He travelled out within the week I lost my relationship with Rontech. He asked me to come see him in the office the following day.

We met. Roberto assured that he would convince Enrico to drop the new procurement plan and revert to my Famalec. A big contract had just landed for Rontech from a new client and my expertise was needed for things to run smoothly. Reconciliation! Soon purchase orders came tumbling in. I was happy, but cautious. I viewed the revival of the Rontech opportunity with detachment, and pressed on in my efforts towards alternative contract sources. Before long two of the construction companies to which I submitted proposals called me, and supply deals were signed. I ploughed back a large chunk of the proceeds from this new turn-around into my hardware outlet, to resuscitate it. It worked. The batteries of sales were supercharged.

In about six months, my account balance had already acquired a new weight. I set a target to raise a certain sum on my own to start up the reality TV programme, having drawn up an expenditure plan. I would contract a production company for technical assistance. It was risky but I thought it was even riskier, as a humanist, to give up on my idea. If I failed and lost my money in the process, I would more easily forgive myself than I ever would for not trying. And, I sensed that putting my money in the idea would make me more serious and determined not to fail. In the background, also, was the fear that the idea could be stolen by the same people to whom it had been exposed in recent times, notwithstanding my ownership of copyright. For, the best and most secure way to technically own an idea, especially in Nigeria, was to have started it. Idea thieves could easily distort the concept, diluting it significantly to escape liability from copyright laws. Collateral to the thought of leaving a legacy through the programme was a new motivation: money. By discussing the idea with experts in the field, I came to realise its massive viability, how the returns could answer most of my prayers, from charity, new businesses to moderate personal comfort.

While I was still saving money towards the project, a friend linked me up with a young man who worked in a firm dealing in television concept and content development. Olaitan had been immersed in the business for close to a decade. He knew what buttons to press and what strings to pull. He studied the proposal and objected to this and that, making suggestions which I applied after the first meeting. Soon we were back to the discussion table.

"What precisely do you want me to do for you in this?" he asked, looking straight into my eyes.

"Sponsors! Get me sponsors."

"That's not a problem," he boasted, "but what do I stand to gain?"

"Well it depends on the value the sponsor is willing to offer me. Based on that, we can discuss."

"I'm talking of percentage. Before anything, we have to define what percent accrues to me."

"What percent does Olaitan want?"

"Sixty for you, forty for me."

"What? That's pretty much!"

"Anyway we'll review it later but first things first: prepare for a presentation, I'll introduce you to my MD. If he likes your idea, you'll bring your lawyer to draw up an agreement with our company. Our company will be dealing directly with the sponsor, with you as an active third-party so you can be involved. Later there might be a need to also draw up a tripartite agreement. My own percentage will come from your share in the whole deal."

"That's ok by me. So when is the presentation?"

"I'll talk with my MD and get back to you soonest."

The presentation went well. Olaitan had earlier worked on his boss so there wasn't much argument. An agreement was later signed between me and the content development firm, which now took over the hunt for sponsors. In three months, a sponsor signified interest and discussions started. A tripartite agreement was later signed, which spelt out what percentage of the initial capital I was deemed to provide. I didn't want to be an idle partner lest that would reflect negatively on my profit accruals. The content development firm took charge of publicity and gave account of disbursements as periodically stipulated. The programme was to take place twice a year. The first episode was a huge success, both financially and in terms of the ripple effect it had in the whole nation. From the proceeds I obtained an international copyright to protect the concept overseas, since I had plans to export the idea beyond the nation.

With the new state of affairs, I became too busy to handle everything: besides Rontech, there were now two other construction companies to which I supplied goods and services; there was the construction hardware outlet to oversee; I had just started my Ph.D programme, and that demanded a lot of time and effort. There was the idea of an advertising agency which I had begun setting up, with Tony and Mimi as partners. I put out an advertisement for a personal assistant. It had to be a very intelligent young man ready to be mentored to impact society. The young man would later prove to be the livewire for the success of my many businesses.

At thirty-two, I felt quite fulfilled. I had given some fellow Nigerian youths a platform to articulate patriotism and change. I had employed a few others. I had changed the fortunes of my family. I made up my mind not to get married, not because I found the institution called marriage wanting, but because I found myself so. Love, anger and all such emotions have the same property as potentially slippery psychological conditions. It was difficult to be certain that I could trust my feelings for another, for life – nor could I be sure of a partner's own commitment in the same breadth. For those who have seen divorce mainly in movies, who have not lived it to know its consequences, it is easy to recommend it when marriage begins to falter. Not me. I would not try what I was not sure of completing. Mature bachelorhood comes with a smothering sense of loneliness. At that stage in a man's life, personal comforts, girlfriends and other forms of company become boring. But I did not care. Life was enough trouble already.

But there was one major item in the to-do list yet to be addressed: institutionalising the charity programme I intended for poor, abandoned children. I later made my testament and willed a large part of my share from the TV programme, part of my equity in the advertising agency, and part of my construction businesses to the yet-to-be-established charity home. That would be my most fulfilling legacy to society. It would have my name embedded in the hearts of those little children – tomorrow's men and women.

The charity institution became my new humanistic torment. Tony took over arrangements to get a location and we finally settled for one in a rural part of Lagos. The cost was affordable compared to the luxury of space and other conveniences in the compound. It was a four-bedroom bungalow with a detached line of rooms for domestic staff, the so-called Boys' Quarters. The plan was to start with five children, a literate matron and two helps and we stuck to that. I needed to groom from scratch a new generation of humans with a huge capacity for thought, intellectuals inspired to transcend the limitations of blind religion, poverty and the hurdles of life. Change must start with one person at a time, and not necessarily with an entire population. A tokunbo van was placed at their disposal. Mimi designed house rules for the matron and staff to ensure that the Home was run like a real family and the children would grow as siblings. There was a small garden at the back of the house, bicycles for sports, a small library in the main building, and a few other amenities for the proper grooming and development of complete humans. The children, all below age ten, were picked from highly underprivileged families after due process, to be on the right side of the law. Tony and his wife coordinated everything.

We had all agreed on a very quiet, brief inaugural party. Apart from the children and staff, the police chief and the traditional ruler of the area, my lawyer, Tony and his wife, there wouldn't be more than ten other guests. I did not want a public show, in my reasoning that even modest publicity would glorify self. But to my surprise, Tony and his lively wife had other plans.

I arrived the Home when the event was already an hour gone. At first I was confused, thinking I was in the wrong place, having visited the place only but twice, once at night. I had proposed an indoor party. But set before me was an uncountable crop of guests sheltered under two spacious canopies. Songs and praises rent the air, with a pastor conducting what seemed like a full-blown church service. Female heads roofed with sprawling head-gears set the mood. I alighted from my car and stood aside watching the unexpected drama staged by Tony and his delectable accomplice. I found myself smiling at the smoothness of their trickery. They found indulgence in my smile and emerged to welcome me.

"So you thought we'd follow your script of a drab, boring event?" Mimi asked amid an expansive grin.

"This is so unfair, but I forgive you guys," I said, embracing both of them, happily.

"Dont be in a hurry to forgive," Tony chipped in, "There are more surprises awaiting you."

After the songs and praises, and refreshment, Tony called on me to give a vote of thanks. From the podium I sighted a lady smiling and waving at me. That was Bimpe. I smiled back at her and continued my speech, briefly narrating my experience to the audience to underscore the spirit behind the setting up of the Home. The narration was real, not mechanical. In my mind's eye cast back to my life in Umuege, I saw the scenes of parental squabbles and divorce; of the bush-trap episodes and of eating ogba n'azu aka, amid other imageries of a survival snatched from the fangs of poverty. I saw my tattered school uniforms and Mother's efforts for me at mechanic village in Owerri; I saw that night in Monica's house, saw Nse in Ajegunle, the lady who gave all; I saw Billy's face and Cerberus, his de facto murderer; there was also the imagery of the Oke-Arin deadly beat, of Chima, and Roberto, and of the pioneer dwellers in our Home, my five little children whose innocence, nay, ignorance of the world ahead of them, touched my heart. Then Nne's image flashed through my mind and my speech got stuck in my throat. Tears! The evocation of her death marked the unplanned climax of that narration. Tears were more eloquent than words in conveying the details of that loss. I mourned her absence in sharing the triumph of the moment, a victory whose realisation was partly incubated in the distant affirmation of a grandmother that loved to a fault. Until that moment I did not know how embarrassingly emotional I was.

But there is nothing unmanly about crying for a thing to which the soul has a deep attachment. It is a loss of humanity, not a mark of manliness, to lack emotions for pity or joy, for sympathy or pain.

After I left the podium upon the end of my aborted speech, two journalists approached me. Tony had invited them. After some reluctance I agreed to be interviewed. I shared with them the story of my reality TV show, and my vision for the Home in the years to come, and they felt very excited about the foundation. I felt so honoured by the interviews when I read them in the newspapers days later.

Generally speaking, efforts at self-immortalisation are not totally altruistic, I agree. Nothing is completely so anyway. Take away divine rewards from religion-induced generosity, and an intrinsic feeling of goodness in gestures of humanism, nothing would get done. But let the individual be entitled to a moderate sense of achievement. I cautioned myself against a certain pulse of self-congratulation that sprouted within me, by holding up the reality that life, with or without the validation of legacy, ultimately brings everyone to the same level by the sheer misery of its vanity. The one who became the president of a nation at thirty, another who became so at seventy; the one the image of whose head is engraved on the national currency, another whose image has never gone beyond gracing a photographic paper; the fruitful and the barren; the king and the pauper; the beauty queen and the ugly lady – all would sooner or later end up in the belly of a little worm. It is not gloom, it is reality. The glory or the lack of it left behind will not tickle or afflict the subjects anymore, and with time even the posterity that whined seemingly irredeemably at their funerals will soon concentrate on more current matters.

Yet in the meantime that both glory and obscurity, or such other paired realities matter, they do not still matter! The one who is chauffeured in limousines and the other who is propelled by his own feet; the glamorously decorated one who dines at palatial tables, and the other whose life wobbles precariously on the daily repetition of cheap starchy meals; the leader and the led – all have their moments of joy and sadness, probably enjoyed or suffered in measures relative to status. The things that excite one may not mean anything to the other. Nature has already shared both goods and evils equally. Envy not the rich man, doctors may be erecting buildings on account of his health. Of course he can at least afford his medication, but who would pay for air when he can get it free? You are bitter that he doesn't share his wealth with you, but why? Charity is a duty he owes himself and God, he doesn't owe it to you, in concept. Therefore hold no grudge against him for refusing to help with your children's school fees. Thank him if he does. And then search yourself; do you really care that much about those less fortunate than you are?

In the final analysis I found fulfilment and inner peace, but not happiness. For man, happiness is a continuing ambition. It is never attained in its entirety, but only supplied by God in instalments to reduce suicide rates. Yes, you can celebrate your recovery from that life-threatening ailment, pop champagne because you survived a terrible accident, but don't yet scream down the heavens, you have not conquered misery for yourself or for humanity. Is it over yet? If only you knew how many other hazards are waiting to ambush that joy! Be delighted, but not too excited. Modesty does not reduce the glow: one must not lose control of self whether in pain or joy. Be grateful. Play your part now for a better world and a happier God. You just have to live here first before you go to heaven. Or hell. Do not exist, live! Recognise the brotherhood of man and have empathy. The next man's predicament is ours. If the poor are hungry, the rich cannot sleep. It is in the performance of these humanistic offices that we can feel adequately utilized, and find a self inured in peace. Godliness is first of all, human relations.

In the face of all the possible beautiful things that life may offer us, it offers also the contrary. The contradiction remains to haunt humanity, such that many of us would not have cared to exist perpetually as inanimate objects. In such status there would be neither gain nor loss. But that is a mere wish, for one cannot, so to speak, determine from here the happenstances in Unborn. Life is still precious. In its vanity lies an opportunity to participate in activity, a chance to debate itself.

As I sit here playing with my five new friends, these children who have given me the opportunity to express my humanity on a special level, I thank God. My investments are doing fairly well and I shall let in more children abandoned by fate, to come share in this diverse family experience, this bond of ethereal oneness. I feel grateful that this life was imposed on me in the first place, for the sense of triumph over poverty and other limitations is such a noble psychological sensation, a thrilling icing on lived miseries. Life is an imposed opportunity to excel.

About the Author

Immanuel James has written extensively on socio-cultural issues that underscore the human condition, constantly raising a voice for youth empowerment through intellectual engagement. A graduate of Mass Communication passionate about humanism, writing, and the study of Philosophy, he writes a column for *The Nigerian Telegraph*, and contributes regular articles to some other national media. He lives in Lagos, Nigeria, where he runs a business outfit, and is presently pursuing post-graduate studies in Multimedia Journalism.